"That woman, the prophetess," General Jondrigar said. "She is a warrior for Lees Obol."

The man, not knowing what to say or if it was wise to say anything, merely nodded, attempting to look alert.

"She needs armor. A fighter needs armor. Tell my armorer. A helmet for her. Made to her measure. And a set of fishskin body armor, such as we wear. And boots. have him plume the helmet with flame-bird plumes, like mine, and make her a spear."

The man presumed to comment. "Can she handle a spear, General?"

"No matter. Someone can carry it at her side. Let it bear a pennant."

The man went away, shaking his head, puzzled, wondering what the prophetess would think of all this.

She, when the armorer came to measure her the next morning, thought it another sign. Neff from his shining cloud approved, and the radiance and the shadow both nodded.

Tor Books by Sheri S. Tepper

Fantasy
DERVISH DAUGHTER
JINIAN FOOTSEER
JINIAN STAR-EYE
NORTHSHORE
SOUTHSHORE

Horror
BLOOD HERITAGE
THE BONES

SHERI S. TEPPER
SOUTHSHORE
THE AWAKENERS
Volume 2

A TOM DOHERTY ASSOCIATES BOOK

SOUTHSHORE: THE AWAKENERS, VOLUME 2

First printing: June 1987
First mass market printing: May 1988

A TOR Book

Published by Tom Doherty Associates, Inc.
49 West 24th Street
New York, NY 10010

ISBN: 0-812-55619-4
Can. No.: 0-812-55620-8

Printed in the United States of America

0 9 8 7 6 5 4 3 2 1

For my children,
Alden, Cheryl, Mark, and Regan
a password

• 1 •

When Pamra left Thou-ne, moving westward along the River road, some thousand of the residents of Thou-ne went after her. Most of them were provisioned to some extent, though there were some who went with no thought for food or blankets, trusting in a providence that Pamra had not promised and had evidently not even considered. Peasimy Flot, for all his seeming inanity, was well provided for. He had a little cart with things in it, things he had been putting by for some time. The widow Flot would have been surprised to find in it items that had disappeared from her home over the last fifteen years or so. There were others in Thou-ne who would have been equally surprised to find their long-lost belongings assisting Peasimy in his journey.

The procession came to Atter, and though some of the Thou-neites dropped out of the procession, many of Atter joined it. Pamra preached in the Temple there, to general acclaim. Then came Bylme and Twarn-the-little, then Twarn-the-big—where the townspeople made Pamra a gift of a light wagon in which she might ride, pulled by her followers—then a dozen more towns, and in each of them the following grew more numerous, the welcome more tumultuous. Peasimy himself began to appoint "messengers" to send ahead with word of their coming. It was something that came to him, all at once. "Light comes," he told them. "That is what you must say." As time went on, the messages grew more detailed and ramified, but it was always Peasimy who sent them.

It was on a morning of threatening cloud that they left Byce-barrens for the town of Chirubel.

The storm did not precisely take them by surprise; the day had brought increasing wind and spatters of rain from very near dawn until midafternoon. Still, when in late afternoon the full fury of the wind broke over them and the skies opened, the multitude were in nowise prepared for it. Some stopped where they were, crawling under their carts or pitching their tents as best they might, to cower under them out of the worst of the downpour. Others fled into the woods, where they sought large trees or overhanging ridges. Pamra, high on her wagon, simply pointed ahead with one imperious finger, and the men who dragged the wagon, half-drowned by the water flowing over their faces, staggered on into the deluge. It was not until they stumbled into the outer wall of the Jarb House that they realized she had pointed toward it all along. Pamra came down from the wagon, and the dozen or so of them, including Peasimy Flot, struggled around the perimeter of the place looking for a door.

It opened when they pounded, warmth drifting out into the chill together with a puff of warm, dry air laden with strange smells and a haze of smoke. Peasimy coughed. Pamra pressed forward against the warding arm of the doorkeeper, the others following, gasping, wetter than fish.

They passed down a lengthy corridor into the main hall to stand there stunned at the scale of the place. It was like standing in a chimney. At one side stairs curved up to a balcony that spiraled around the open area, twisted up, and up, kept on going around and around, smaller and smaller, to the seeming limit of their eyes, where it ended in a dark glassy blot, a tented skylight black with rain. It was, Pamra thought, like being inside the trunk of a hollow tree with an opening at the top and all the tree's denizens peering down at you. Heads lined the balconies, went away to be replaced by others, and throughout the whole great stack of living creatures came a constant rustle and mumble of talk, a bubbling pulse of communication that seemed to be one seamless fabric of uninterrupted sound.

From some of the balconies nets hung, littered with a flotsam of clothing and blankets. From other balconies long, polished poles plunged to lower levels. A brazier was alight at the center of the floor, its wraiths rising in dim veils in this towering, smokestack space.

"Come in," said the Mendicant ironically. "So nice to have you."

"It is raining out there," announced Pamra evenly, no whit aware of the sarcasm. She drew back the cloak that had covered Lila to disclose the child, not at all discomfited by the soaking she had received.

"Wet," affirmed Peasimy. "Dreadful wet. A great flood out of the skies. Mustn't let *her* drown. Too important."

"Ah," assented the Mendicant. "And you are?"

"The crusade," said Peasimy. "We are the crusade. Light comes! She is the Bearer of Truth, the very Mother of Truth."

"Ah," said the Mendicant again, frowning slightly. He had heard of this. All this segment of Northshore had heard of this, one way or the other. As one of the Order's more trusted messengers, he had more interest in it than most. A message had come through Chiles Medman, Governor General of the Order, from Tharius Don asking the Order to assist in procuring information.

"Trale," he introduced himself. "Mendicant brother of the Jarb. What can I offer you by way of assistance?"

"Towels," said Pamra simply. "And a fire to dry ourselves. Something hot to drink if you have it conveniently by." She stared around her, up at the endless balconies where people came and went, staring down at her, leaving the railings to others who stared in their turn. Pale blots. Mouths open. Hands moving in beckoning gestures. Something distressed her, but she could not identify it. Something was wrong, missing, as though she had forgotten to put on her skirt or her tunic. She looked down at herself, puzzled. She was damp but fully dressed. Why, then, this feeling of nakedness?

Trale led them across the hall, through an arch beneath the balcony and into a wide, low room that curved away just inside the outer wall. A refectory. Pamra shivered. It was not unlike the refectory at the Tower of Baris. The smells were not unlike those smells. Cereals and soap, steam and grease, cleanliness at war with succulence. Trale beckoned to them from an angled corner, a smaller room opening off the large one, where a fire blazed brightly upon the hearth.

"I'll return in a moment," he murmured, leaving them there.

Those who had drawn the cart stood back, waiting for Pamra to approach the fire. She gestured them forward. The room was warm enough without baking herself. She took off her outer clothing and spread it on a table. Her knee-length undertunic was only damp, clinging to her body like a second skin. The men turned their eyes away under Peasimy's peremptory gaze, one of them flushing.

Trale was back in a moment with towels and a pile of loosely woven robes over one arm. He did not seem to notice Pamra's body under the clinging fabric but merely handed her one of the robes, as impersonally as a servant. Behind him came a man and a woman, one bearing a tea service, the other a covered platter at which Peasimy looked with suspicion.

"Jarb," said Trale. "It is our custom."

"We won't—" Pamra began.

"No. It is *our* custom. With any visitor. Call it—oh, a method of diagnosis."

"We are not ill."

"The diagnosis is not always of illness. Do take tea. This is a very comforting brew. It has no medicinal qualities aside from that."

They sat steaming before the fire, moisture rising from them and from their discarded clothing in clouds. Rain fell down the chimney, making small spitting noises in the fire. The wall at their side reverberated to the thunder outside, hummed to the bow-stroke of the wind. In the great hall the voice murmur went on and on. Beside the fire Trale knelt to scrape coals into a tiny brazier. Beside the brazier lay three oval roots, warty and blue, each the size of a fist. Jarb roots, Pamra thought. Trale peeled the roots carefully, dropping the peels into a shallow pan. When all three were peeled, he laid the roots into the ashes and began to dry the peels over the brazier, stirring them with a slender metal spoon. The woman who had brought in the tea buried the peeled roots in the ashes and turned to smile at Pamra.

"It is only the peel which has the power of visions. Jarb root itself is delicious. The Noor eat it all the time. Have you ever tasted it?"

Pamra shook her head, oppressed once more by the sense of something missing. "No." She ate less and less as the crusade wore on. Hunger seemed scarcely to touch her. Now, for some reason, however, she felt ravenous. Perhaps it was the smoke. Perhaps the smell of food. "I am hungry, though."

"They only take a few moments to steam. Some scrape the ashes off, but I like the taste." She drew a pipe from her pocket and handed it to Trale, who filled it with the powdery scraps from the pan. All three had pipes, and in a moment all three were alight, seated before the fire, the smoke from the pipes floating out into the room, into the refectory, away into the chimney of the great hall. The fragrance was the same one that already permeated everything. Sweet, spicy. Pamra folded her arms on the table and laid her head upon them, suddenly both hungry and tired. She had not felt this hungry, this tired, in months. Why was she here? She thought briefly of the *Gift of Potipur*, wishing she were aboard, translating the murmur of Tower talk into the murmur of tidal current, the thunder outside into the creak of boat timbers. She could be there. With Thrasne. Instead of here. Beside her Lila chortled and said, clearly, "Over the River. Thrasne went over the River."

Peasimy turned, his little ruby mouth open, cheeks fiery red with the drying he had given them. "She talked!"

Pamra nodded sleepily. "She does, sometimes."

"I hadn't heard her before."

"She talks about the River a lot. Mostly that." She rubbed her forehead fretfully. The sweet smell of the Jarb had soaked into the top of her nose and was filling it, like syrup. She turned to find the three smokers knocking the dottle from their pipes onto the hearth. The immediacy of the smell was dissipating.

The woman raked the baked Jarb root from the fire, brushing it off and placing it upon a little plate. This she placed before Pamra with a spoon. "Try a little."

Pamra spooned off a bite, blowing on it to cool it. The root was sweet, too, but delicious. The slightly ashy taste only complemented it. She took another spoonful, then hesitated.

"Go ahead, eat it all," the woman said. "There are people bringing plenty of food for you and for the others."

By the fire, Trale sat, rocking back and forth.

"Did you have a vision?" asked Peasimy curiously, studying the man's face.

"Oh, yes."

"What was it of?"

"Of you, Peasimy Flot. And of Pamra Don. And of what is to come."

"Oh!" Peasimy clapped his hands, delighted. "Tell us!"

Trale shook his head. "I'm afraid it can't be told. There are only colors and patterns."

"Red and orange and yellow of flame," said the woman. "Black of smoke."

"Red and orange and yellow of flowers," said the man. "Black of stony mountains."

"Red and orange and yellow of metal," said Trale. "Black of deep mines."

"That doesn't sound like much of a vision," pouted Peasimy.

"Or too much of one," said Pamra, one side of her mouth lifted in a half smile. The Jarb root had settled into her, making some of the same kind of happiness Glizzee spice often made. Not rapture. More a contentment. Warmth. It had been a sizable root, and her sudden hunger was appeased. She smiled again, head nodding with weariness. "I'm so sleepy."

"Come with me," the woman said. "We'll find a place for you to rest."

They went out into the great hall again and up the spiraling balcony. A twist and a half up the huge trunk, the woman pointed into a room where a wide bed was spread with gaily worked quilts. The door was fastened back with a strap, and the woman loosened it now, letting the door sag toward its latch.

"Sleep. When you've slept enough, come back down to the place we were. I'll be there, or Trale. Will the baby be all right, here with you?"

Pamra nodded, so weary she could hardly hold her head up. She heard the latch click as she crawled into the bed, felt Lila curl beside her with a satisfied murmur, then was gone into darkness.

Outside the room people moved to and fro, some of them pausing to stare curiously at the door before moving away to be replaced by someone else. Inside the room, Lila squirmed out of Pamra's grasp, turned to let her feet drop off the edge of the bed, then stagger-crawled to the door to sit there with her own hands pressed to its surface, smiling, nodding, sometimes saying something to herself in a chuckling baby voice, as though she watched with her fingers what transpired outside the wooden barrier.

Below in the firelit room, the three Mendicants crouched before the fire, staring into the flames. Peasimy had fallen asleep where he sat, as had the men with him.

"Mad," said Trale at last. "There's no doubt."

"None," agreed the woman. "She hasn't eaten for weeks or months. She's all skin and eyes. She's an ecstatic. A visionary. The fasting only makes it worse. The minute the smoke hit her, she felt hungry. She's half starved herself."

"How long do you think we can get her to stay?" the man asked.

"No time at all. Tomorrow morning, perhaps. If the storm goes on, perhaps until the rain stops."

"Not long enough to do any good."

"No."

"It's too bad, isn't it?"

Trale nodded, poking at the fire. "Well, a time of changes is often unpleasant. I don't see the Jarb Houses seriously threatened. Or the Mendicants."

"There will be a need for more houses." The woman made a spiraling gesture that conveyed the wholeness of the edifice with all its murmurous inhabitants.

"Perhaps some of the people in residence will be able to leave," the man said. He sounded doubtful of this.

"Some are ready to leave as Mendicants." Trale sighed. "Taking their pipes with them, as we do. The others—if they go, they go into madness once more. More houses will be needed, but it's unlikely we'll be able to build them."

"We could keep her here."

"By force?" It was a question only, without emotion. But the woman flushed deep crimson. "I thought, persuade her, perhaps."

"Try," Trale urged her. "By all means, Elina, try. It has not a hope of success, but you will not be content unless you try."

Late in the day a bell rang and people began filing down from the chimney top toward the refectory. Children leapt from the railings into nets and from these into other nets below. Some whirled down tall poles. A train of whooping boys came spinning down the spiraling banister, loud with laughter. The tables filled, and there was a clatter of bowls and spoons. Out in the chimney hall, Elina pared Jarb-root peels onto the brazier, renewing the pale wraiths of smoke which filled all the space to its high, blind skylight. Pamra opened the door of her room and came out onto the balcony to look down, Lila held high against her shoulder. Elina beckoned to them, and Lila squirmed out of Pamra's arms, over the railing, plunging downward, arms spread as though to fly. Elina caught her, without thinking, only then turning pale with shock while the child chortled in her arms and Pamra, above, put hands to her throat as though to choke off a scream.

"All right," said Lila. "You caught me."

"Did you know I would?" the woman asked in an astonished whisper.

"Oh, yes," said Lila. "The smoke is nice."

Pamra was coming slowly down the twisting ramp, her eyes never leaving the child below. Lila squirmed to be put down and staggered toward the foot of the ramp, face contorted in the enormous concentration necessary to walking. She did not fall until the ramp was reached, and Pamra scooped her up.

"Lila, don't ever do that again." In her voice was all the anguish of every mother, every elder sister, all imperiousness gone. She smiled at Elina, shaking her head, and they shared the moment. Children! The things they did! It lasted only a moment.

"I should be getting back to my people," Pamra said. "They will be wondering what has happened to me."

"They know you are here," the woman responded. "It is still raining. They will be more comfortable if they believe you are comfortable. Do not add your discomfort to their own by going back into the wet."

"You're right, of course. And it will not hurt to have a warm meal." Pamra was amazed at herself, but she was hungry again. She looked around her curiously. "I got only the general impression before. Are all Jarb Houses built this way?"

"Yes. So the smoke can permeate the whole structure."

"The smoke? I see it does. But why?"

Elina took her by the arm, drawing her close, as though they had been sisters, used to sharing confidences. "The Jarb smoke is said to give visions, you know? But in reality, Jarb smoke erases visions and restores reality. For those disturbed by visions of madness, the Jarb smoke brings actuality. You see that woman going into the refectory? The tall one with the wild red hair? On the outside, she is a beast who roams the forests, killing all who pursue her, sure of their ill will and obsessed by the terrors of the world. Here she is Kindle Kindness, a loving friend to half the house."

Pamra peered at the woman, not seeming to understand what was being said.

"Outside, she has visions of herself as a beast, of herself hunted. In the house, the smoke wipes those visions away. In here, she is only herself."

Pamra stared at her, awareness coming to her suddenly, her face paling. "Neff," she cried. "Neff!"

"Shhh," said Elina. "Shhh. There is no need to cry out."

"Neff! Where is he?"

Trale came from the refectory, joining them, taking Pamra's other arm. Wearily, pointedly, with a resigned look at Elina, he said, "Your visions wait for you outside. They cannot come into a Jarb House."

Pamra drew herself up, regally tall, becoming someone else. "Truth cannot exist in this place, can it, Mendicant? Light cannot come here? Only darkness and smoke?"

He shook his head. "All your—all your friends are waiting for you. Come now. There is food waiting, also."

She shook her head at them, pityingly, but allowed them to take her to the place where Peasimy stood impatiently with the others, all standing beside their chairs, waiting for her to be seated; then all waiting until she began eating. She nodded at the others, saying, "Eat quickly, my friends. We must leave this place."

"Dark comes?" asked Peasimy, glaring at the Mendicants. "Pamra?"

She shook her head. "They are not evil, Peasimy. They are only misled." She had been hungry, but now she began to toy

with the food before her, obviously impatient to be gone. Elina
laid a hand upon her shoulder, tears in the corners of her eyes.
"Pamra! Courtesy! 'Neff' is not impatient." Pamra took a bite,
chewed it slowly, watching them with that same pitying gaze.
Now she knew what had been missing since she had entered the
house. Neff, and Delia, and her mother. Them and their voices.
Gone. As though they had never been except in her memory.
Did these poor smoke-blinded fools think she would let them
go? Though she could not see them in this smoky haze, the
center of her being clung to what she knew to be true. They—
they were true. Neff was true. She took another bite, smiled at
Peasimy and encouraged him to eat.

From the side of the room, Trale watched, eyes narrowed in
concentration. Elina came toward him. "She did not make the
connection with her own condition at all."

"Oh, yes. She knows what we tried to do. But she has
rejected it."

"Why, Trale?"

"Because her madness is all she has. Whatever else there
might have been once has been taken away. Whatever else there
might be in the future seems shoddy in comparison. Who would
wed a man when one might wed an angel? Who would live as a
woman when one might rule as a goddess?"

"We could keep her here by force."

"Setting aside that we would break all our vows, yes. We
could."

"In time, she would forget."

"Ah."

"She would grow accustomed."

"Elina."

"Yes, Trale."

"Clip the flame-bird's wings if you must, Elina. Set it among
your barnyard fowl. Tell yourself you do it to save the flame-
bird's life. But do not expect it to nest, or to sing."

She bowed her head, very pale. At the table behind her,
Pamra rose, her hand shaking as she wiped her mouth with the
napkin. "Where are my clothes?" she asked.

Peasimy found them for her, beside the fire, and she put them
on. They were warm and dry.

"Won't you stay until it stops raining?" Elina asked her. "Only until morning."

"No," Pamra said, her eyes darting from place to place in the high dwelling, marking it in her memory. Another time—there might be converts to be had in places like this. "No. Neff is waiting. Mother and Delia. They're waiting. We have set our feet upon the road and must not leave it. This is a bad place, Elina. You should come with us. You can't see the road from in here, Elina. Come with us. . . ." Her face lit from within, glowed, only for a moment, but for that moment Elina felt herself torn, wrenched, dragged to the gate of herself. Fear struck at her and she drew back.

"No, Pamra. It is safe here. The people here find much joy and comfort."

"Joy," said Pamra. "Comfort!" The scorn in her voice was palpable, an acid dripping upon those words. "Safety. Yes. That is what you have here."

Peasimy was suddenly beside her, swallowing the last bite of his supper. Then they were moving toward the entrance, out across the open chimney, through the hallway, pulling at the great doors. They went into the night, a night miraculously cleared of storm, with the moons lighting the sky. Potipur, half-swollen and sullen above them to the west; Viranel a mere sickle dipping beyond the western horizon; Abricor a round melon, high in the east.

"You see," said Pamra. "Neff has arranged it. Here he comes now." And she turned her radiant face to the woods, from which some invisible presence moved to join her. Elina, in the doorway, gasped, for she saw it, for that moment saw it, a towering figure of white light, golden wings outstretched, its breast stained with red.

Trale was behind her. "Come in, Elina."

"Trale, I saw . . ."

"Saw what she sees. As do all those who follow her. Come in to the fire, Elina."

Behind Pamra and the others, the doors of the Jarb House shut with a solemn clang. From the forests came the multitude, and Pamra's heart sang. "Crusade," she called. "Let us go on."

• 2 •

Thrasne thought of what he was about to do somewhat as he might have regarded taking the axe to himself if he had been touched by blight. He would have rejected the intention to lop off his own leg with horror, yet he would have done it because the alternative was more terrible still.

So, he fell in with the plan to go with a group of Medoor Babji's Melancholics on a voyage of exploration to find Southshore without enthusiasm, with a kind of deadly reluctance. He resolved upon it because staying anywhere near Pamra was more horrifying than leaving the world in which she moved. If he stayed, he would have to follow her. And it would be terrible to watch Pamra, to hear of her, to be told of the crusade. Any of these were more repugnant to him than risking his own life. He told himself he would welcome death if it meant he need not realize the danger Pamra ran and go in apprehension of that terror.

"I love her," he said to Medoor Babji. "Whether she is mad or not. I love her." And he did. His loins quivered at the thought of her. He knew every curve of her body, and he dreamed of that body, waking in a shaking sweat from agonies of unfulfilled passion.

And Babji, having observed his obsession over the days that had just passed, was wise enough to hold her tongue, though she thought, Stupid man, at him, not entirely with affection. How could she blame him for this unfulfillable desire when she had a similar one of her own?

Here, in the city of Thou-ne, on the same day Pamra cried crusade in the Temple of the Moons, Medoor Babji came to Taj

12

Noteen and gave him the tokens she carried with few words of explanation about the seeker birds, watching his face as it turned from brown to red to pallid gray, then to brown once more.

"Deleen p'Noz," he said, sinking to one knee. "Your Gracious Highness." The secret Noor language was used these days only for names and titles, little else.

"We need none of that," she told him firmly. "This is not the courts of the Noor. I do not need to hear *'Deleen p'Noz'* to be recalled to my duty. We are not in the audience tent of the Queen. Though I am the Queen's chosen heir, we are here, Noteen, in Thou-ne, as we were this morning when you whacked me with your whip stock. I've told you what we are to do. I want you to pick me a crew to go. Thrasne will need his own boatmen, and we cannot expect to live on the deck if there is storm or rough weather. We must limit our numbers, therefore, to the space available. Thrasne kindly offers us the owner-house. There are three rooms for sleeping, with two bunks in each room. There is an office and a salon. Not large. We can have none among us who will cause dissension."

"Not Riv Lymeen, then," he mused. "How about old Porabji?"

"He has a good mind," she assented. "Which we may need far more than a young man's strength. Yes."

Noteen thought about it. "Do we need a recorder? Someone to keep an account? A journal of the voyage?"

She thought a moment, then nodded. Queen Fibji had not commanded it, yet it was something that should be done.

"Then Fez Dooraz. He was clerk at the courts for ten years as a younger man. He looks as though a breath would blow him over, but he's the most literate of all of us."

She suggested, "Lomoz Borab is sound. And what about Eenzie?"

"Eenzie the Clown?"

"I'd like one more woman along, Noteen. And Eenzie makes us all laugh. We may need laughter."

He assented. "Six, then. Porabji, Dooraz, Borab, and Eenzie. You, Highness. And me."

"You, Noteen?"

"I will send the troupe back to the steppes. Nunoz can take them."

"I had not thought of you, Noteen."

"You object?" He asked it humbly enough.

She thought of this. He had not bullied her more than he had bullied anyone else. She could detect no animosity against him in herself. "Why not. And I have a thought about it, Noteen. You will command our group. So far as they are concerned, Queen Fibji's message came to you."

He thought on this, overcoming his immediate rejection of the idea as he confronted her thoughtful face. It might be better, he thought to himself, if no one knew who Medoor Babji was. "It might be safer for you," he murmured.

"I was not thinking of that," she said. "So much as the comfort of the voyage. We have done well enough with me as a novice. Why complicate things?"

"Thrasne owner doesn't know?"

"I told him we were ordered to go. I didn't tell him the seeker birds came to me, or what words they carried."

"Do you have enough coin to pay him?"

"Strange though it may seem, Taj Noteen, he isn't doing it for coin, or at least not primarily for coin, but yes. I have enough." Among the tokens she carried was one that would open the coffers of money lenders in Thou-ne. The Noor had accounts in many parts of Northshore.

"We'll need more yet for stores. How long a voyage do we plan?"

"Queen Fibji commands us to provision for a year. A full year. We will need most of the hold space for stores. Thrasne knows that."

"Well then, I'll get Dooraz and Porabji ready. They're good storesmen, both of them."

And it began.

Thrasne talked to the crew. He didn't give them his reasons, just told them they'd be well paid. Several of the men told him they'd go ashore, thanks for everything but they were not really interested in a voyage that long. Thrasne nodded and let them go. The others chewed it over for a time.

"You'll want me to replace the ones that left," Obers-rom said at last. "We'll need full crew, Thrasne owner. I don't suppose those blackfaces will be up to much in the way of helping on a boat."

"I don't suppose so. And we'd better get in the habit of callin' 'em by their names, Obers-rom. Or just say 'Noor.' They count that as polite."

Obers-rom agreed. He hadn't meant anything by it. Boatmen weren't bigoted. They couldn't be. They'd never make a copper if they couldn't deal with all kinds.

And it was Obers-rom who worked with Zyneem Porabji and Fez Dooraz—they were Obbie and Zynie and Fez within the day—to fill the *Gift of Potipur*'s holds. From the purveyors and suppliers they ordered dried fish and pickled fish and salted fish, grain in bulk, grain in dry cakes, and grain in flour, dried fruit, jam, hard melons, half barrels of slib roots—ready to sprout salad whenever they were wet down, even with the brackish River water. They ordered smoked shiggles, procured by Fez from some unspecified source along with kegs of Jarb roots. They bought sweetening and spices and kegs of oil, both oil for cooking and for the lanterns and stove. They paid for bolts of pamet cloth and coils of rope, extra lines for fishing, and bags of frag powder. They sought a pen of fowl for the rear deck with snug, watertight nesting boxes, and the cooper began making an endless series of kegs for fresh drinking water.

They ordered spices and medicines, a set of new pans for the cook, and supplementary tools for the carpenter's locker.

Not all of this was available in Thou-ne. Some of it was mustered mysteriously by the Noor and arrived as mysteriously on other boats coming from the east. This meant delay, and more delay, but the Noor were patient, more patient than Thrasne owner, who wanted only to put some great challenge like an impenetrable wall between himself and the way Pamra had gone. The harder he worked, the less he thought of her, yet he could not give up thinking of her entirely and went each day to the marketplace, asking for news of her, unable to tell truth from rumor when news was given.

And in between times he sat in his cubby or alone in his watching place and distracted himself by writing in his book. Though, as it happened, sometimes the things he wrote were not a distraction at all but led him deep within himself to the very things he would rather not have thought of.

• 3 •

Talker of the Sixth Degree, by the grace of Potipur articulate, Sliffisunda of the Gray Talons perched in the entryway of his aerie waiting for the approach of the delegation. He had asked for a report on the herd beasts, and the keepers had told him they would send a delegation. From the northlands somewhere, wherever it was they kept the young animals they had taken. So, let them send their delegation and be quick about it. Sliffisunda was hungry. They had brought him a new meat human just that afternoon, and he could hear it moving about in his feeding trough. It made him salivate disgustingly, and the drool leaked from his beak onto his feet, making them itch.

Rustling on the rampway. Wings at far aperture. So, they were assembling. Now they approached. Stillisas, Talker of the Fifth Degree. Two fours, Shimmipas and Slooshasill. He knew them, but then . . . he knew all Talkers. There were only some fifteen hundred of them in the whole world, divided among the Gray, Black, Blue, and Red Talons, the only four that had not been allowed to fall into ruin at time of hunger. Well.

"Uplifted One." Stillisas bowed, tail tucked tight to show honor. The others, one on either side, bowed as deeply.

"So," Stillisunda croaked. "Stillisas. You have something to report to me."

"About young thrassil and weehar, Uplifted One. We have six of each animal. One male, five females of each. They are carefully hidden. I have just come from place. By next summer they will be of age to breed. Slave humans say we must capture

17

other males, next year or year after, if herds are to grow strong. No more females are needed.''

"And how long, Stillisas, before we may dispense with shore-fish?" Many of the Thraish had adopted the Noor word for the human inhabitants of Northshore. It conveyed better than any other word his feelings for humans. Shore-fish. Offal. To be eaten only when one must.

"Realistically, Uplifted One, about fifteen years. And then only under most rigid controls. There is already some trouble with fliers assigned to me as help. Fliers must be prepared for restraint. Fliers must be sensible!"

Sliffisunda twitched in irritation, depositing shit to show the extent of his offendedness. "You may leave that to Sixth Degree, Stillisas. To those of us who no longer share meat.''

Stillisas flushed red around his beak. It was true. Stillisas did share meat with others, one wriggling body for four or five Fifth Degree Talkers instead of having one for each of them. Only the Sixth Degree could eat in dignified privacy, without the stink of others' saliva on their food. He should not have spoken so. He abased himself now, crouching in the female mating position while Sliffisunda flapped twice, accepting the subordination.

"If all goes well, there will be herd of some sixty to eighty thousand in thirteen years, Uplifted One. Weehar females often throw twins, according to *sloosil*, captured humans. At Thraish present numbers, fifty thousand animals will be needed annually to feed Thraish people. In fourteenth or fifteenth year, that many may be slaughtered.''

"Enough if *horgha sloos*, sharing meat,'' sneered Sliffisunda. He shat again. "And if Thraish do not share?''

"Many years longer, Uplifted One. One and one-half million animals each year would be needed if all are to have fresh meat, without sharing.''

"At Thraish present numbers.''

"Yes, Uplifted One.''

Sliffisunda hissed. There were only seventy some-odd thousand of the Thraish. Only fifteen hundred of them were Talkers. At one time there had been almost a million fliers. But it would take two hundred million weehar and thrassil slaughtered a year to support that many. Dared he dream of that?

Power. Power over many. What power was it to be Talker over this pitiful few? He dreamed of the ancient days when wings had filled the skies of Northshore, when wings had flown over the River, perhaps to the fabled lands of the south, in the days before the fear came to prevent their flying over the River at all. But why not? There had been that many once. If the fliers had stopped breeding when the Talkers suggested it, all would have been well. So, somehow the fliers must be brought under control. It would require some new laws, some new legends. The opaque film slid across his eyes as he connived. *An elite order of fliers to carry out will of Talkers. Breeding rights given as awards for service. Eggs destroyed if flier did not obey. Number carefully controlled. And yet, that number could be larger than at present. Much larger.*

He came to himself with a shudder. Those crouched before him pretended not to notice his abstraction, though he glared at them for a long moment, daring them to speak.

"Tell me of disturbance among the *sloosil*," he asked at last. "I hear there is disorder among humans, near Black Talons, in places called Thou-ne and Atter."

"It is same person as before," murmured Slooshasill. "Uplifted One sought same person in year past. Human called Pamra Don."

So. Human called Pamra Don. Human who emptied pits in Baris. "Rivermen!" Sliffisunda hissed. It took him a time to recognize that the three before him had not replied. Contradiction? "Talkers do not agree?"

"Pits are full," ventured Shimmipas. "Full. Fliers gorge."

"Not Rivermen." Sliffisunda almost crouched in amazement, catching himself only just in time. "Tell!"

"Procession." The Talker shrugged. "Many humans walking. At sunset Pamra Don speaks to them."

"Words?"

"Tells of Holy Sorters in sky. Tells of Protector of Man. Says humans must know truth. Says will tell Protector of Man."

"*Shimness*," snorted Sliffisunda. It was the name of a legendary Thraish flier, one who had always accomplished the opposite of what he tried. In common parlance it meant "crazy" or "inept," and it was in this sense Sliffisunda used it now.

"Pits are full," Shimmipas repeated stubbornly. "If procession goes on, more pits will be full."

Sliffisunda looked narrowly at the others. They dropped their eyes, appropriately wary.

"See with eyes," Sliffisunda said at last. It was all he could do. In the room behind him the chains in the meat trough rattled, reminding him of hunger. He drooled, dismissing the delegation, and returned to his own place. They had brought him a young one this time. Soft little breasts, tasty. Tasty rump. The Tears had softened it nicely, and the mindless eyes rolled wildly as he tore at the flesh. It screamed, and he shut his eyes, imagining a weehar in his claws. It, too, would scream. Why, then, did these human cries always annoy him? He tore the throat out, cutting off the sound, irritated beyond measure, no longer enjoying the taste.

He went to his spy hole and looked out upon the sky. The delegation was just leaving, three Talkers and three ordinary fliers, flying east along the River against a sky of lowering storm. *Foolish to fly in this weather. They could be blown out over water.* Sliffisunda postulated, not for the first time, where the fear had come from that prevented the Thraish from flying over water at all. *Survival,* he told himself. *During Thraish-human wars, many Thraish ate fish. Other Thraish killed them. Only Thraish who did not eat fish survived. Perhaps reason some Thraish did not eat fish then was fear of water.*

It was possible. Anything was possible. Even this thing in Thou-ne and Atter was possible.

He would go to Black Talons. He would see for himself.

• 4 •

The Council of Seven was gathered in the audience hall of the Chancery, the round council table set just outside the curtained niche where Lees Obol lay. By an exercise of willful delusion, one could imagine the Protector of Man as part of the gathering. The chair nearest the niche was empty. Perhaps the Protector occupied it spiritually. Or so, at least, Shavian Bossit amused himself by thinking.

As for the other six, they were present in reality. Tharius Don, fidgeting in his chair as though bitten by fleas. Gendra Mitiar, driving invisible creatures from the crevasses of her face with raking fingers. General Jondrigar, his pitted gray skin twitching in the jellied light. Koma Nepor, Ezasper Jorn. And, of course, Shavian himself. A second ring of chairs enclosed the first, occupied by functionaries and supporting members of the Chancery staff. So, Tharius had invited Bormas Tyle to attend, though Bormas was a supporter of Bossit's and Tharius knew it. Gendra had her majordomo, three district supervisors, and her Noor slave to lend her importance, though Jhilt squatted on the floor behind the second ring of chairs, conscious of her inferiority in this exalted gathering.

Koma Nepor and Ezasper Jorn supported one another. And Chiles Medman, the governor general of the Jarb Mendicants, was there—supporting whom? Shavian wondered. The Jarb Mendicants were tolerated by the Chancery, even used by the Chancery from time to time, but they could not be considered a part of the hierarchy. So what was Medman here for? Supporting some faction? There were three factions, at least. Tharius, the enigma, who would do the gods knew what if he were in power.

21

Gendra, advocate of increasing the elixir supply and the power
of the Chancery with it, and of increased repression. She enjoyed that. And Bossit himself, practical politician, who plotted
enslavement of the Thraish and no more of their bloody pre-
sumption. And old Obol, of course, behind the curtains, lying
in his bed like a bolster, barely breathing.

The general had no faction. His Jondarites stood around the
hall as though carved of black stone. The scales of their fishskin
jerkins gleamed in the torchlight; their high plumes nodded ebon
and scarlet. Their axes were of fragwood, toothed with obsidian. Only their spear points were of metal. From time to time
the general pivoted, surveying each of them as though to find
some evidence of slackness. He found none. The soldiers in the
audience hall were a picked troop. If any among them had been
capable of slackness, that tendency was long since conquered.

"Let's get to it," Shavian muttered at last, tapping his gavel
on the hollow block provided for it. It made a clucking, mina-
tory sound, and they all looked up, startled. "We are met today
to consider the matter of this 'crusade'—preached and led by
one Pamra Don. I might say, this person is the same Pamra Don
who caused us some difficulty a year or so ago." He stared at
Gendra, letting his silence accuse her.

She bridled. "You know we've set Laughers after her, Bossit.
Including that Awakener from Baris. Potipur knows he would
give his life to get his hands on her. His search must have been
out of phase. Evidently she has been behind him the whole
time."

"Behind him, or on the River, or hidden by Rivermen, what
matter which," Shavian sneered, annoyed with her. "The fact
is, she avoided him, him and all the others who were looking
for her. She came to surface in a town where no Laughers were,
a town from which your representative had only recently departed, a town ripe for ferment because of some damned statue
the superstitious natives had found in the River."

"The Jondarites should have stopped it," growled Gendra
through her teeth, glaring at the general. "Why have Jondarites
in all the towns otherwise. . . ."

"The Jondarites have no orders concerning crusades," said
the general in an expressionless voice. "They are ordered to put

down insurrection. There was no insurrection. They are ordered to punish disrespect of the Protector of Man. No disrespect is being shown, rather the contrary. They are told to quell heresy. There has been no heresy they could detect. The woman spoke of lies told to the Protector, of plots against the Protector.'' His eyes glowed red as he spoke. Who knew better than he of the lies that surrounded Lees Obol. Who knew better than he of the actuality of conspiracies. Scarcely a day went by that Jondrigar did not uncover a plot against the Protector. The mines had their share of Chancery conspirators he had unearthed.

"Enough," rapped Shavian. "Recriminations will not help us."

"Where is the crusade now?" Tharius Don asked, knowing the answer already but wishing to get the conversation away from those around the table and onto something less emotionally charged. He was rigid in his chair, yet twitchy, full of nervous energy. New adherents to the cause were being reported almost daily. For reasons he could not admit even to himself, he had been delaying the strike for months, and it could not be put off much longer. With every week that passed, the fear of discovery grew more imminent and compelling. In his heart he thanked the gods for the crusade, even though it had put Pamra Don at risk. It had drawn the Chancery's attention, for a time. "What's the name of the town?"

"A few days ago, she was in Chirubel," Bossit answered in a weary, irritated voice. He did not want the fliers stirred up any more than they were, and though this matter had not yet seemed to upset them, who knew what it might mean in the future. And with Lees Obol failing so fast . . . though he had only the Jondarites' word for that. No one else could get nearer to him than across the room. He shook his head and rasped, "A watchtower relay brought word. The pits in Chirubel are full. There was a great storm there, and many of her followers died."

"Died?" Tharius had not heard this.

"Old people, mostly. The great mob of them have no proper provision of food or shelter. The towns have been instructed to put their own surplus foodstuffs under guard, and the Jondarites have been ordered to prevent looting. So, there is a good deal of hunger. Which begets a regrettable tendency to eat off the land, as it were.''

"Violence?"

"Some. Fights break out. Mostly the deaths are old people dying of lung disease brought on by cold and hunger. Some younger ones, too, through accidents or violence. Some children and babies, the same.''

"So, the pits are full," Gendra mused. "Well, the fliers wanted the quota of bodies increased. They should be happy.''

"Ezasper Jorn," queried Bossit, "what mood are the fliers in?''

Jorn, huddled in his chair wrapped in three layers of blankets, blinked owlishly at them from his cavern of covers. "Voiceless as mulluks. They may not understand what's going on so far as a crusade is concerned. They don't seem curious, but then they've seen these little skirmishes before. We've had intertown wars; we've had rebellions put down by the Towers. That kind of thing has filled the worker pits from time to time over the centuries, so they might not think much of it. In short, they do not seem to be concerned. It's a local phenomenon, after all.''

"They'll scarcely change their reproductive habits on the basis of this temporary glut, which, at most, affects ten or a dozen towns." Koma Nepor was using his best pedant's voice, reserved for meetings such as this where chortle and giggle would not serve. "I agree with Jorn. They'll stuff themselves for a time; then the movement or whatever it is will fizzle out as these things always do; and they'll go back to normal.''

"Hungry normal," commented Gendra with a vast grinding of teeth. "In those towns, at least. With all the oldsters gone, the death rate will be low for a time." She reflected upon this. There was no reason the average lifespan should not be somewhat shortened. For parents, say, fifteen years after the birth of the last child. Or even twelve. For nonreproducers, earlier, unless they filled some important niche in the town economy. She would send word to the Towers. Fuller pits around the world would please the fliers, and if she could start currying the favor of the Talkers even now . . .

"So, the Talkers will tell the fliers to move across town lines and share." Shavian was heartily weary of the entire discussion.

"The point is not what the fliers will or will not do, though it may come to that later. The point is, what are we to do?"

Tharius stirred uneasily. He had been arguing the proper course of action with himself for days now, first yes, then no, both sides with reasons that seemed equally good. Now he must choose.

"Have her brought before me," he said firmly, nothing in his voice betraying either how little faith he had in his own recommendation or how deeply he was invested in its success. "Have her brought here. We know where she is. We do not need to wait for Laughers to find her. They were instructed, had they found her, to bring her here, so let us get on with it. Send word to the Jondarites in—what's the next town west, Gendra?" He knew perfectly well. Pamra Don had surfaced in a hotbed of the cause. The dozen towns west of Thou-ne were all rife with rebellion, and their Towers were full of Tharius's men.

"Rabishe-thorn," she responded absently, even as she peered at him with searching eyes. What was he up to? "Rabishe-thorn, then Falsenter. If we send word now, they should be able to intercept her in one or the other."

"Send word she is not to be harmed," Tharius went on in an emotionless voice, praying the quivering of his hands clasped in his lap could not be seen. "As Propagator of the Faith, I need to know everything she knows, and I won't get it if she's too frightened or abused or—forbid it—dosed with Tears. It will take months for her to reach us overland. During that time, the crusade will be effectively stopped since she will not be there to lead it." And this was the bait he hoped would bring them. Though he was thankful for the distraction she had provided, he wanted Pamra safe. With the day of the strike approaching, with his own inevitable mortality close at hand, he wanted to know she was well. I want to leave something behind me, he told himself, as though talking to Kessie. Kessie, I want to leave a posterity—silly though that may seem. I want it.

None of this was the business of the gathering. He pulled himself into focus and said again, "The crusade will dissipate while she is on her way here."

Gendra would have liked to find something wrong with his reasoning, but she couldn't. Gendra wanted Pamra Don killed, both because it was her nature to dispose of wild factors in that way and because some instinct told her it would be a very good idea. Pamra Don and Tharius Don. And the lady Kesseret. An odd group, that. An untrustworthy group. When she, Gendra, became Protector of Man, her first order to the Jondarites would be to do away with certain of the Chancery staff. And certain Tower Superiors. And others. She smiled, a rare, awful smile, showing her teeth.

Shavian, his eyes darting between them as though watching a game of net-ball, nodded in approval. The general glared but did not object. Why would he? He would sooner believe in plots than in no plots.

Ezasper Jorn and Koma Nepor simply watched, listened, said little. Having plans of their own, they didn't care about these things. And as for Lees Obol, his voice came to them plaintively from the curtained niche behind them. "Somebody get me my pot."

The Jondarites outside the niche moved to the Protector's service. Gendra stood up and ordered tea in a loud voice, at least partly to disguise the sounds emanating from the curtained room. There was general babble for a few moments, for which Tharius Don was very grateful. A Jondarite brought the Protector's teapot into the hall and set it upon a distant table, over a lamp, ready when the Protector asked for it. Behind it, the curtain glowed red as blood in the light of the warmer. Tharius found his eyes fixed on it, as though it were an omen.

He joined the babble, adding to it. When they came to order once again, his suggestion would be remembered, but his own connection with it would be somewhat overlaid by later conversation. A subtlety, he felt, but nonetheless acceptable. Even subtlety was welcome.

And yet, except for his own emotional needs, why bother? He had asked himself this more than once in the preceding days and weeks, ever since the first word of the crusade had come via seeker bird and watchtower. Servants of the cause had passed the word along, knowing Tharius Don would want to know. Mendicants of the Jarb had passed the word along, for Chiles Medman had asked them to. The Jarb Houses were firm supporters of the cause, to Tharius's amazement, though Chiles had explained why.

They had met by chance on one of the outer walls of the Chancery compound, brought there by a day of inviting sun and more than seasonable warmth, encountering one another quite by accident and remaining together because not to have done so would have looked suspiciously like avoidance or disaffection. Avoidance was as suspect as propinquity. There were always watchers. They had fallen into conversation, the first they had ever held outside the context of the conspiracy. They had spoken of the nature of fliers.

"Look at a flier through the smoke sometime, Tharius Don." Chiles Medman had held out his pipe, as though inviting Tharius to do it then and there. There were no fliers closer than Northshore that anyone had reported, though there might have been a dozen of them spying from the high peaks for all anyone knew.

"What do you see, Medman? A differing reality?" Tharius was touchy about this.

"We see them stripped of our own delusion, Tharius Don. Through the smoke they look like nothing much except winged incarnations of pride."

"Pride?" He had not really been surprised. Everyone knew how stiff-necked the Talkers were.

"They would be happy to see every human dead if they did not need us for food. They would rend all intelligence but their own. They kill, not out of bloodthirstiness, but out of pride. They have a word for sharing, *horgho*. It means 'to abase oneself.' Their phrase for sharing food, *horgha sloos,* means also 'dirtying oneself.' Did you know they call us *sloosil*?"

Tharius Don could not help snorting at the word. "No. What does it mean?"

"Meat. Simply that, in the plural. Meat. I met one of the Fourth Degree Talkers at a convocation once. His name was Slooshasill. 'Meat manager.' He was responsible for providing bodies for Fifth and Sixth Degree Talkers."

"So you don't think they respect us?"

Chiles Medman had shaken his head, lit his pipe, and considered Tharius through the smoke. "Why should they?"

"They've borrowed our craftsmen. They've learned writing

from us." Why shouldn't they? his hope had insisted. Why shouldn't they respect us?

"Well, they don't. If they didn't need us for food, they would slaughter us all tomorrow. They would not even keep us for slaves, because we remind them of *horgha sloos*. We remind them of abasement. They had an oral tradition and adequate housing for thousands of years before we came. Why do they need our writing? Or our craftsmen?"

Tharius had glanced around, assuring himself they were alone, then said softly, "And yet you support the cause? Not, seemingly, because you share my dream of sharing this world in dignity?"

"You know I don't, Tharius. I support the cause because I believe it's the only chance for humanity. The track we are on is madness. We're a flame-bird's nest, waiting for the spark. Our self-delusion grows greater every generation. We are moving farther and farther from our own truths."

"We have twenty-four hundred townships. Every township has about forty thousand people in it. There are almost a hundred million of us and fewer than a hundred thousand of them," Tharius had said in a mild voice.

"There are a hundred million blades of grass, and yet the weehar graze upon them all. The fliers could double their numbers in one year, Tharius. They're keeping their numbers down by breaking their eggs. They only incubate seven or eight a year in any given township, and they could incubate fifty or more. There's fifty percent mortality among the chicks. When the population grows too large, the Talkers kill the male chicks. If they could breed as they like, there would be a million of them in four or five years. All young. In fifteen years, when those came to breeding age, there would be hundreds of millions, all at once. The young may not be able to breed, but they can fight. They're carnivores, for gods' sake."

"Necrovores, rather."

"Not the Talkers. And none of the Thraish like eating dead meat."

"How do you know all this about them? Their numbers? Their habits?"

"We look, Tharius. We listen. We pay kids to climb rocks

and spy on their nests. We send spies into Talons and listen to what they say."

"In contravention of the Covenant?"

"Oh, shit, Tharius. Come off it. Don't go all pompous on me. Who else is going to do it? Who except the Jarb Mendicants could be trusted to do it?"

Tharius's face had reddened. "I get sick, sometimes, of your assumptions of omniscience, Medman. You see everything through the smoke, and that's supposed to be reality. It is not necessarily my reality, which I tend to believe has an equal right to exist!"

"We've never said it was the only reality," Medman had said, putting away his pipe. "We've only said we see without delusion. Without preconception. Without prejudice. The Jarb pipe does that for us. For some of us."

"But only for you madmen." It was unkind, and Tharius had repented of it at once.

"Yes." Softly. "Yes, Tharius Don. Only for us madmen. The smoke only works for those of us who are capable of alternate visions." Chiles Medman had left him then, a little angry, only to return, speaking in a vehement whisper.

"Tharius Don, you have not been among the people of Northshore for a hundred years. When I am not here in the Chancery—which I am not, most times—I see them every day. I see those who are told to believe in Potipur and Abricor and Viranel. Potipur the Talker. Abricor the young male Thraish. Viranel the female Thraish. Three gods, Tharius Don, made in the likeness of their creators—the Thraish. Who eat humans. And I see mankind trying to believe in that. . . .

"I see them trying valiantly to believe in the Sorters. Virtually every human knows in his heart it's a lie. They have seen the workers. You think boys don't sneak into the pits and look at the dead ones, just on a dare? You think people don't follow the Awakeners out to the pits sometimes, spying on them? You think people don't know? Aren't aware? Even those who believe the most, you think they don't suspect, down deep, that something is awry, that they are being fed on lies?"

"The Awakeners tell us most people believe," Tharius had answered. It was lame, and he'd known it.

"The Awakeners tell you most people believe, and they tell the people the Holy Sorters exist, and they tell their colleagues one thing and their Superiors something else. I only knew one Awakener in all my years who would tell the truth. He's a man named Haranjus Pandel, from Thou-ne. He's a cynic, Tharius, and an honest man.

"But as for the rest of Northshore, it's a tinder pile, as I said. People have no hope for the future. They are ready to immolate themselves if it would hatch that hope. We have more Jarb Houses now than we had a hundred years ago, and we need twice as many. People see the workers shambling around, and something—perhaps the way one of them moves or the tilt of a head—makes them think maybe Mother is under that wrapper, or Daddy, or sister or daughter or son. Or they think of themselves there, not peacefully laid away but staggering around, stinking, hated by everyone. Then madness, Tharius Don. Madness. And only the pipe gives them any hope then."

"Your hallucinogenic pipe." Tharius had smiled a little bitterly.

"The inverse of that," Chiles Medman had replied. "An inverse hallucinogenic, Tharius Don. A pipe that lets them see the dead for what they are, and the moons for what they are, and the fliers for what they are, so that they need not struggle to believe what their eyes and noses tell them is ridiculous. It is the struggle to believe which maddens, Tharius Don. The wildest of the Jarb House Mendicants come from the most devout homes. . . ."

Something had happened then to interrupt their conversation, and Tharius had not talked with him since except for the odd word at ceremonial events. Still, and despite Tharius's own rudeness on that occasion, he counted on Medman's support. When the time came.

"If the time comes," he said to himself bitterly. "If the time comes." The strike was as prepared at this moment as it would ever be. He was making excuses these days to delay it as he had been for months. He knew it. He didn't know why. "When the time comes," he said again, not convincing himself.

The council members resumed their places, now with tea steaming before them. The niche was silent. Shavian rubbed his forehead, reminding himself. "Ah, what were we saying? Yes. Pamra Don to be summoned to the Chancery. Any comment?"

Chiles Medman rose, was noticed, said, "I would support a meeting with Pamra Don here in the Chancery. The fact that this crusade has moved the people with such fervor indicates a level of dissatisfaction among them we should be aware of. For our own sakes, as well as theirs." He sat down again, having started them off like hunting birds after a swig-bug, darting here and there.

"Dissatisfaction," bellowed Gendra Mitiar. "I'll give them dissatisfaction!"

"Hush," Bossit demanded. "The governor general of the Jarb Mendicants has not said there is an insurrection. He has said 'dissatisfaction,' and I agree we should know of any such. What do you hear of dissatisfaction, Mendicant?"

"Murmurings," Chiles replied, as though indifferent. "The 'disappearances' seem more noticed of late. Taken more account of."

"They have been no more than usual," Gendra said stiffly. "About two a month from each township. Mostly old people."

"They used to be mostly old people." Chiles nodded. "Of late, there have been many young ones. When old people vanish, it is a short wonder. When young ones go, people grieve longer. And talk longer."

"The Towers have strict orders . . ." She fell silent, suddenly suspicious. Indeed, the Towers had very strict orders concerning those recruited for Talker meat. And yet, if the Talkers offered . . . if the Talkers offered a sufficient reward directly to the Superior of a Tower, might not that Superior be bought? The idea was shocking, and terrible and inevitable. Her eyes narrowed.

"Do you allege malfeasance?" she challenged Chiles Medman. "If so, where? What Tower?"

He shook his head, took his pipe from his pocket, and lit it to peer at her through the smoke. What he saw evidently reassured him, for he smiled. "I have no knowledge, Dame Marshal of the Towers. Only murmurings. Which is why I suggest bringing Pamra Don to the Chancery. Let us ask her."

Gendra subsided, her teeth grinding. Shavian looked from

one to the other of them, awaiting further comment. Koma Nepor assented, Ezasper Jorn nodded. The general merely pivoted, keeping his eye on his men. "No objection to that?" Shavian asked. "Then let it be done."

Now, Tharius thought to himself, let us send them off yet again in some other direction. "Has any word come from the herdsmen? When last I spoke with you, Jorn, you said it was thought that fliers had made off with young weehar and thrassil. Is it still assumed that fliers have stolen a breeding stock? And did I hear there were herdsmen missing as well?"

Shavian reddened with chagrin. He could not fault the question, but it reflected upon his own purview. As Maintainer of the Household, the household herds were his responsibility. "Yes," he grated. "There are herdsmen missing as well. Three of them, and among them the best men we had for understanding of the beasts."

Tharius mused over this, looked up to catch Chiles's eye upon him through a haze of smoke. "What do you see, Mendicant?" he asked.

"Herds," the Jarbman replied. "Stretching over the steppes of the Noor, in their millions."

Koma Nepor snorted. "From ten beasts? Hardly likely, Governor. The Talkers may guard a small herd. They will not be able to keep the fliers from depredations upon a large one. Eh, Jorn? Am I right?"

Ezasper Jorn nodded from his cocoon. "Likely. They are voracious beasts, the fliers. Not sensible of much, according to the Talkers. I have been told that before the time of Thoulia they were warned to curtail their breeding and yet ignored the warnings until all the beasts were gone. What sensible beast would outbreed its own foodstock?"

"And yet," brooded the Mendicant, "I see herds."

"And Noor?" asked the general, suddenly interested. "If there will be herds, where are the Noor?"

The Mendicant put out his pipe, shaking his head. "I see no Noor, General Jondrigar. None move upon the steppes in my vision. But then, who is to say when my vision will come true? In a thousand years, perhaps? Or ten times that."

Tharius Don cleared his throat. "It would be wise, General,

to ask your balloon scouts to keep their eyes open for weehar
and thrassil. If they are found upon the steppes, they should be
slaughtered, at once. And I suppose a guard has been set upon
the herds here behind the Teeth?''

Shavian gnawed his cheek, asserting to this without answering. Did the man think him a complete fool? Of course a guard
had been set. Not only upon the household herds, but upon
every herd in the northlands. All were being driven here, close
by, where they could be watched.

"Have we anything more?" he asked, hoping fervently that
what had already been discussed was enough.

"Hearing none," he said, tapping the gavel perfunctorily
once more, "we are adjourned."

"Somebody," came a plaintive voice from behind the curtain. "Bring me my tea." The Jondarite across the room picked
up the pot he had placed there and brought it forward. Ceremo-
niously, he entered upon service to Lees Obol.

They left the audience hall to go their various ways. Gendra
Mitiar took herself off to the archives to harass old Glamdrul
Feynt. The master of the files had not been diligent. When the
time came, soon, she wanted proof or something that looked
like proof, some reason for doing away with Tharius Don.
Self-righteous prig! Staring at her as though she were less than
nothing! She would show him who was nothing. Him, and his
pretty cousin Kesseret, and his descendent, too, that Pamra
Don. . . .

Shavian Bossit went to his own suite and sent a messenger to
Koma Nepor. It was time to talk seriously about what could be
done to keep Talkers alive, but passive, while the elixir was
made from their blood—not in these piddling quantities, but by
the gallon! His spies told him Koma had been experimenting
with the blight. Perhaps . . . He grinned in anticipation, a
wicked mouse grin, then sat himself down to wait. . . .

And Tharius Don took himself to the tower above his own
quarters in the palace and brooded. He felt caught in a wrinkle
in time, a place in which time was both too long and too short.
Too short to do all his raging imagination told him he should
have done long since; too long to wait, too long a time in which

too many obstacles might be thrust up before the cause to inhibit
the last great rebellion. . . .

"Rebellion," he whispered to himself. "Since you were only
a child, Tharius Don, you have dreamed of rebellion." And yet,
what else could he have been?

He could have been nothing else, born into the family Don
with its strong tendencies toward both repression and ambition.
There had been many old people in the household. His mother's
parents, the Stifes. His father's parents, the Dons. His own
parents. An aunt. Seven of them, all artist caste. And against
the seven of them, only Tharius and an adored, biddable younger sister who was happy to do whatever anyone said, at any
time.

And they did say. Continually; contradictorily; adamantly.
The Stifes were at knife's point with the Dons. The Stifes were
clawing away at one another. The Dons elder were at the throats
of the Dons junior, and the alliances among the seven swung
and shifted, day to day. There was only one thing that could be
depended upon, and that was that young Tharius would be both
the weapon they used on one another and the battleground over
which they fought. He was petted, praised, whipped, abused,
slapped, ignored, only to be petted once more. He was of their
nature, if not of their convictions, and at about age nine or
ten—he could not remember the exact year, or even the incident
that had provoked it—he had repudiated them all. He remembered that well, himself rigid against the door of the cubby in
the attic which was his own, his face contorted as he stared into
his own eyes in the mirror across the room, his utter acceptance
of his own words as he said, "I renounce you all. All of you.
From now on, you can fight each other, but you will not use
me." Or perhaps those words had only come later, after he had
had time to think about it. The renunciation, though, that had
happened, just as he remembered it.

And from that time he was gone. An occasional presence. A
bland, uninteresting person, hearing nothing, repeating nothing,
unusable as a weapon because he did or said nothing anyone
could use or repeat to stir up enmity or support. Useless as a
battleground because he did not seem to care. Not about anything at all.

As for Tharius, he did not care about them anymore. He had discovered books.

There had always been books, of course. There always were books, in the shops. Holy books. Accepted books. Bland histories in which there was never any violence or deviation of opinion. Devotional books in which there were never any doubts. Even storybooks, for children, in which obedient boys and girls obeyed their elders, learned their lessons, and became good, obedient citizens of their towns.

Life wasn't like that. Looking around him, Tharius saw hatred and violence, pain and dying. He saw workers. Awakeners. Grim, stinking fliers in the bone pits. Men and women vanishing, as though swallowed by evil spirits. None of that was in the books. Not the accepted books.

But there were other books.

A few days before Tharius's repudiation of his kin, the poultry-monger's shop across the alley was raided by the Tower. A great clatter of Awakeners and priests of Potipur came raging into the place, all blue in the face with their mirrors jagging light into corners. Tharius Don was on the roof above the alley when it happened, hiding from his grandmother Stife. There was noise, doors slamming, some shouting, some screaming, people moving around in the attics opposite him, barely seen through the filthy glass. Then the Awakeners burst through the back door and began throwing books into a pile. They were screaming threats at the poultry-monger and his wife, both of whom were protesting that they had only bought the house a year ago, that they'd never looked into the attic, that they didn't know the books were there. It was likely enough true. Tharius had never seen lights in the windows opposite his own.

"It's only that saves your life for you now, poulterer," snarled an Awakener. "That and the dust on these volumes. Don't touch them. There'll be a wagon here in an hour or so to haul them away for burning."

They left a blue-faced priest of Potipur at the head of the alley to keep watch, but he got bored with the waiting and fell asleep. Most priests were fat face-stuffers anyhow, half-asleep on their feet a good part of the time. Tharius had stared down at the pile of books, silent as a stalking stilt-lizard, judging how many of them he might take away and how long he had. His own attic room was at the top of a drainpipe, and getting them back would be a difficulty. . . .

Inspiration struck him, all at once. He found a sack, put all his own books in it, hung it over his shoulder, and climbed down the protruding drainpipe, his favorite road to freedom. The exchange was quick—his dull books for the ones in the alley—and he was back up the drainpipe again, sweating and hauling for all he was worth, hearing the creak of the wagon wheels even as he slid over the parapet onto the roof beside his own window.

When the wagon arrived, the books were loaded by some flunky who did not even look at them. From the roof, Tharius watched him as he took them down to the stone wharf at the Riverside and burned them. Everyone pretended not to notice, even one old man who was choked by the smoke and had to act as though it were from something else. So. There were books, and books. The forbidden books went on the shelf in the corner, just where the others had been. No one ever came up here except Grandmother Stife, once a month or so, to peek in the door and then shout at him to sweep the place out.

Tharius was hooked, confirmed in rebellion. The books were real ones. Stories of people as they were. A history of Northshore. A little book about the arrival, called *When We Came*. Tharius had been taught certain things as true, but they had always seemed senseless. Now, suddenly they began to connect.

Time went. Tharius became a book collector. Hidden in the attics of the Don home was a collection that would have condemned all the family to death had an Awakener got wind of it. Tharius found them in other attics, entering from the roofs, prowling dusty spaces by lantern light, old, shut-up places where no one came anymore but where books were sometimes found. In corners. Under floorboards. He found them in houses where people died, before the Awakeners or the kinfolk came to take inventory. He found them in the rag man's yard, buried at the bottom of stacks of old clothes. Fragments more often than whole volumes, but of whole volumes, three or four a year, perhaps. By the time he was eighteen and subject to the procreation laws, he had almost thirty of them.

Which was bad enough in itself. Worse, so far as Tharius was concerned, was the fact that in these thirty books were references to hundreds of others. Somewhere on Northshore there were, or had been, more!

Sometimes late at night, when the moons lit the alleyway, Tharius Don had a waking dream of all those books. More and more. All the answers to all the questions anyone had ever asked would be there in the books.

And the books, he was convinced, were in the Towers. Why else would the Awakeners be so agitated about books, if it were not some kind of secret knowledge only they were supposed to have? Knowledge about how things really were. How things used to be. How they had been in some other place before humans had come here.

Influenced by a bit too much wine, Tharius broached that subject at dinner one night, hearing the words fall into a horrified silence.

"Before what?" his father snarled. "Before what?"

"Before humans came to Northshore," Tharius stuttered.

"Where did you get an ugly idea like that?"

"I just—I just thought we must have come from somewhere else, you know. Because there are so many things we can't eat." Even in his half-drunken surprise at the words that had come from his own mouth, he was wary enough not to mention the books. "It seemed obvious. . . ."

He was sent from the table, in disgrace. Doctrine was clear on that point. Humans had always lived on Northshore and had always been governed by the gods. His bibulous remark was occasion for a loud, screaming battle among the Dons and the Stifes. Two days later when he returned home from a foray, he found a young woman named Shreeley at the table. He had seen her before. Not often. She was the daughter of a friend of his father's, a pamet merchant from the other side of Baris.

"Your wife-to-be," his father said in a stiff, unrelenting voice. "You have had entirely too much time on your hands to sit around dreaming up obscenities."

Tharius Don was more amused than anything else. The girl wasn't bad looking; she had a sweet, rounded body, and Tharius

Don had had some experience with sweet, rounded bodies. It would not be a bad thing to have one of his own to play with.

What he had not foreseen was the sudden loss of privacy. No more attic room. He had only time to hide the books before all his belongings were swept up and reinstalled in a room two stories below, one he would share. And after that, he found it difficult to be alone for a moment.

Shreeley made sure of that. She slept with him. She rose with him in the morning and walked with him to the job his grand-parents Stife had obtained for him. "You show none of the family talent for art, Tharius Don," said Stife grandfather. "We have apprenticed you, therefore, to Shreeley's father, the pamet merchant."

"I thought it was custom for young people to choose their own professions," Tharius complained.

"Had you done so in your fifteenth or sixteenth year, as is also customary, we would have acceded to your choice, Tharius Don. Since you did not do so, you lost that opportunity."

Shreeley came to walk home with him after work. She ate with him. She sat with him or walked with him after dinner. Went to bed with him. He tried to read one of his books only once, but Shreeley caught him at it. "Read to me," she begged sweetly. "Read to me, Tharius Don." He made up something about Thoulia, and she fell asleep while he was reciting. He hid the book away, sweat standing on his brow.

Still, for a time it was not impossible. Sex was more than merely amusing. Tharius had a great deal of imagination about sex, and Shreeley was compliant. Until she became pregnant, at which time everything stopped.

"No," she said. "It might hurt the baby."

"It won't hurt the baby. And you like it."

"I don't like it. I only did it to get pregnant and comply with the laws, Tharius Don. I hope you don't think I *enjoyed* all that heaving about."

"Shreeley's father says you have been neglecting your du-ties," his father admonished. "With a baby on the way, you'd better start attending to business."

It was that night Tharius Don went to the Tower of Baris and begged admittance as a novice. When the family learned of it, they never spoke of him again. When Tharius's son was born, they named him Birald. When Tharius heard of it he uttered a heartfelt wish for the boy's sanity, but without much hope considering that he, Tharius, might be losing his own.

He had sacrificed everything in hope of books, and there were no books in the Tower except those of a shameless falsity and unmitigated dullness. There were no books, and there was no leaving the Tower. For a time Tharius considered killing himself, but he could not think of any foolproof way to do it. And as time wore on, one factor of Tower existence saved him—the rigid, unvarying discipline which allowed much time for thought. Tharius was in the habit of thought. And as the months wore away, he began to find links in the behavior and beliefs of the Awakeners to things he knew from books.

And he saw early on a thing that many in that place never saw. He saw that the seniors did not believe what the juniors were told to believe.

It was evident, once the first piece fell into place. There was knowledge here. Not among the juniors. Not taught to the juniors. Withheld from them, rather. Given to others, later on.

With a grim persistence that would have astonished all factions among the warring Stifes and Dons, he persevered. Years went by. He achieved senior status, learned what he could, learned there was more yet that could be learned, in the Chancery!

He was thirty-eight, a cynical member of the trusted circle that actually ran the Tower of Baris, and a personal friend of the Superior, when he was responsible, all unwitting, for bringing Kesseret to the Tower.

One of his duties was the enforcement of the procreation laws. Women over the age of eighteen who were not readying for marriage or were not already mothers, whether married or no, came under his jurisdiction. A wealthy man—whose wealth did not exceed his age, decrepitude, or hideous ugliness—presented a petition together with a generous gift to the Tower. Tharius Don signed it as a matter of course. It ordered the nineteen-year-old woman named Kesseret to marry the merchant at once or present herself to the Tower as a novice. It was routine. Rarely did anyone come into the Tower as a result. Sometimes the one under orders made a generous gift and the petition was revoked for a time. Sometimes not. It was simply routine.

Except in this instance. Kessie had been unable to buy herself free. She had been unwilling to submit. She came to the Tower.

To the Tower, to Tharius Don, who asked for and received mentorship in her case. She was older than most novices, as he had been. It was harder for her than for most, as it had been for him. She rejected much of what she was taught, as he had done.

So he told her the truth. From the beginning. Comforting her, urging her, meeting her in quiet places away from the Tower, keeping her away from worker duty as much as possible. And one day she had said, "You can protect me all you like, Tharius Don. That doesn't make it right, what we do."

He had agreed. And from that the cause had been born. Not right away, not all at once. They did not know enough yet.

"I'm told the answers are at the Chancery," he said. "I'll have to get there."

"How long?"

He shrugged. "Twenty years, minimum, I should think. I'm in line to be Superior when Filch dies or moves up. If they don't give him the elixir pretty soon, there'll be no question about his moving up. Say five years there, either way. Then I have to make some kind of reputation for myself. In something."

"Something safe," she whispered. "Apologetics, Tharius. The apologetics they feed us juniors is awful. It's dull. It's ugly. It wouldn't convince a swig-bug. Make your reputation in defense of the faith, Tharius. In scholarship. It takes only cleverness and a way with words. It's all mockery, all lies, but we can do it. I'll help you."

And she had helped him, and he her. They had been lovers for twenty years, sometimes impassioned, never less than fond. Kessie was forty when she took Tharius's place as Superior of the Tower in Baris and he moved on to the Chancery. They had not known then that it was the last time they would make love to one another. Once at the Chancery, Tharius had advanced rapidly. He had been given the elixir. And after that was no passion, only the remembrance of their coupling, their ecstasy, though that remembrance had been full of nostalgic longing.

The books he had sought were at the Chancery. The palace

was full of books, very old books. No one cared except Tharius. He read his way through centuries of books. Of all those at the Chancery, only Tharius knew the truth of the Thraish-human wars in all their bloody, vicious details. He rebelled against that viciousness. Only Tharius knew of the Treeci and dreamed of that gentle race—for so he interpreted what he read—as an answer not only for the Thraish, but for man. From these books came the cause, and in that long, long remembrance the cause had grown.

And now, now he had delayed long enough, and it must all soon come to pass. He leaned his face into his cupped hands and evoked the memory of Kessie. Kessie as he had seen her last, carried away over Split River Pass, smiling bravely back at him. Her life had been given to this thing. This secret thing. His own had been given, also.

For the two of them there could be no future, but perhaps he could save Pamra Don for some better fate. Perhaps she could live the life he and Kessie had not been able to live. Perhaps she could find someone to love; perhaps she could bear children as he and Kessie had never been allowed to do.

With such simple hopes he comforted himself, believing them. He would give up everything, the world itself, for this cause. But even while doing that, he would try to save Pamra Don.

• 5 •

Midday in the Temple on the first day of first summer, the year's beginning. In the wide, carved sand urns, sticks of incense burn away into curling smoke, gray-white wraiths, rising into the high vaults of blackened stone. On the floor the murmuring multitude shifts from foot to foot with a susurrus of leather upon rock. All is muted, the color leached away, all sharpness of sound reduced to this soft, formless whisper which runs from side to side of the Temple, like liquid sloshing in a bowl. "Truth," it says, "Light," lapping at the walls of the place like surf, returning again and again, tireless as water.

A pale blur of faces, staring eyes, gaped mouths, nostrils wide for the heaving, phthisic breath, indrawn by bodies that have forgotten to breathe for a time. Wonder piled on wonder as the crusaders parade with their blood-bright banners to the rumble-roar of the drums, rhythmless as thunder, rhymeless as pulse. Oh, Peasimy Flot has an eye for spectacle and an ear for the wry, discordant sound to set teeth on edge and wrench the ears away from ordinary concerns. See what drums he has manufactured from kettles and hides, what robes he has managed to scrounge from what can be begged or stolen; see what gilded crowns and jeweled scepters he has set in the followers' hands to confound and amaze the multitudes. Glass and shoddy may glitter with the best in the dim Temple light, as they do now, among the hundreds half-drunk on fragrant smoke.

And Peasimy himself, now mounting the steps of the Temple to stand as he always stands, as Pamra always stood, before the carved moon faces, turning in his high coronal and rich-appearing vestments to call into that breathing silence.

42

"Thou shalt follow no creature except the Bearer of Light,"
he calls in his little piping voice, from the Temple stairs in the
twentieth town west of Rabishe-thorn. "Thou shalt not earn
merit except by crusade. Thou shalt not give to the Temple and
the Tower what belongs to the Protector of Man."

His voice is shrill, the high treble sound of a whistle. It cuts
through the crowd murmur like a knife, leaving a throbbing
wound of uncertainty behind. The voice is not of a piece with
the display. They had expected other than this.

"Where is she?" someone brays in a trumpet voice. "Where
is the Light Bearer?" They have heard of her. Every township
on this quadrant of Northshore has heard of her, and though the
entertainment thus far has been better than expected, some few
are irritated that she has not come herself, that this pumped-up
little creature has come in her stead.

"Gone to the Protector of Man," Peasimy replies, irritated to
be so interrupted. "Long ago. With many following after her to
testify to truth." He pauses, trying to remember his place in the
usual speech, counting the thou-shalts in his head. "And those
who have gone will be first in her kingdom, and those who
come later will be last, but even to the last will gifts be given
which are greater than any gifts these devils have ever pretended
to give." His gesture at the carved moon faces is almost like
Pamra Don's gesture, and these words are almost exactly something Pamra Don has said. Most of what Peasimy says is almost
what Pamra has said. She has never referred to "her kingdom,"
though she has spoken of the kingdom of man. Peasimy points
to the carved moon faces, flier faces, and waits until the babble
dies down.

"Thou shalt not revere the Awakeners," says Peasimy. "Thou
shalt not walk in darkness."

"What does he mean?" a rugged, doubtful man grumbles to
one of the followers. "What does he mean about walking in
darkness?"

"It's symbolic," whispers the follower. "At night, when the
lanterns are lit, you must walk in the patches of light as though
splashing them into the darkness. It's symbolic of the Light
Bearer."

"What the hell good does it do?" the doubter persists.

"It's pious," snarls the other. "The Light Bearer does it. To concentrate her mind on the truth." So Peasimy has said, and they have had no reason to doubt him. Perhaps. Or maybe what Peasimy said was that the Bearer of Truth had been found in that way. The follower can't remember. It doesn't matter.

"Oh." The other subsides, twitching. None of this sounds like good sense to him, and he wonders what all the fuss has been about.

"Thou shalt love the Protector of Man with all thy heart," Peasimy shouts. "Thou shalt keep him safe from lies."

"That's what the Light Bearer is going to the Chancery for," the follower instructs. "To advise Lees Obol of the lies which are done in his name." The doubter grunts, unconvinced, though in this case the follower has quoted correctly.

"Thou shalt give generously to the followers of truth, in order that the world may be enlightened," Peasimy goes on, ticking the commandments off on his fingers. Sometimes he remembers ten, sometimes more than that. Tonight the crowd is restive, he will only give them ten. "Thou shalt not withhold food from those on crusade." He is hungry, very tired, and his throat is sore from all the shouting. Tomorrow they will go on to a new town, and his voice can rest. He takes a deep breath. "Thou shalt not make fuk-fuk."

An embarrassed titter runs through the Temple, a break of laughter, like light coming suddenly through clouds to astonish those beneath with a benison of gold. "What the hell?" the doubter growls, doubled with laughter. "Baby talk. What the hell!"

"The Mother of Truth commands it," the follower says through gritted teeth, embarrassed himself by the word Peasimy always uses and weary of having to explain it. "If you want to be really Sorted Out, you don't do *that*."

"Well, if we didn't do *that*, there wouldn't be any of us to be Sorted Out." The man laughs in genuine amusement. "Where the hell does he think babies come from, pamet pods?"

In which he is closer than he knows to Peasimy's true belief. The widow Flot had never found it necessary to tell Peasimy other than the pleasant myths of childhood, and Peasimy, who has discovered the facts beneath other myths by following and spying through windows, has never found the facts of this one. He has never seen a baby born. He would not believe the connection between that and the other were he told. Pamra Don, Mother of Truth, has said the strange, frightening act he has so often observed through windows at night is a mistake. It is therefore a perversion. A darkness.

The follower, elderly enough to have forgotten the urgencies of passion and much puffed up by his new position as expositor of truth, defends the revealed word. "There's a lot more fucking going on than necessary for babies. That's what the Light Bearer means. The Mother of Truth says we don't do it, so we don't do it. Not and be a follower of hers."

The questioner laughs himself out of the Temple, his healthily libidinous nature rejecting all of it. But in the vast echoing hall, there are others to whom the ideal of abstinence appeals. There are disenchanted wives who can do well without a duty that seems to consist mostly of discomfort, grunting, and sweat. There are husbands who consider it an onerous and sometimes almost impossible performance which seems to be demanded—in pursuance of the procreation laws—too frequently and at inconvenient times. There are young ones, drawn to a life of holiness like moths to a flame, easily willing to give up something they know nothing of. There are spinsters being forced into marriage or pregnancy by the procreation laws, and men being forced into unwanted associations by the same. There are those who resent the Tower saying yes and therefore choose to follow the Bearer saying no. For every lustful lover there is at least one juiceless stick, anxious to have his lack made into virtue. Thus, in the departing footprints of each mocker, a follower rises up, and Peasimy Flot leads them on to the next city west while a trickle of the formerly recruited ones move northward, then west, where Pamra Don has gone. The crusade has steadily been approaching Vobil-dil-go, the township through which Split River runs, the most direct route from Northshore to the Chancery.

"How long do we carry the word before we follow the Bearer?" one of the followers asks Peasimy. He is one of the dozen or so who have accumulated the status of leaders in the crusade, those to whom Peasimy habitually talks, those who know what is going on.

"Pretty soon now," Peasimy answers him, though somewhat doubtfully. "Pretty soon now I'll take some and go after the Bearer, and you must take some and go on." He has dreamed this. The Bearer had gone a way, then turned north. Now Peasimy must go a way and then turn north. And so on, and on, like a chain. As he says it, he begins to like the idea. "A chain," he repeats. "Like a chain. One, then another one, then another one."

The follower to whom Peasimy speaks is an excellent speaker who has often itched to take Peasimy's place upon the Temple stairs. He has a loud, mellifluous voice, and, since he finds both women and sex utterly repugnant, he has wholly adopted Peasimy's doctrine. He will have sense enough not to speak of his repugnance directly to the multitudes, as he knows he must include women among his followers if he is to acquire the kind of power—and service—he desires. In his satisfaction at considering this not-so-distant future, he forgets to answer Peasimy's suggestion.

"You will do it if I tell you," Peasimy asserts, interpreting the man's silence as unwillingness. "Yes, you will."

"If the Bearer of Light commands," the man says, silently exulting. "When you leave us, how will you know which way to go?"

"North, until we see the mountains. Great tall mountains," Peasimy replies proudly. The Jondarites had told him that, when they had taken Pamra Don away. Now he quotes them in a singsong voice, certain of the way he will go. "Keep the mountains on the right." He pats the arm on which he wears his glove. That is his right arm, Widow Flot had told him. "The arm with the glove is your right arm, Peasimy. You eat with your right hand." So he pats it now, quite sure. "Keep the mountains on the right. Until we come to a big river with some high places with flat tops. That's Split River Pass, where we go through, to the Chancery."

Joal makes note of it. He has no plans to lead the crusade anywhere but where he wants it to go, and at the moment that does not include going anywhere near to the Chancery.

• 6 •

Sometimes I wonder what I'm doing when I write these things down. I read what I wrote about what happened, and then I try to remember what happened, and sometimes I can't remember whether I'm remembering what really happened or only what I wrote about it. The words have a way of doing things on their own. They sneak around and say things I'm not sure are real.

I wrote something the other day about an order of food that came in from the east, and later I heard Taj Noteen talking with Medoor Babji about it as though it had been some other thing entirely. I always figured me and the men saw things pretty much the same way, but now there's others here who seem to look at this world as though they had eyes different from mine. If I hadn't written it down, I wouldn't have thought again about it, figuring I'd just missed something about it at the time. But I did write it down, and what I wrote wasn't what the Noor were saying at all.

Of course, I'm only an ignorant boatman. Maybe priests and Awakeners are taught to do it better, but words written down seem to me could be very dangerous things.

From Thrasne's book

While the *Gift* and the Noor waited for stores, Thrasne passed the time by doing things to the *Gift*. A new railing on the steering deck. A small cabin below for himself since the Melancholics would be using his house. Reinforcement between the ribs in the fore and aft holds. And, though it cost him much thought and argument with himself, a tall mast mounted on the main deck, just behind the owner-

47

house. This was decided soon after Obers-rom hired three new men who knew about sail.

"Used to run back and forth among the islands out there," one of them told Thrasne. "There's chains of islands out there, out of sight of Northshore, farther out than the shore boats go, Owner."

"You ran *up*-River?" Thrasne asked in astonishment.

"Well—what I'd say about that would depend who I was talkin' to."

And thus did Thrasne owner learn of whole tribes of boatmen who paid the tides no more attention than they paid the little pink clouds of sunset.

"You don't know how the tide works as far out as you plan to go, Thrasne owner," the man said. "You don't know and I don't know. You'll never row this flat bottom across World River, that's for sure, and I'm suggestin' it would be a good idea to have another way to move it."

Thrasne regarded the mast with a good deal of suspicion, but he could not argue with what the man said. They surely couldn't row the *Gift* across the World River.

By the time they were ready to depart, Pamra had been gone for months. Still, word of her came to Thou-ne. The Towers evidently had a way of getting information, and Haranjus Pandel had conveyed certain information to the widow Flot, who conveyed it to half the town.

"She was in Chirubel," Thrasne said to Medoor Babji in a carefully unemotional tone. "There were thousands and thousands following her when she got there. I wonder how all those people are fed?" He wondered how Pamra herself was fed, but he did not mention it. Thoughts of her were like a wound which he knew could not heal unless he quit picking at it.

"Way I hear," said Medoor, "some aren't fed. Many dead, Thrasne. The worker pits in the towns between here and Chirubel are full. Some of the Towers are recruiting extra Awakeners, so I hear it."

"I'll bet the old bone eaters love that," Thrasne said, turning his eyes to the wide wings that circled above the town.

"Well," she said abstractedly, watching his face, "if there

are more dead people, there could be more fliers hatched, couldn't there? Probably the fliers like that idea.''

"You're not saying they think?'' Thrasne objected. "You mean more of their little ones would survive, that's all.''

"Did you ever hear of fliers who can talk?'' she asked.

And he, driven into memory, remembered a time when old Blint had said something very much like that. Just before he died. He mentioned it to her, wondering.

"Talk to the Rivermen sometime, Thrasne. They know things.''

It was all she would say at the time, but it gave him something else to concern himself about. What was Pamra doing? Hadn't that Neff been a flier—well, sort of? Was she doing the will of the fliers? Without even knowing it!

These concerns were driven away in the flurry of departure.

It was almost at the end of first summer. The mists and breezes of autumn were beginning. Alternate days were chill and windy, and it was on one such that the *Gift* left the docks at Thou-ne. So far as the standabouts were concerned, the boat had been hired by the Melancholics for a Glizzee-prospecting voyage among the islands. It departed properly downtide, and only when it was out of sight of the town did it turn on the sweeps and press away from Northshore. Once well away, the new boatmen—sailors they called themselves—put up the bright, unstained sails and the boat moved on its own, cross-current, the wind pushing at it from up mid-River and yet somehow moving it across. It was the way the sail was slanted, the new men said, and Thrasne paid attention as they lectured him.

In the weeks that followed, he learned about tacking, though the new men laughed at the lumbering *Gift*, calling her "fat lady" and "old barge bottom." When Thrasne objected, they offered to show him the kind of boat that skipped among the islands, and he gave them leave to stop at a wooded isle they were passing at the time to spend two days cutting logs for ribbing and planks. It was to be a small thing, one that could be put together on the top of the owner-house. Thereafter the voyage was livened for all of them by their interest in the new boat.

Once they had passed the braided chains of islands, it was livened by little else.

Except for the sailors, none of them had ever been out of sight of land. Even the sailors had experienced this seldom and briefly, for the islands were thickly scattered in their chains, few of them isolated enough to require long sailing without a few rocky mountaintops or rounded hills in view. Now, however, they were beyond the last of the islands.

Each day at dusk, the winds began to blow from behind them, from Northshore. Then the sails would be set to take the wind almost full while the rudder slanted them against the tide, and all night long the watch would stand, peering ahead into nothing but water. In the mornings, the wind would reverse, blowing toward them, and the sailors would curse, setting the sail to let them move slightly forward and downtide. Thus they moved always away from Northshore, sometimes a little east, sometimes a little west, cleaving to a line that led southward— southward into what? None of them knew.

"This man who saw Southshore—Fatterday? Why didn't the Queen of the Noor hire him for this voyage?" Thrasne asked after a particularly frustrating bout of tacking.

"When they sought him, to send him to us, he was gone, Thrasne. Noor scouts looked everywhere for him. All the Melancholics were sent word to watch for him, but he has not appeared."

"Sounds like a madman. Perhaps he is in a Jarb House somewhere."

Medoor Babji shook her head at him. "Then he will never come out, except as a Mendicant."

"You won't know him then, if he does. All dressed up the way they are, with those pipes in their mouths most of the time."

"Only when madness is about, Thrasne owner. So they say. They smoke the Jarb root only when madness is about, for they are vulnerable to visions."

"The Mendicants? Truly? I thought they were supposed to be the only certifiably sane ones."

Medoor Babji perched on the railing, teetering back and forth with a fine disregard for the watery depths below, setting herself to lecture, which she often enjoyed. "The way I have heard it is this: There are two types of people in the wide world, Thrasne owner. There are those like you, and me, and most of those we know, who see the world the same. I say there is puncon jam on the bread, and you say it, too; we both taste it. Then there will be one who says there is an angel dancing on the bread, and another who says there is no bread at all but only starshine in the likeness of food. Those are the mad ones. So, the mad ones go to a Jarb House and live in the smoke, and they become like you and me, eating puncon on their bread. But if they come out of the house, they see angels again, or lose their bread entirely. But some of them come out with pipes in their mouths which they light when madness threatens. And they go throughout the world selling their vision of reality to those who are not sure whether they are mad or not.''

"And with the money they build Jarb Houses," concluded Thrasne, amused despite himself. It was the first time he had been amused in a very long time.

"Don't laugh! It's all true. Moreover, those who come out as Mendicants can see the future of reality as well as the present. That's what they are paid for. So it is said. Now, I said don't laugh."

"I wasn't laughing," he said. "I was wishing Pamra could come into a Jarb House, somehow."

"No." Babji shook her head, sending her tightly twisted strands of hair into a twirling frenzy around her back and being sure he heard what she said. "That is a vain hope, Thrasne. She would not stay. It is not our world she wishes to see."

Upon the River day succeeded day upon the *Gift*. At the end of the first week they had made a modest festival, and this habit continued at the end of each week that followed. On the morning after one such celebration, a hail from the watchman brought them all on deck.

The creatures came out of the oily swell of the water like hillocks, lifting themselves onto the surface of the River to lie staring at the *Gift of Potipur*, a long row of eyes on a part of each one of them, that part lifted a little like a fish's fin, large eyes down near the body of the strangey and smaller eyes out at the tip. They blinked, but not in unison, those eyes, so that the people gathered at the ship's rail had the strange notion they were confronting a crowd, a committee rather than one creature. One of the oily hillocks swam close to the *Gift*, dwarfing it, and spat strangey bones onto the deck. "A gift," it sang in its terrible voice, turning onto its back and sinking into the River depths with a great sucking of water and roil of ivory underside, like a bellying sail of pale silk.

"What is that?" asked Medoor Babji, seeing how quickly the crew of the *Gift* moved about picking up the strangey bones.

"Glizzee spice," said Thrasne. "It grows within them. They spit it onto ships, sometimes, or into the water near where ships are floating. Old Blint said they mean it as a gift. Strangeys watch ships a lot. Sometimes if a man falls overboard, a strangey will come up under him and hold him up until the boat can get to him, or even carry him downtide to the boat if it's gone on past."

"They don't look like fish."

"Oh, they aren't fish, Medoor Babji. Not shaped like them, not acting like them, not the size of fish. One time when old Blint was still alive, I saw one the size of an island. The whole crew could have gone onto his back and built a town there."

"I never knew Glizzee was strangey bones."

"Most people don't. They think it grows somewhere on an island, and that's why the boatmen have it rather than some land-bound peddler. And you know, there's some ships a strangey will not come near. Strange in look, strange in habit, strangey by name. That's what we say, we boatpeople."

"How marvelous," she breathed. "And probably it isn't bones at all."

"Likely," he agreed. "But it is something they make in their insides or swallow from some deep place in the River."

He knew there was more to it than that. When night came, he wrote in his book, all his wonderings about it, but he said nothing of these to Medoor Babji.

• 7 •

Baris Tower shone in the light of first summer sun, its stones newly washed by rain. About its roof the fliers clustered, perching on the inner parapet, keeping watch as they had been commanded to do. Something about Baris had been doubtful for a considerable time now. From faroff Chancery to the Talons, word had come. Baris was suspect. The one called Gendra Mitiar had sent the word. So much all the fliers knew. What was suspected, they did not know, except that it was something to do with the Superior of the Tower, with the human called Kesseret.

And yet it was Kesseret who had told them of the expedition over the River, to Southshore. "It's only the Noor who are going," she had said. "And they are of no use to you, anyway. However, it might give other people bad ideas. You had best take word to the Talkers of this. . . ."

This word had gone to the Talons, Black Talons and Gray, Blue and Red. In each it had led to much screaming argument on the Stones of Disputation. If a human was guilty of heresy, surely she would not have given such important information? If she had given such important information, then could she be guilty of heresy? Such nice distinctions, though they were the stuff of life to Talkers, were beyond fliers' comprehension or interest. They had been told to watch. Unwillingly, they watched.

Kessie, well aware of their constant surveillance, paid no more attention than was occasionally necessary. The story about the expedition of the Noor had done its planned work of distraction. She saw fliers constantly at the Riverside, spying on the boats that came and went. Reports would be going back to the

Talons; speculation among the Talkers would be rife. So, their attention was where Tharius Don had wanted it. Now she had only to hang on, letting time wear by, praying he would not delay much longer, trying to figure out why he had delayed so long. Did he fear death that much? Surely not; surely not the idealist, Tharius Don. She could not answer the question that came back to her, again and again. Why had he delayed so long?

The business of the Tower crept on at the pace of a tree's growth, slow, unobservable. She tried to keep up appearances, with everything as it had been before. She let herself become a bit negligent in recruiting, but that could be laid to her experiences with the traitor junior, Pamra Don. Her servant, Threnot, seemed to spend more time than ever walking around Baristown in her veils and robes, but if the Superior wished to gather information, no one would question that too strongly. The Superior herself looked unwell, old, somehow, which might be explained by the strain of the long journey that had returned her to Baris.

Or could be explained by the fact that the elixir, sent from the Chancery through the office of Gendra Mitiar, was not efficacious. It seemed to have been adulterated. Kessie sent frantic word through secret routes. She did not mind dying, but she did not want to do it until after the strike. Her life had been given to the cause. She must see its fulfillment.

In time, another vial of elixir arrived from Tharius Don, but the damage had been done. She looked in the mirror at the lines graven around her eyes and mouth, the fine crepe of her skin. No pretense would convince her ever again that she was young. She regretted this. When the end came, she had wanted both of them to appear, at least for a time, as they had when they loved one another so dearly. It had been a culmination, a picture in her mind. A honeymoon. Ah, well; ah, well. She offered it up to the cause, along with her twisted fingers and toes.

"How long, lady?" begged Threnot. She was an old woman, eighty at least. She wished to live long enough to see the end, to see the Thraish confounded, to see the pits emptied. She was glad to see the lines around Kessie's eyes. They were like the lines around her own, confirming them sisters grown old in the cause.

"Soon, Threnot. Tharius Don tells me that Pamra Don is only a few weeks' journey from the Chancery. He admits to selfishness, but says he wishes to have her in his protection before the strike. There are one or two other things he's waiting on. If possible, he wants to locate the stolen herd beasts and eliminate them- from consideration. He thinks if the Thraish have any beasts at all, they may place great weight upon some impossible future and delay acceding to reality." And when he has done that, she thought despairingly, he will find some other reason for delay.

"They would." Threnot nodded. "Those filth bags would rather do anything than what good Tharius Don expects them to do." Threnot had never met Tharius Don, but she had long been Kessie's confidante.

"When they are Treeci, they will not be filth bags anymore," Kessie admonished, surprised that she had come to believe this. She had longed for this faith, the faith of Tharius Don, and perhaps it had come as a reward for her suffering. "When they have become Treeci," she said again, rejoicing in the calm confidence of her voice.

· 8 ·

In the Tower at Thou-ne, Haranjus Pandel reflected on transiency. The sun was far sunk in the south. First summer had gone, and the rainy winds of autumn gathered about the tower, making the shutters creak and cold drafts creep through the stone corridors. Thunderheads massed over the River and surged over Northshore, sailing away into the north in mighty continents of cloud. Ill luck gathering, he thought. Like fliers. Dark and ominous. For days, weeks, fliers had been gathering upon the Black Talons to the east of the town, coming and going. He had never seen so many, not even at Conjunction when they came, so he believed, to breed. It was not the only strange thing to have happened recently.

A few weeks ago had come a Laugher, down from the northlands, cut off from further travel east, so he said, by the towering height of the Talons.

"I demand your assistance, Superior."

He was like all of them, hot and bitter, his eyes like burning coals in the furnace of his face.

"How may I assist the servant of the Chancery?" Haranjus had asked, taking refuge in formality. It would not do to be indiscreet to a Laugher. It was not smart to relax convention or ritual. "The Laugher's need is my command."

"I need to get word to the Talkers, up there," and he had pointed to the heights of the Talons, looming at Thou-ne's eastern border.

"I . . . I can summon a flier," Haranjus had stuttered. He had expected anything but this, anything at all. "What is it you wish me to say?"

56

"I will say it myself. Just take me to the roof and summon one of them, however it is you do it."

There was a way, of course. Twice each month, Haranjus was expected to provide a living body for the Talker's meat. He saw that these bodies were taken, almost always, from among the travelers through Thou-ne. The town was too small to accommodate the loss, otherwise. Certainly it was too small to accommodate it without comment. Now that the Temple attracted so many travelers, it was no trick to abduct one here, one there, as they traveled on westward. His few trusted seniors had become expert at the exercise.

And when the living bodies were ready, they were trussed up on the roof of the Tower and fliers were called. At evening. In the lowe of sunset, so the fliers might return to the Talons with their burden well after dark.

"Yes. There is a bell," Haranjus said. "But I don't have . . . I mean, there's no reason to call them. They may be very angry."

"Leave their anger to me," said Ilze. "They will be more angry yet when they hear what I have to tell them."

He went with Haranjus to the roof, not unlike the roof at Baris, surrounded by a low parapet, fouled with shit, littered with feathers, and reeking with the musty, permeating smell of Thraish. They waited there, not speaking, Ilze because he had no inclination to speak, Haranjus because he was afraid to. When the blaze of sunset was at its height, Haranjus struck the bell.

The plangent tone stole outward, away from the Tower, rising like a bird, lifted upon the air, winging to the Talons tops, a reverberation now softly, now loudly feeding upon itself, intensifying its own sound with echoes. When the blaze of the west began to dim, dark wings detached themselves from the distant peaks and came toward the tower. When those wings folded upon the tower top it was almost dark. The flier croaked, "It is not time for meat."

"This man asked for you," Haranjus said. "I have brought him at his command, as I am sworn to do." He turned then and left the roof. Whatever it was, he didn't want to be involved in it. Nothing could have stopped him from listening at the door, however. He leaned there, ear applied to the crack, holding his breath.

"I have a message for Sliffisunda of the Talons," Ilze said. "There is heresy abroad upon Northshore, and Sliffisunda of the Talons must be told of it."

The fliers gabbled, croaked, not sure of whether they would or would not.

"Sliffisunda will command it if you tell him I am here," Ilze said at last. "He knows me. Return and ask him."

Sliffisunda, it appeared, could be asked. He was at Black Talons. He had come there fairly recently. The fliers would return and ask him, albeit unwillingly. Sliffisunda was evidently in a temper.

"Tell him to send a basket for me!" shouted Ilze as the great wings lifted from the Tower. He stumped to the door and down the stairs, finding Haranjus somewhat out of breath in the study at their foot.

"Give me food," Ilze commanded. "And something to drink. They'll be back within the hour."

"You're going to the Talons?" He could not help himself. Despite all promises to himself not to ask questions, his traitor tongue did it for him.

"One way or the other," Ilze sneered. "It was here the crusade started, wasn't it. I shouldn't wonder if you were involved in it."

"Oh, no. No. A man came from the Chancery. He said I did right to ignore it. . . ."

"Fools! What do they think is happening here? The roots of our society are being nibbled away, and they say to ignore it?"

"It seemed very—innocent."

Ilze barked. It could have been a laugh. Like a stilt-lizard, ha-ha, ha-ha. "When all the fliers are dead and the elixir gone forever, then tell me how innocent it was, fool." Ilze, like many of the lower ranks of the Chancery staff, was naive enough to suppose that all Tower Superiors received the elixir. Haranjus Pandel did not disillusion him. Belatedly, firmly, he shut his mouth.

In an hour the fliers arrived with a large basket clasped in their claws. Moments later, the Laugher was gone, carried away in that same basket. Shortly after that, Haranjus sent a full account of his visit, via the signal towers, to Gendra Mitiar, knowing it would reach others as well.

· 9 ·

Ilze was unceremoniously tumbled from the basket to sprawl upon a high, dung-streaked shelf of stone. Half a dozen fliers stood about, shifting from foot to foot and darting their heads at him as though he were prey. Ilze drew his knife and made a darting motion in return, at which there was a great outcawing of mockery. This, in turn, brought a Talker, who dismissed the fliers—to their evident annoyance—and escorted Ilze through a jagged opening in the cliffside along a rough, narrow corridor that appeared to be a natural cleft in the stone only slightly improved by artifice. A number of small rooms opened from this cleft, rooms with smoothed floors and blackened corners showing where fires had been laid in the past. Rough hangings closed each of these niches from the corridor, and piles of rugs along the walls made it clear the rooms were for the use of human visitors. Or slaves, Ilze told himself. Or meat.

He was left alone here, the Talker taking himself off without a word. Ilze was content with this. If they were interested in what he had to say, they would listen to him sooner rather than later. Though he feared them, it was worth the gamble to find and hold Pamra Don. He could not go on living until that was done.

A scrape at the doorway drew his attention, and he regarded the pallid man who entered with suspicion.

"Who are you?" They both asked it, at once. It was impossible for both of them to answer, and there was an itchy pause during which each waited for the other.

"You!" grated Ilze with an impatient gesture. "Who are you?"

The pallid man answered, words tumbling over one another as though long dammed up behind the barrier of his throat. "My name is Frule. Which tells you nothing much. I am a scholar. A student, you might say. I live here. I study the Thraish."

Ilze snorted. "And they allow that?"

"They might not, if they knew that's what I was really doing. However, I am an acceptable stonemason and a fair carpenter. The Thraish have a need for both."

"For what?" Ilze stared around him, making an incredulous face. "Do they live better than their guests?"

"Differently." The other shrugged. "Who are you?"

"I am Ilze, formerly of the Tower of Baris. I've come to bring the creatures news of something that much affects them," he said in a challenging voice. "In return for which I hope they will help me with my business."

"Which is?"

"Finding and avenging myself on one Pamra Don."

"Oh. The crusade woman." The pallid man nodded wisely. "We've heard of that business, even here. What has she done to you?"

"That's my business." Had he tried, Ilze would have been unable to answer the question. It was one he had never asked himself. Pamra had been the cause of pain and unpleasantness. She was, therefore, fit subject for vengeance, no matter that she had done nothing at all to Ilze. "My business," he repeated abstractedly.

"Let it be your business, then," said Frule. "I only asked because it helps to know what brings humans here. The Thraish have few human visitors. I have seen only one or two. There are a few others like me, who pretend to be craftsmen. And a few who really are craftsmen, not that the Thraish can tell the difference."

"Stupid animals," Ilze snorted.

"No," said the other in a calm, considering voice. "Not, I think, stupid. Simply not very interested in most of the things humans are interested in. Though I can understand much of

what they say to one another, when one has been here a time,
one longs for human speech. And yet, as I remember it, we
humans spend much time talking of sex or politics—that may
not be true in the Chancery, of course." This was a polite aside
with a little bow to Ilze. "The Talkers have no sex, and their
politics are rudimentary. They do not talk of things most of us
would find interesting. They talk of philosophical things. The
nature of reality. The actuality of God. How Potipur differs in
his essential nature from Viranel. Whether perception guaran-
tees reality. Things of that kind. . . ."

"I find that hard to believe," Ilze said with a sneer. "They
do not look or behave like philosophers."

"But then, how should philosophers look or behave? We
cannot expect the Thraish to behave as if they were human. If
human philosophers perched on high stones, engaging in screaming matches, shitting on each other's feet the while, they would
be discredited, but for the Thraish that's ordinary enough
behavior."

"And they talk only of philosophy."

"And food, of course. They talk a great deal about food."

"Dead bodies," snorted Ilze.

"No. They scarcely mention what they eat now. All their talk
is of what was eaten long ago, when there were herdbeasts on
the steppes. They recall the taste of weehar with religious
fervor. There is something deeply and sincerely religious among
the Thraish, and it wells up from that belief they call the
Promise of Potipur." The man nodded to himself, reflecting.
"Do you know that promise? 'Do my will and ye shall have
plenty.' That seems to be the core of it. And the will of Potipur
involves breeding large numbers of themselves, too many for
this world to sustain, which destroyed their plenty before. I
think sometimes how hard it must be for them to keep to that
belief when there have been no herdbeasts on the steppes for
centuries. But, I understand, there may be beasts soon again."

Ilze had not heard this rumor. Frule enlightened him, telling
him what had been overheard. "They don't seem to care what
we overhear. Sometimes I don't think they believe we are
sentient," he commented, shaking his head. "They don't seem

to consider what we might tell other humans about them when we leave here.''

"Perhaps they have ethics which would make such a thing impossible," Ilze suggested with a sneer.

"Possibly." The man shrugged. "It is true that the Thraish cannot conceive of a nest sibling giving anything of value to others outside that nest, and that would probably include information. They cannot conceive of it because no Thraish would do it, for any price. Perhaps they consider us human workers as a kind of next sibling because they feed us. Perhaps they consider us an emotional equivalent to nestlings. On the other hand, there is a kind of scavenger lizard, the ghroosh, which lives in Thraish nests, feeding on the offal that is left there, and perhaps they consider us in that light. Perhaps we are merely tolerated. Ah, well, whatever the truth of that may be, it is interesting to meet you, good to see a new face."

"How many humans are there here? And what do you eat?"

"Oh, we bring some food with us. And the fliers catch stilt-lizards for us, or we climb down to the River to catch fish. Though we have to eat it there. The Thraish will not allow it in the Talons. As for how many of us? A dozen or so, sometimes more, sometimes fewer. I've been here two years myself, building perches and feeding troughs, mostly. Though it's interesting, I've stayed long enough. It's getting time to go."

"Go where?" Ilze was suddenly very interested. Did the Chancery know of these human lice, creeping among the feathers of the Thraish?

"Back home," the scholar said with a vague gesture. He peered closely at Ilze, not reassured by what he saw in the Laugher's face. "You wouldn't be of a mind to make trouble for me with the fliers, would you, Laugher? For my saying I'm studying the Thraish."

"Is it in accord with doctrine?"

"I've never been told it's forbidden."

"Which is not the same thing," Ilze sneered. "I've other stuff on my plate just now, *student*. I will remember you are here, however, when my current task is done." He turned away in contempt, and when he turned again, the man was gone. Ilze threw himself down on the piled rugs and waited, not patiently.

When the day had half gone, a flier pushed into the room, perhaps the same one who had led Ilze here.

"Sliffisunda of the Talons will see you, human. Follow me."

Which Ilze was hard-pressed to do. Twice he had to be lifted in the claws of the fliers before he was deposited at last on an elevated ledge above a yawning gulf. A jagged hole led to a space among the stones where Sliffisunda stood before a curtained opening. Ilze was not invited to enter, and he shivered in the chill wind of the heights.

"You wish to report heresy," it croaked at him. "Heresy, Laugher?"

"There's that woman, Pamra Don," Ilze snarled without preliminary chat. "She's guilty of heresy. This crusade of hers is a heresy. The Talkers—all the Thraish—will soon learn to regret it."

"We have listened to what she says, Laugher. It is nothing much. Meantime, pits are full. Fliers find much meat."

"You have listened to what she says in the public squares, Sliffisunda. You have not heard what she says in the Temples."

"Tower people tell us, nothing much."

"Then Tower people lie."

Sliffisunda hissed, head darting forward as though he would strike. "Why would they lie?"

"Because they have been corrupted, stolen from the faith. They are not believers in Potipur. They dissemble, Talker. Pamra Don is a heretic, and she leads a band of heretics."

"And yet pits are full."

Ilze gestured impatiently. "Of course. For a little time. Until she gains strength. Then there will be no more bodies in the pits at all."

Ilze had expected rage. There was no rage. The Talker hissed once more, then turned his head away. For a time there was silence. "How long, Laugher, before this crusade does, as you say, 'gain strength'?"

"Years," Ilze admitted. "It moves slowly, true. And yet, not many years. It will get all the way around the world in twelve or fifteen years, if it continues at its current pace."

"And in that time, we may expect pits to be full?"

"Probably. But that's temporary, and purely local. Only where the crusade is passing at any given time."

"Ah." The Talker turned away again, hiding his face so the human would not see his expression. One might let the crusade alone. In fifteen years, when it had rounded the world, the Thraish would be ready to strike at them all. In the meantime, many humans would have died and been eaten, the fewer to fight later. However, Thraish numbers could not be increased on the basis of purely local plenty, and if some accident happened, if breeding stock were lost to winter cold, then fifteen years might be too soon.

On balance, it might be better if the crusade were stopped. On balance, it might be better if things were as usual for the next few years. Peaceful. The humans kept biddable and quiet. It was something for the Stones of Disputation, something he could discuss with his colleagues of the Sixth Degree.

"You wish to stop this thing, Laugher?"

"I can stop it, yes."

"How?"

"Pamra Don is being taken by Jondarites to the Chancery. You Talkers must demand she be turned over to you. It was she, after all, who emptied the pits at Baris. You have just ground for complaint. Demand she be given to you. Then give her to me!"

If Sliffisunda could have smiled, he would have done so. Transparent, this one. And still as fiery as when the Talkers and Accusers had done with him, before he was made a Laugher. Set on the trail of Pamra Don, nothing would stay him, not even his fear of the Talkers.

"Do you not fear us?" he asked now. "We gave you much pain."

"Necessary," Ilze said with an angry flush. "It was necessary. Not your fault. Pamra's fault." There was a little fleck of foam at the corner of his mouth. He felt it there, wiped it away, struggling to remain calm.

"And if we took this Pamra Don, but did not give her to you?"

"You owe her to me," Ilze whined, the words vomited out unwillingly in a detested, shameful tone he could no more control than he could withhold. He willed himself to silence and heard his own voice once more. "You set me looking for her. You owe her to me."

"Perhaps," soothed Sliffisunda, chuckling inwardly. "Perhaps we do. We'll see, Laugher. Remain with us for now, while we discuss this matter."

"If you will provide for me." Sulkily, this.

"Oh, we will provide." This time chuckling audibly, Sliffisunda turned away through the heavy curtain. In time some fliers came to take Ilze back to his room.

In a high, narrow shaft cut into the bones of the mountain, Frule edged himself away from the hole leading to Sliffisunda's aerie. It had taken him a year and a half to open the cleft wide enough that he could climb it. It was hidden on three sides and from above. Only the fourth side gaped toward the north, and Frule braced himself against the stone as he withdrew a small mirror from his pocket, breathing upon it, then polishing it vigorously upon his sleeve. He cocked an eye at the sun, then tilted the mirror to catch it and fling the dazzling beam into the empty northlands. Flash, flash, again and again, long and short, spelling out his message. After a time he stopped, waiting. From a distant peak came an answering flash, one, two, and three.

Frule sighed, hiding the mirror once more in his tunic. He had had more excitement in this one morning than in the last two years put together. Gratifying, in a way. There had been very little to report to Ezasper Jorn since the Ambassador to the Thraish had recommended him to Sliffisunda as a competent workman, luring his spy, Frule, to take the job by promise of much reward when the duty was done.

Much reward.

There could be only one reward. The elixir. Something of that magnitude was what it would take to pay him for these two cold, comfortless, stinking years! And yet, it would have been difficult to argue for such a reward had there been no results, no juicy, blood-hot information.

He shivered, half anticipation, half cold, drawing his cloak more closely around him. It would be some time before his message could be received at its ultimate destination and new instructions transmitted. Still, better wait where he was. Getting into the cleft required a hard climb up a rock chimney with his shoulders and feet levering him upward in increments of skin-scraping inches. He had managed to get into position today barely in time to hear the conversation between the visitor and the Talker. Better stay where he was. He lost himself in dreams of fortune, eyes glazing with thoughts of the elixir. He dozed.

He did not wake even when the claws dragged him out of the cleft and over the cliff to bounce upon a hundred projections before his pulped body came to rest far below.

"A spy," said Sliffisunda mildly. "I knew he was there, somewhere. I heard him breathing. And I smelled him. He was very excited about something."

· 10 ·

Looking at my carvings today, wondering which ones I ought to give away, I came across the little boat I'd carved, oh, fifteen years ago, maybe. The Procession boat. Always meant to get some gold paint for it, but never did.

I remember that Procession. I saw the Protector of Man with my own eyes. I don't know where I was when he came around before—I'd have been old enough to remember if I'd seen him, so I suppose I didn't. The golden boat was as long as a pier, and it shone like the sun itself, all full of Chancery people in robes and high feathers. It was a wonderful thing to see, and all the shore was lined with people chanting and waving. But when I saw it, I remember wondering what it was all those people did, there in the Chancery, there in the northlands. No farmers among them, that's for sure, nor boatmen, either. Soft hands and pale faces, all of them, so they aren't people who work. So I said to Obers-rom, what do you suppose they do with their time, those people? And he said, whatever it is, it won't help you or me, Thrasne. And I suppose that's right.

But I still wonder what they do.

From Thrasne's book

Word reached Ezasper Jorn late in the evening, carried down endless flights of stairs, through door after door, shut against the cold of polar winter, the message carefully transcribed onto handmade paper, the missive properly folded and sealed. Jorn liked these little niceties, the sense of drama conveyed in folded, sealed documents, ribbons dangling from the wax, the color of the ribbons betokening what lay within. These ribbons were red. Something vital. Something bloody, perhaps. He played with the heavy paper for a moment, sliding his thumbnail beneath the seal, teasing himself.

So, Frule had at last acquitted himself well! Ezasper Jorn had almost given up hope of receiving any sensible information from the man, not that it was his fault. Ezasper had visited an aerie in the Talons, once. They were not made for two-legged spies, and Ezasper had no source of winged ones. Frule must have carved himself a spy hole somewhere. Ezasper grinned, for the moment almost warm enough in the flush of his enthusiasm.

Now. Now. Where could the information best be used? He peered into the corridor for a long moment before slithering along to Koma Nepor's suite, knocking there for an unconscionable time before the Research Chief heard him and let him in. Ezasper gave him the letter, reading it again over his shoulder, jigging with pleasure.

"I think we'll give it to Gendra, don't you? Part of a package? Later we'll get old Glamdrul to tell her there's heresy all right, started in Baris. She'll like that. She's dying for a reason to get rid of the Superior in Baris, dying to rub Tharius Don's face in it, too. Then we'll suggest it would be a good idea if she went there herself."

"She won't leave the Chancery," Nepor objected. "She won't leave the center of power when the power is looking for a center, old fish. No. Never. She won't."

"Ah, but might she not go in order to obtain the support of the Thraish for her candidacy?"

"How would she do that?"

"Read what's in front of you, nit. She will gain the support of the Thraish by delivering Pamra Don into their claws. In return for supporting her, of course. All other things being equal, it's a strategy which just might work. The assembly likes things peaceful between us and the Thraish. It would get her some votes, if she were around to get them—which she won't be."

"Because while she's gone, we'll do away with Obol and see that you, old fish, that you're named Protector, is that it?"

Nepor rubbed his hands together, jigging from foot to foot in his excitement. "Oh, that will be a turn."

Ezasper Jorn sat down ponderously, pulling his cap firmly down to cover his ears and stretching his legs toward the fire. Even in these vaults, far below the earth, the cold crept in as the winter lengthened. "Well, Tharius will vote for himself, you may be sure of that. Obol will be dead. Gendra will be gone. That's three."

"Bossit will vote for himself. You and I will vote for you, Jorn. That's six, and two votes for you."

"Leaving Jondrigar."

"Oh, that's a difficult one. I should think the general will not vote for anyone."

"Ah, ah, but you see, I have this letter."

"A letter? What letter, Jorn?"

"This letter from Lees Obol. To the general."

"When did Lees Obol last write anything? Come now, Jorn. Would you try our credulity?"

"Nepor, if you ask the general, 'Can the Protector of Man write a letter?' what will the general say?"

"He would say the Protector could write a letter, or ride a weehar bull over the pass, or thump down a mountain with his fists. He would say the Protector could do anything at all. I think he believes it, too."

"He does, yes. He has that happy faculty of never confusing reality with his preconceptions. General Jondrigar will believe in the letter, leave that to me."

"And the letter will say?"

"That Lees Obol, feeling himself fading away, chooses to recommend to the general that he vote for Ezasper Jorn as the next Protector of Man."

"That's three of you," said Nepor admiringly. "And only two against."

"But a very strong two," Ezasper mused, holding out his hands to the fire. "Bossit. And Tharius Don. Perhaps I can find some reason that Tharius Don would consider it wise to support me. . . ." He stared into the dancing flames, lost in contemplation. Koma Nepor, familiar with this state of reflective trance in his companion, snuggled more deeply into his chair to consider which of the several strains of blight he had available to him would be best to use in ridding themselves of Lees Obol.

Ezasper Jorn carried the message to Gendra Mitiar the following morning, wending his way through endless tunnels from the roots of the palace to the roots of the Bureau of Towers, finding Gendra Mitiar at last in a room warmed almost to blood heat by a dozen braziers, ventilated by the constant whir of great fans turned by her slaves. Gendra was undergoing a massage at the hands and feet of Jhilt, the Noor. Though Jhilt was sweating and panting from her exertions, the sheet-covered heap that was Gendra's ancient body showed no signs of perceiving her exhaustion.

"Message from the Talons," he said, trying to fit his words between the slap, slap, slap, wrench, crunch, grunt that Jhilt continued.

"Ahum," Gendra responded.

"Important, Gendra. You should listen."

"Don't care about the stupid fliers."

"Don't care about being the next Protector of Man, perhaps?"

"Enough, Jhilt," Gendra said, slapping the woman's hands away. "Get out of here." She sat up, wrapped in the sheet, her ravaged face peering from the top of it like the head of an enshrouded worker, looking no less dead than many did. "What was that you said?"

"I merely asked if you were not concerned with the possibility of being our next Protector. Koma Nepor and I have talked it over. In return for some arrangement which we can undoubtedly agree upon, we two would be willing to support you for that position. Entirely quid pro quo, Gendra. You know me well enough to know I am not altruistic." He made a long face, appearing both shamed and somehow ennobled by this admission, sighing deeply the while. She regarded him suspiciously, and he made a disarming gesture. "I have no chance at the position myself, and making an arrangement to support you would be more profitable for me than seeing Tharius Don as Protector." He turned away, watching her from the corner of

his eye. It was not necessary to see her, for she ground her teeth
at the mention of Tharius Don. He went on, "Of course, this is
all somewhat premature. I have every reason to believe Lees
Obol will live for two or three years yet. Still, it is not too early
to plan. Proper planning will, I am sure, assure your nomination. However, nomination by the council is only a first step.
Election by the assembly is necessary. As Ambassador to the
Thraish, I feel it would be important to convince the assembly
you have the endorsement of the Thraish as well."

"And how is that happy eventuality to be achieved?"

He handed her the message, its open seal still dripping red
ribbons across the words. "My spy, Frule, has overheard a
conversation between the Laugher Ilze and our old friend
Sliffisunda."

She took the paper from his hand, screwing her eyes into it,
pulling the content of the words out of the paper like a cork
from a bottle, weighing, evaluating. When she had read it once,
she cast Ezasper Jorn a suspicious glance and read it again.

"What here can be used to my advantage, Jorn? I don't see
it."

"If you were to deliver the woman to them yourself, Gendra?
Having made somewhat of a bargain with them? Their support
for yours. Tharius Don won't let this Pamra Don go easily, you
know. He wants her in his own hands. So much was clear at our
last meeting."

"True. He has some unexplained interest there. I've asked
Glamdrul Feynt to look into it, but the old bastard dithers and
forgets. Still, I'll threaten Feynt a bit and see what emerges. So.
So. You think my turning the woman over to them would gain
their favor, eh?" She had quite another reason for wanting the
favor of the Thraish, but she did not intend to discuss that with
Ezasper Jorn.

"Something for something, Gendra. If you want our support,
Nepor's and mine, you'll have to offer something. We'll talk
again." He left her chewing on that, figuring how to outwit him
in the long run, so taken with her own cleverness she couldn't
think for a moment he had already outwitted her.

The corridors of the Bureau of Towers were long and echoing, the stairs even longer. When he came to the bottom of the sixth flight, three levels below winter quarters, smelling the opulent dust of the files, he was too out of breath to summon Glamdrul Feynt for a time. He contented himself with leaning on a table while his heart slowed, then banging the nearest door in its frame three or four times, hearing the echoes slam down the endless corridors, ricocheting fragments in an avalanche of sound.

When the sound died it was resurrected, coming from the opposite direction, another door slammed somewhere far away, and the sound of Feynt's voice, "Hoo, hoo, hoo," as he stumbled nearer. When he saw who it was, he straightened and stopped limping. "So, Jorn. What's on your mind?"

They sat on a filthy bench, staring at dust motes like schools of silver fish in a slanting beam that struck from a high lantern into the well of the files, talking of Gendra Mitiar, of fliers, of this and that.

"So you've got it all planned, have you?"

"If you'll tell her there's heresy in Baris, yes. That'll do the trick. She'll trot off to the fliers with Pamra Don, and she'll keep right on going. Oh, she can't wait to set her claws into that woman in Baris."

"And you'll be the next Protector, then?"

"Sure as can be. We count three votes for it, against two at the council. Of course, the assembly's something else, but we can manage that."

"And what's in it for old Feynt, Jorn? Oh, I know you've talked dribs of this and drabs of that, but what's in it for me, I want to know?"

"Elixir, Feynt. All of that you want. What else can I do for you? Some other job? No reason you have to stick down here, is there?"

"Nobody else knows where anything is, you know that, Jorn." It was said with a kind of belligerent pride.

"Does it matter?" It was said all unheeding, Jorn so drunk with his own plotting he didn't think. He was watching the dust motes, thinking of himself on the royal Progression, dressed all in gold and held up by the Jondarites to the acclaim of the mobs. He did not see the wrinkle come between Feynt's old eyebrows or the hateful gleam that winked once across his eyes. *Did it matter?* Did a man's life matter? Over a hundred years spent on these files, and did it matter?

When Ezasper Jorn left in a little time, he did not know he had made an enemy of what had been, at worst, a malicious but disinterested man.

· 11 ·

A mong the more respected followers of the crusade were several scribes, including a light-colored spy sent by Queen Fibji and at least one adventurer from the island chain. Night found these assigned recorders, among others who kept records for their own various reasons, hunched over their individual campfires or crouched into the pools of their lantern's light, scribbling an account of the day's sayings. Some of them had not seen Pamra Don herself, so they wrote what others said of her, of her and Lila.

"She shines with a holy radiance," some wrote, confusing the shining statue that had appeared in Thou-ne with the woman it had likened. "The child is a messenger of God, sent into her keeping, an unearthly being, of an immortal kind." In which they were more accurate than they realized, though Lila's unearthly nature came from a source closer to them than the God of man.

"The Noor are personifications of the darkness," they scribbled. Queen Fibji's spy gritted his teeth as he made note of this particular doctrine. It was a new teaching. Peasimy Flot had been stopped by a troop of Melancholics in a town market square as they were passing through. Unwisely, the Melancholics had suggested the crusaders be whipped for holiness's sake. Peasimy had peered into their dark, grinning faces and had turned away with revulsion, shivering. "These are devils," he cried. "The darkness creeps out of their skins." The word had spread rapidly through the following, and since that time, the crusade had gone out of its way to surround and brutalize troupes of Melancholics, beating them with their own whips.

When the spy for Queen Fibji had written it all down, he rolled the account into a lightweight tube made of bone and attached it to the legs of a seeker bird. The Queen would soon have this news to add to her many burdens. The writer considered it more ominous than most information he had provided.

After sending the bird off, he went back into his little tent and shaved his head. His skin was light enough not to appear Noorish, but nothing could have disguised the long, crinkly strands of Noor hair. He would follow yet awhile. The whole movement had a feeling about it, as before a storm when the quiet becomes ominous. He slept badly, dreaming of that storm but unable to remember its conclusion when he wakened.

• 12 •

Out here, on the water, I think about things a lot, things that didn't bear thinking of when we were closer to shore. The nights are bigger here, and the daytimes, too. Space is bigger. I feel as though the inside of me—what's in my head—is bigger out here than it was on Northshore. Perhaps because it's quieter, here. Perhaps the quiet entices the shy thoughts out, ideas that never come out when there are people around. . . .

Like the truth of what I felt . . . feel for Pamra Don. When she came, it was like there was a woman-shaped hole in my life, just waiting. Like a flower waits for a beetle to come along and land on it. Not doing anything, you understand. Just blooming, all that color around an emptiness. The emptiness has to be there, ready for something to move into. That's the way it was with me; all my bloom surrounded this Pamra-shaped hole. When she came along, that was the space that was empty. I guess things always nest or build or roost in spaces that are unoccupied, so that's where she roosted. You can't expect the beetle to love the flower or the bird to love the branch. The branch and the flower are just there, that's all. Does the flower need the bug? Maybe so. Maybe the branch needs the bird, too. But the bug and bird don't know that. Or care.

Maybe what happens between people, men and women, is often like that, one having a certain place that needs filling and another coming along who seems to fill it—for a while, at least.

From Thrasne's book

77

When Pamra Don arrived at the Split River Pass it was the beginning of second summer, the seventh month. Behind the Teeth of the North, polar winter had given way to thaw and the promise of spring. On the steppes, the rains of autumn made room for the balmier days to follow. Pamra went crowned with flowers, for each day some one among her followers created a chaplet for her, a task begun as one follower's happy inspiration and continued thereafter as custom. Each night the faded wreath was taken away by its creator to be pressed between boards and kept forever. Or so it was thought at the time.

The Jondarite captain, commander of her escort, had orders to bring her only so far as the cupped, alluvial plain at the foot of the pass. No one had known how long the journey would take, and it had been thought possible they might arrive during polar winter when the road to the Chancery was impassable. He sent word, therefore, upon arrival at the edge of Split River, and set up camp to await a reply. Pamra's followers, who had been strung out in a procession many days long upon the road, began to agglomerate on the banks of Split River and around the tall, flat-topped buttes that dotted this stretch of steppe with brooding, sharp-edged cliffs. Soon the vacant lands had the look of a settlement, with tents springing up like mushrooms, fishermen and washerwomen at the waterside, children climbing rocks and chasing birds, and small groups constantly coming and going from their search for food in the surrounding foothills and valleys.

When word came to the Chancery of the arrival of this mob, Tharius Don, after some deliberation, sent word for the Jondarite captain to see that the multitude was fed from the Chancery warehouses at the foot of the pass, "for the prevention of disorder, and lest hunger lead large numbers of people to attempt an ascent of the pass."

Not that the Jondarites weren't quite capable of killing several thousand of them, but disposal of the bodies would be a problem, and there was no sense in letting scavengers ruin the surrounding countryside. So Tharius Don said, at some length, whenever anyone was inclined to listen.

Only then did he send a litter for Pamra Don, instructing the Jondarite captain to escort her to him, at the palace, as soon as might be. This order was countersigned by General Jondrigar. The captain would have ignored it, otherwise.

"What're you going to do with her?" the general wanted to know. "Stirred up a lot of trouble, evidently, and showed up here with a mob. Better let me have the lot of 'em put down." He said this with a flick of his curiously reptilian eyes. "Save trouble."

Tharius shook his head. "No! We need to know many things about this crusade, General. We will not find them out by violence. Just get the young woman here, safely into my hands, please. As Propagator of the Faith, this is my province, and I have Lees Obol's instructions to take care of such matters." As indeed he did, though the last such order had been issued fifty years before. Still, none of Obol's orders had ever been rescinded, and the least word of the Protector was supposed to be considered a command forever. Tharius used the Protector's name now in order to assure obedience from Jondrigar, knowing that unless Lees Obol himself contradicted what Tharius had just said, Pamra Don was as good as in his hands.

In which intention, Tharius succeeded better than he had planned. The general was so impressed by the use of the Protector's name—little enough referred to in recent years—that he decided to go over the pass and fetch the woman himself.

He set out upon the morning, riding a weehar ox, his plumed headdress nodding in time with the slow stride of the beast, as unvarying a pace as the sun's movement in its ponderous half circle above the mountains, from twilight to twilight. Soon this half-light would pass, and the Chancery lands would lie beneath a sun that did not set, but the general was content to relish this season of spring dusk. In it his accompanying men moved like shuffling shadows, their individuality lost, becoming one multilegged beast which tramped its way up the long, winding road toward Split River Pass. At such times the general knew the immortality of now. There was no past, no future, and he was content to let time fade into nothing. There was only this plod, plod, plod, his own pulsebeat magnified into something mighty and eternal. Armies, he thought, turning the word over in his mind as though it had been the name of God. Armies. Mighty, inexorable, obdurate. It was as though his own body had been multiplied a thousand times, and he felt the multiplied strength bursting through his veins at each beat of the footfall drum. It was better, even, than battle, this slow marching, and in the dim light below the plumed helm, the general could have been seen to be smiling.

Behind him in the palace, Tharius Don supervised his servants in making ready the suite Pamra Don would occupy, vacant since Kessie's departure. It was chill from the winter, dusty from disuse. Out the window he could watch the slow snake of Jondarites as it wound its way up the pass. A day to the top, a day down the other side. A day there, changing the guard, seeing to the warehouses. Then two days to return.

"The cover on this chair is split," he said to the house-keeper. "Have it recovered and returned here within three days. Oh, and Matron, the paint on that window needs to be redone." The window frame was blackened by fire. The ledge below, also, where the flame-bird's nest had burned. As he stood there, a flame-bird darted down the wall, the first bird of summer, shimmering across his sight like a vision, blurred by tears. "Stupid," he cursed at himself, wiping the moisture away. "Stupid." He had been thinking of Kessie.

Someone else at the Chancery also thought of the lady Kesseret. In her high solarium, still too cool for real enjoyment, though the view was, as always, enthralling, Gendra Mitiar stood peering out at the marching Jondarites. Shifting from bony buttock to bony buttock on a bench nearby, Glamdrul Feynt pretended a lack of interest. A litter of paper scraps around the bench testified to the fact he had been there for a time he considered unnecessary and unconscionable.

"I have to get back to the files, Mitiar," he whined. "Things are stacking up."

"Oh, hush," she snarled impatiently. "I'm thinking."

"Well, I can be doing my filing while you're thinking."

"I want you here!" She ran her fingers down the crevasses of

her face, once, twice, then scratched her balding pate vigorously, as though to stimulate thought. "Tell me again, Feynt.
You found evidence of heresy in Baris. . . ."

"Some evidence there may be a hotbed of heresy in Baris,
yes. I've said that. Go back a few generations and you find all
sorts of things happening in Baris that spell unorthodoxy. Dat-
ing from the time of Tharius Don, when he was Superior of the
Tower there. That was before you were Dame Marshal." As it
had been, though not by much, and Tharius had continued in
that job for some time after Gendra had acquired her current
position. Glamdrul Feynt did not dwell on that. Suspicion thrown
on Tharius Don was merely lagniappe, thrown in for effect.

"Aha," she muttered for the tenth time. "Aha. And you
have documentary evidence?"

"Sufficient," he said. "Sufficient." He did have. Or would
have, if he decided it was necessary, though chances were it
would never be needed. Gendra was lazy. She wouldn't ask to
see it. She was content to let underlings do the work, at risk of
their heads if she was later displeased.

"All right," she snarled. "You can go."

He closed the door behind him emphatically, then crouched
to peer through the keyhole. Inside the solarium Gendra Mitiar
was flinging her ancient body from side to side, jigging wildly,
as though something had gotten inside her clothes and was
biting her. It took him a moment to figure out what she was
doing.

Gendra Mitiar was dancing.

The master of the files stumped away, limping ostentatiously
until he was around the corner and a good way down the hall.
The servant he had left there was sitting dejectedly on a bench,
staring at nothing, and he snapped to attention when the old
man struck at him.

"Wake up, you stupid fish. What do you think this is, your
dormitory?" He fished in his clothing, shedding paper like
confetti, finding the folded, sealed packet at last in the bottom
of a capacious pocket. "Now, you take this to Tharius Don.
Now. Not five minutes from now, but now. Got that? Then you
come tell me you've done it or bring me an answer, one."

He watched the man scurry off, then took himself below.

"So, Ezasper Jorn," he snarled happily. "So, Gendra Mitiar. So and so to both of you. Old shits. Old farts." It became a kind of hum, te-dum, te-dum, and he sang it to himself as he went down the endless stairs. "Old shits. Old farts. So and so." Occasionally he interrupted this song to mutter, "Does it matter?" to himself, screwing up his mouth in a mockery of Ezasper Jorn's usual speech. "Does it matter, old fart? Does it, eh?"

Glamdrul Feynt was on his way to keep a very important, and secret, appointment with Deputy Enforcer Bormas Tyle, and with Shavian Bossit, Lord Maintainer of the Household.

When Feynt's servant arrived, Tharius was still at the window. Somehow he had not been able to leave it. He did not leave it when he opened the sealed packet, putting it before his blind eyes but not seeing it for long moments.

"Today Gendra Mitiar sends word to Jondarites in Baris for the arrest of Kesseret, Superior of the Tower at Baris." He saw it without seeing it, and then it blazed into his consciousness all at once. *Arrest. Kessie.* Unsigned. He whirled. The man had gone. He ran to the door, looked down the hallway. Gone. He couldn't remember the man's face. Not one of his own servants. Whose? The packet was anonymous.

It was from someone in the Bureau of Towers, then. Someone Gendra had antagonized, perhaps. What matter who?

He left the room hastily, setting all thoughts aside but those of the message he must send. "Highest priority, immediate attention, to Kesseret, Superior of Tower at Baris, Jondarites have order for your detention. Go at once to Thou-ne." The message would be sent through his own secret channels, of course.

And then another. "Highest priority, immediate attention, to Haranjus Pandel, Superior of Tower at Thou-ne. Provide secret refuge for Kesseret, from Baris. Patience. Soon. Tharius Don."

Only when these messages were sent did he sit down to try and figure out what was going on. The only message to reach Gendra lately, he assured himself, was one from Thou-ne saying that Ilze, the Laugher, had gone to the Talons. All messages from Haranjus Pandel—as from any member of the cause—

were surreptitiously obtained and copied to Tharius as a matter of course. What other messages? What other messengers? In winter? None he knew of.

Ezasper Jorn was thought by Tharius—indeed, by everyone—to be so complete a fool that Tharius did not even consider him in passing.

At the top of the pass, General Jondrigar dismounted his beast and let the handlers take it away. Now that it was assumed the fliers knew there were weehar and thrassil behind the Teeth of the North, the general chose to ride an ox whenever he liked. Since last year's depredations on the herds, he had had crossbowmen stationed with the herdsmen, ready to bring down any flier who presumed to try such theft again. Making off with a weehar calf wasn't something that could be done quietly. One flier couldn't lift the creature, unless it was newborn, and the newborns were now carefully guarded. It would take two or three fliers, together with straps or some kind of basket, to carry a young beast, and that meant a certain amount of noise. The crossbowmen were alert. The general was fairly confident the fliers would get no more.

As for the beasts already gone, Koma Nepor had provided some clear flasks filled with a clinging liquid. Whenever the abducted herdbeasts were found, this liquid was to be thrown among them. "It contains a special strain of . . . ah, let us say biological material? Eh? No matter what, exactly. It will do the job on the beasts. Additionally, it will infect any of the fliers who come into contact with them."

Which, being a derivative of the blight, it would do. Nepor had not been successful in determining the life cycle of the blight. Something in it escaped him and his ancient microscopes. He had been able, however, to make from blighted fish a long-lived distillation that was very effective. This distillation, modified in various ways, had remarkable effects on people, and Koma Nepor had no reason to believe it would not work as well on weehar and thrassil.

Seeing the clutter on the plain below, the general's hand twitched as he considered using the flasks upon the herd humans gathered there. "Trash," he muttered, reassuring himself with a glance at the expressionless Jondarites around him. "Trash." Indeed, the multicolored splotches at the foot of the pass could as well have been fruit rinds, paper scraps, shells, bones, and chips. It heaved like a garbage pit, too, alive with human maggots squirming along the River and among the buttes. "Where is the woman?" he asked the messenger who awaited him. "Pamra Don?"

The messenger pointed, offering his glass. On a slight hillock overlooking the River a wagon stood with a tall tent beside it. All around the hill, banners bloomed like flowers; red, green, blue, and Jondarite tents surrounded the whole. "There," said the messenger.

Through the glass, General Jondrigar stared into Pamra Don's face. At this great distance he could see nothing but the pale oval. A woman, carrying a child. Why was it, then, he asked himself in irritation, that she seemed to be looking directly into his eyes?

He did not hurry his trip down the pass. At the bottom of the pass there were warehouses to inspect. He received a report that worm had gotten into one that stored dried fish as well as roots and grain captured from the Noor. He specified the materials in that particular warehouse be used to feed the multitude. He was told what the spy balloons had seen from on high, a great number of approaching Noor, also crusaders, the steady trickle rising from Northshore into the northlands and thence to the place they stood.

"And a war party of young Noor, General. Just above Darkeldon. We could have a troop there in two days."

The general shook his head. "Not now, Captain. Not with all this nonsense going on. I want a battalion here, spaced out around this mob. I want crossbowmen stationed on the slopes of the Teeth and on some of those buttes. You'll have to scale some of them and let rope ladders down. No threats, mind, Tharius Don doesn't want this flock of nothings injured. Nonetheless, we won't take chances," and he grinned his predator's smile, hard as iron, his gray, pitted skin twitching as though insects were crawling on it.

Only when all that business was attended to did he go on out onto the plain and to the tent his aides had set up at the foot of

one of the buttes, protected from the wind. Evening was drawing down, and the cookfires were alight. They bloomed around
him like stars, many nearby, fewer farther away, only a scatter
at the far horizon and beyond, showing where the stragglers
were.

A large fire marked the hill where Pamra Don's tent stood.
He looked at it for a time, scornfully, then sent word to the
commander of the troop guarding her. He wanted the woman
brought to him tonight. As soon as he had eaten.

He had not finished when they brought her, carrying the
child. He pointed with his chin at a chair across the tent, far
from the fire. The soldiers escorted her there and stood at either
side, calm and alert. General Jondrigar stared at her over his
wine cup, waiting for her to say something. Prisoners always
said something, started pleading sometimes, or offering themselves. Pamra Don said nothing. The child stared at him, but
Pamra was not even looking at him but at something else in the
room. The general swung his head to follow her line of vision.
Nothing. A bow hung on the tent pole. His spare helmet. His
spare set of fishskin armor, with the wooden plates. She wasn't
looking at those, surely. Nodding in that way. Seeming to
murmur without actually making a sound. He went on chewing,
suddenly uncomfortable.

"You can go," he muttered to the soldiers. "Wait outside."
For some reason he did not want them witness to this . . . this,
whatever this was. Not rape. Even without Tharius Don's command, he would not have done that where anyone could see or
hear him. Not good for discipline. When the men had gone, she
still did not seem to see him.

"Do you know who I am?" he asked her at last.

She turned toward him eyes that were opaque, almost blind.
They cleared, very gradually, and she focused upon him. "I
. . . they said you were General Jondrigar."

"Do you know what I am?"

"You . . . no. I don't know."

He rose to walk toward her, leaning forward a little, thrusting
his face into hers. "I am Lees Obol's right arm, his protection,
leader of his armies. . . ."

Her face lit up as though by fire. She leaned forward, across the child, to take him by the shoulders, and by surprise. He could not remember a woman ever having touched him willingly. Aunt Firrabel, of course, but only she. And now this one. Where she touched him burned a little, as though he were pressed against a warm stove, and he could not take his eyes from hers.

"General Jondrigar," she said, "the Protector of Man has need of you. Lees Obol has need of you."

Of all the things she might have said, only this one could have been guaranteed to draw in his whole attention, focused as by a burning glass upon a radiant point. He lived for nothing but to meet the Protector's needs. Who could tell him what those needs were better than his own eyes, his own ears? Still, her eyes burned into his own with a supernatural glow. Perhaps some messenger had conveyed something to her. Perhaps the soul of Lees Obol had spoken to her.

"What need?" he gurgled, barely able to speak. "What need has the Protector?"

"The Protector has been misled by evil men," she said, fulfilling all his fears and hopes at once. Had he not suspected plots against the Protector? Had he not prayed to forestall them all? "They have told him that the fliers are more important than men, have told him some men are more important than others. They have made his great title a trivial thing."

"No," he croaked. "They would not dare."

"They have," she asserted, her face radiant with truth. "I tell you they have! What is the Protector of Man if any man is nothing? Have you thought of that, General? If even a single man is nothing, of what value is the Protector of Man?"

"Man?" he asked, uncertain how she had meant it.

"Northshoremen," she whispered, "Jondarites. Chancerymen. Noor. Yes. Even the Noor. For if the Noor are made less, then their Protector is made less. A blow at the Noor is a blow at Lees Obol. . . .

"And the workers, too, General. Were they not once men? If they are used and eaten, is not Lees Obol minimized by that?"

"Who does these things?" he asked, still a little uncertain, his slow, ponderous mind finding its way among the things she had said. Part of it had been clear the moment she said it. If a treasure was of no value, then he who guarded it was of no value, either. He could grasp that, all at once. It needed no explanation. "Who?"

"You know who. Who here in the Chancery treats with the fliers, General? Who here in the Chancery maintains the Towers? Who goes ravaging among the Noor?"

"We?" he asked, uncertain, in growing horror. "I?"

"You have said." She nodded to him. "You have said, General. All of you, here in the Chancery. You have betrayed Lees Obol!"

He roared then, striking her hands away, glaring at her with red, righteous eyes. How dared she? How dared she? And yet. Yet. The roar died in his throat. She stood there still, glowing, totally unafraid, looking at him with pity.

"It's not your fault," she whispered. "You didn't know. Not until I told you."

"I know now," he growled. It was a question, but it came forth as a statement of fact. "I know now."

"Yes." She waited for a time while he stood there, immobile, the child on her shoulder, then turned and left him, without another word, walking out through the tent flaps where the soldiers waited. One of these men called, uncertainly, "Shall we take her back to her tent, General?"

He muttered something affirmative, unable to form words, standing there in silence, brooding beside his fire, slowly building the edifice his nature demanded, the structure that must properly house the Protector of Man. It could have no window or door to admit error. Monolithic, it must stand forever. Lees Obol must be better served, and he could be better served only if man were better served.

What had she said to him? There were only those few words. He said them over to himself, again and again, seeking more. There must have been more. And yet, had she not said everything?

Late, past midnight, he sat there, getting up from time to time to add a stick to the fire, sitting down again. Very late in the night he rang the bell that summoned his aides. When they came, he astonished them with the messages he gave them, each signed with his own seal.

When only one was left, he said, "That woman, the prophet-ess. She is a warrior for Lees Obol."

The man, not knowing what to say or if it was wise to say anything, merely nodded, attempting to look alert.

"She needs armor. A fighter needs armor. Tell my armorer. A helmet for her. Made to her measure. And a set of fishskin body armor, such as we wear. And boots. Have him plume the helmet with flame-bird plumes, like mine, and make her a spear."

The man presumed to comment, "Can she handle a spear, General?"

"No matter. Someone can carry it at her side. Let it bear a pennant. Tell the armorer. He will know. And bring one of the weehar oxen over the pass for her to ride, one of the young ones."

The man went away, shaking his head, puzzled, wondering what the prophetess would think of all this.

She, when the armorer came to measure her the next morn-ing, thought it another sign. Neff from his shining cloud ap-proved, and the radiance and the shadow both nodded.

· 13 ·

Tharius Don's frantic message came to Baris at first dark. Each evening at this time, Threnot went for a walk along the parklands. From time to time on such forays she encountered wanderers who might, perhaps, have been accounted a little furtive if anyone had been inclined to care who a servant talked with during her frequent strolls. The wanderer encountered this night was less furtive and more in a hurry than most. Threnot returned swiftly to the Tower. Only an hour or so later, she might have been seen to leave once more, going down to the town on some errand, her veils billowing in the light wind. The flier detailed to watch such comings and goings nodded, half-asleep. When Threnot was later seen to leave the Tower yet again that night, the flier scratched herself uncomfortably, for she had not seen the woman return from her second trip. Three trips in one night was not unheard-of, but it was rare. Perhaps she would mention it to the Talkers. Perhaps not. The ancient tension between Talker and flier had in no sense been changed by recent history.

Actually, only the first and third veiled women had been Threnot. The second had been Kesseret herself, fleeing to the house of a Riverman pledged to the cause. Threnot joined her there some hours later, and when dawn came, both women were on a boat halfway to the next town west. In the hours between Kessie's leaving the Tower and Threnot's leaving it, word had been spread in the Tower that the lady Kesseret was ill of a sudden fever, that she would stay in her rooms until healed of it, keeping Threnot with her to nurse her. Kesseret's deputy had

89

been told to take charge of Tower affairs and asked not to bother the Superior for five or six days at least.

"I have taken water and food and all things needful to her rooms, Deputy," Threnot had said in her usual emotionless voice. "The Superior is anxious the Tower should avoid infection." "Infection" was a word generally used to mean any of several nasty River fevers that were occasionally epidemic and frequently fatal.

"She asks to be left alone until she is well recovered, which I have no doubt will occur in time." Threnot looked appropriately grave, and the deputy—not an adherent of the cause—entertained thoughts of a possible untimely demise and his own ascension to the title.

Therefore, on the morrow when Jondarites came bearing orders for Kessie's arrest (emanating from Gendra, but countersigned by the general), the officious deputy told them of the Superior's illness in such terms as did not minimize the likelihood the sickness might prove fatal. The word "infection" was used several times again, at which the Jondarites had second thoughts and departed. They would return, they said, in a week or so. Nothing in their instruction had indicated sufficient urgency in the matter to risk infecting a company of troops.

On board the *Shifting Wind,* the lady Kesseret, Superior of the Tower of Baris, became simply Kessie, marketwoman, one of the hundred thousand anonymous travelers on this section of River and shore. Her hair was not braided in the Awakener fashion; her clothes were ordinary ones long laid by for such a need; when she looked in the mirror, she did not see the lady Kesseret. If Gendra had looked her full in the face, she would not have seen Kesseret, either.

And Kessie amused herself bitterly, hour on hour, wondering whether Tharius Don would recognize her if he ever saw her again.

Rumor spread through the palace like a stain of oil on water, at first thick and turgid with unbelief, becoming thinner and brighter with each retelling, until at the end it was a mere rainbow film of jest, an iridescent shining upon the surface of the day.

The general, accompanied by a woman? The general's weehar ox harnessed with another? His banner companied with another banner? Laughter burst forth at the thought, jests abounded, giggling servitors lost their composure when confronted by glum-faced Jondarites, themselves privy to the rumor but unable, because of the exigencies of discipline, to show any interest in it.

"True," the palace whispered, cellar to high vault, "it's true. The crusade woman has converted Jondrigar. She has put flowers on his head!"

Tharius Don shook his head, incredulous. Typical, he thought. The more outrageous the rumor, the more quickly it would spread in the Chancery, where excitements were few and urgencies infrequent. Any titillation was worth its weight in metal, and a laugh at the expense of the general was worth ten times even that. Flowers on his head, indeed. Tharius made his way to the high Tower, his powerful spyglass in hand, wanting to judge the progress of the procession now coming toward Highstone Lees, along Split River from the pass.

The drummers first, then the spearmen. Then the banner carriers—with two banners. And then . . .

Then, Tharius Don's eyes told him, then the general on a weehar ox with flowers on his head.

They came marching through the ceremonial gate, drummers, spearmen, banner carriers, then the general and Pamra Don, walking side by side while the weehar oxen were led off to be fed hay and groomed for another such occasion. Tharius Don so far recovered himself as to put on hierarchical garb and come out to meet them. While nothing had prepared him for this unlikely event, he had managed to survive the political climate of the Chancery for a hundred some years by reacting quickly to events no less improbable.

"General." He bowed, waiting some explanation and trying not to stare at the chaplet of flowers that both the general and Pamra Don wore around their helms. Pamra Don carried a child. The child stared at him, smiling.

"Tharius Don," boomed Jondrigar, "Propagator of the Faith. This young person is a strong warrior for the faith, Tharius Don. She is a great soldier for Lees Obol!" This said, he peered intently at Tharius Don to see how it was received. The general had already determined that his view in the matter was to be the only one permitted.

From a window above them in the palace, Gendra Mitiar and Shavian Bossit stared down, Gendra's nails raking her face in agitation; Shavian, as usual, was inscrutably calm. Behind them in the room, Bormas Tyle strained for a glimpse of the ceremonial group assembled in the square, but his line of sight was obscured by the fountain which threw a curtain of spray across the assemblage. He grimaced, his knife sliding ominously in and out of its sheath as he stared at Gendra's back. No matter. Soon things would be arranged differently. Soon enough, no one would place himself so impolitely relative to Bormas Tyle, so carelessly respecting his dignity. Shavian Bossit turned from the window and winked at him, only a twitch in that impassive face, but enough for Bormas Tyle to understand. He took his hand from his knife and went to find another window. Soon it would not matter. Meantime, he, too, would observe the spectacle.

In the square below, Tharius Don blinked away the spray of the fountain and replied, "I know she is a soldier for Lees Obol, General. Pamra Don cares greatly for the Protector of

Man." He stared at the child. It looked deeply into his eyes, making him uncomfortable.

The general shifted from foot to foot a little uncertainly. His imagination had carried him no further than this formal declaration, though he now felt that something more was warranted. He had feelings inside himself for which he had no name, feelings of anxiety, perhaps even of fear, as though recent events presaged dangers that would be inevitably derived from them, yet which he could not foresee.

"What is she to do here?" the general demanded, coming to practical matters.

"She is to be my guest," said Tharius Don. "She and the child. I have had a suite prepared for her . . . them. We will talk of her crusade. Perhaps she should meet with Lees Obol."

"Yes." The general nodded, his face clearing like a lowering sky after storm. "Oh, yes, she should meet with Lees Obol." Thus relieved of responsibility, he stepped back, satisfied for the moment, though Tharius Don knew his natural and chronic paranoia would overtake him before much time had passed.

Tharius Don offered his hand, courteously. Pamra Don took it, shining-faced. She turned to bow toward the general. "Thank you for my armor, General Jondrigar. We will talk again of this great war we fight together."

In the guest suite, high above the courtyard, Pamra Don went immediately to the windows to fling them wide. Neff had not followed her through the corridors, as her mother and Delia had, but he stood at once on the ledge outside the window, smiling through it at her, his radiance lighting the room.

"Would you like to put the baby down and put on something a little more comfortable?" Tharius Don suggested.

"I didn't bring any clothes," she said simply, not seeming to care.

He opened the armoire, showing her a rack of soft robes and shoes. "These would fit you, Pamra. They belonged to the lady Kesseret, of Baris. She wore them when she was here."

"The Superior!" Her eyes flashed and her lips twisted. "Liar!"

Tharius sighed. He had wondered whether Pamra held some such opinion. "When did Kesseret ever lie to you, Pamra?"

"The Awakeners lied. About the Holy Sorters. They lied."

"When did Kesseret ever lie to you?"

"Full of lies and filth about the workers, none of it true. I have come to appeal to Lees Obol, the Protector of Man. It is better if man knows the truth."

"When," Tharius repeated patiently, "did Kesseret ever lie to you?"

The glaze left her eyes and she looked at him uncertainly.

He said it again. "When did Kesseret ever lie to you?"

"She was Superior."

"When did she ever lie to you?"

"Not she," Pamra admitted, "but . . ."

"Kesseret would never have lied to you," he concluded. "Ilze lied to you, I have no doubt. But it is unfair of you to blame the lady Kesseret, my dear friend, your cousin."

"Cousin?" She had not expected this, this homely word from a long-ago childhood, before the Tower. "Cousin."

"Cousin, yes. Can you remember your grandmother?"

Pamra's lips twisted again, but she nodded, yes.

"Her father was my son. And Kesseret is my cousin."

She did not make the connection at once. It came only gradually, almost against her will. "You are—you are my great-great-grandfather?"

"Say merely 'ancestor,' it is easier. Yes. Which is one of the reasons I have brought you here. We are family. Indeed, we are the only remnants of the family. Your half sisters are dead, so I am told. Without children. You and I, Pamra, are all the Dons." He did not want to talk with her about her crusade. He did not want to talk with her about the lies told in Towers or the obscene stupidity of the workers. He did not want to defend the status quo or to tell her the truth about the cause, for she might blurt it all out, unwittingly, even angrily, and then where would they be? He wanted to talk to her about the Dons, about Baris, about easy, sentimental things. It was a need in him.

But Pamra did not help him. She turned to the window where Neff blazed in the air, hearing his voice ringing in her ears. "I must see Lees Obol," she said, putting aside everything Tharius had said as though it had been wind sound, the chirping of swig-bugs, meaningless. "Since you are family, you will help me see him."

"Of course." He sighed. "Tomorrow. He is a very old man; he sleeps much of the time. Tomorrow morning, very early." If one was to get any sense out of Lees Obol, the very early morning was the only possible time, though in recent months even that was unlikely.

"Not now?" She was disappointed, but not angry at the delay. She had come almost to welcome delay, so long as it was inevitable. Things had gone at such a pace, such a headlong plunge, that at times she felt she could not encompass all that was happening. Delay gave a space. Inevitable delay could not be questioned, not even by the voices. Sighing, she sat down.

"Would you like to take off your armor?" Tharius Don asked again. "Put on one of these robes, Pamra Don, and we will have something to eat together. It is time you and I spoke, don't you think?"

Yet still she looked past him to the window, not seeing him, and he gave it up, sending in one of the servants instead, a heavy-bodied woman who would peel Pamra out of the tight fishskin armor and the high helm at Tharius Don's command. As she did, coming grim-lipped from the room.

"That's no dress for a woman. What kind of heretic is this? What's the matter with that child?"

"Never mind, Matron. Just see that the luncheon I've ordered is sent up promptly." The thought of food made him slightly ill. He had not eaten for days, perhaps for weeks. His body refused food, even though he was light-headed sometimes from hunger. He told himself it was only the imminence of the strike, the ultimate victory of the cause, but even telling himself this could not make his tongue enjoy the taste or his throat want to swallow. He had always felt his vision was clearer while he was fasting. Perhaps he fasted instinctively now, desiring the resultant clarity. Still, Pamra had to eat. The child had to be fed. Pamra seemed to be mostly skin stretched over slender bones. He did not look into the mirror to see how this description suited himself as well. "Send up the luncheon," he repeated to the servant's departing back.

She was gone with a fluster of skirts and a tight-lipped grunt. To spread more rumor, no doubt, thought Tharius. Rumor, the blood of the Chancery. Which we suck together, more, and yet more.

They sat together at a small table set by the window. The child drank water. Pamra ate almost nothing, and that little without any indication of enjoyment.

"What is the child's name?" he asked her.

"Lila," she answered. She told him about Lila. He understood about one-tenth of what she said, and disbelieved most of that. The child was very strange. Its expression was not childlike. The way it moved was not childlike. It could not be her sister, and yet it could not be what she said it was, either. Tharius turned his eyes away to poke at the food without tasting it, watching this year's flame-bird as it built its tinder nest on the ledge, flying back and forth across the window with beakfuls of fiber from the pamet fields.

"Do you see him?" she asked suddenly, her eyes fixed on the open window.

"The flame-bird, yes."

"Flame-bird," she said. Yes. Neff was a flame-bird, born from the flame of his funeral pyre. How clever of this man, this ancestor, to have known. She reached out to take his hand, wanting to share with him what she knew, what she felt, about Neff, about Delia, about the God of man. Words poured from her, a spate of words, tumbling over one another in their haste to be spoken.

"Tell me," he asked finally, marveling at what he thought she was saying to him, "is Neff in the keeping of the God of man?"

She nodded urgently. "Yes, oh, yes."

"But he is not a man. Neff, I mean. Treeci, didn't you say. Not human at all." Treeci! His heart pounded. The Treeci existed. They really did. Just as the books had said, just as they needed to be. Beautiful. Civilized. As the Thraish would be, too. "Neff was a Treeci. Not human?"

"Not then, no," she said. "But now, now he is . . ." She had not thought of this before, but of course he was. She saw

him, radiantly winged, not the Neff of Strinder's Isle, but Neff
with arms to hold her and a mouth that spoke to her, kissed her
gently through the flames. "He's a man now. Not like I am, or
you, Tharius Don. Something finer than that."

"An angel, perhaps." He was trembling, awed, feeling himself in the presence of something exalted and marvelous.

She considered this. "Angel" was a very ancient word, but
one that every Northshoreman knew. A kind of beneficent
spirit. Without sex or identity or kind. Suddenly she knew that
was exactly what he was. "An angel, yes," in a tone of ringing
rapture that made him want to weep.

"And the general saw all this, when you explained it to
him!"

She tried to explain this as well, and Tharius Don's soul, ever
eager for proof of his thesis, took it in like water upon sun-
parched earth. Even in this unlikely soil, goodness would grow!
Oh, if Pamra Don could find a soul in Jondrigar and warm it to
thaw, what might she not do for the Thraish! He longed for
someone to discuss this with. Kessie. Kessie had told him the
girl had this talent. Why had he not understood what Kessie
meant? She had called it "recruiting," but it was so much more
than that! Oh, if Kessie were here. But she was not! No one
was. Only himself, and Pamra Don, and the world out there
waiting a message from him.

Which he had dreaded to send. Which he had put off sending
for some little time. The cause had been ready for a year or
more, ready as it would ever be, and yet he had not sent the
word. Why? He had asked himself this, morn and evening,
wondering whether his own dedication was as great as it once
had been. Was it failing purpose? Or did he fear his own
inevitable death when the elixir was no longer available?

Or was his delay, his procrastination, foreordained, perhaps,
in order to allow this thing, this miraculous thing, to happen.

"You told the general the truth," he urged, "and the general
accepted that?"

She nodded. That was what had happened.

He shook his head, awestruck into silence. She had told the
truth, and the general had accepted it. Tharius Don had never
doubted the existence of the divine, and her statement con-

firmed his belief. Yes. He had delayed in ordering the strike because something greater than himself had chosen that he do so. Perhaps the Dons had indeed been chosen for something marvelous, for some great purpose. But it might be Pamra Don, not Tharius, who was to accomplish this great thing. He stared at her, watching the glitter of her eyes as though it had been stars, moving in the heavens to spell out a command.

There was a knock at the door, a knock too soft to break through his reverie, which was then repeated until he heard it.

A messenger with a letter from Shavian Bossit.

He broke the seal and read it, read it without really seeing it. "The Jondarite captain at Split River Pass has received a delegation of Talkers, and they bear a written message as well. Sliffisunda demands Pamra Don be sent to him. The Thraish want her at the Talons for questioning. Gendra and I are inclined to agree it is a good idea, and Gendra offers to escort her and oversee her safety."

Pamra was saying something, but he didn't hear her. He read the message again. At first it made no sense, but then its purpose bloomed in him like some gigantic, fiery flower, its perfume enwrapping him, spinning him in a sudden delirium. Pamra Don was wanted at the Talons, by the Thraish. Pamra Don, who had done a thing for the cause that Tharius Don had never thought of doing. Pamra Don, who had converted the general in one day. Pamra Don, who saw the souls of Treeci and people reborn as angels.

And yet, how could he know? How could he be sure? He turned to her with a fierce and longing love to demand the answer.

"If you were to speak to the Talkers—to the fliers, Pamra. If you were to tell them the truth, would they believe?"

She looked at him uncertainly, past him at the glowing figure of Neff, outside the window. Radiant. Breast stained with red, nodding to her as he always did. Yes, yes, anything was possible, anything was conceivable. Yes.

"Talkers?" she asked.

"The fliers. The fliers who talk. You know."

She did not know. Still, anything that talked should be told the truth. "It's better to know the truth," she said. Neff would know. Wasn't he kin to the fliers? Wouldn't he know?

"If I send you to them, Pamra? Can you convert them as you did General Jondrigar?"

"It's better when people know the truth," she said again, a thing she often said when nothing else seemed to fit, for that is what Neff often said to her. Her voice was calm, her face serene, still colored by the rapture that often came over it. "It's better to know the truth."

He took it for affirmation.

"Rest," he told her with an exultant glad smile. "I'll come back and talk with you more later."

He went down to the council meeting, where Jorn and Mitiar, with their arguments for sending Pamra to the Thraish well rehearsed and arranged, were amazed to find such disputation unnecessary.

"I agree Pamra Don should go to the Thraish. Take her," Tharius said. "Keep her safe, Gendra, but take her along. Take her, and the child, but be sure she talks to Sliffisunda himself."

"I think Sliffisunda will require that," Shavian interjected in a dry voice. "There will be no problem." He wanted to ask Tharius what had happened to him. The man was dizzy with joy, like a child on festival morning when the Candy Tree had grown in the night. Like a young Chanceryman at his first elixir ceremony. Full of light. Buoyed up. It was almost tempting to delay the meeting a little in order to find out why, but Gendra's offer to leave the Chancery was too much a godsend to risk losing. Easier on everyone if she's away for a while, he assured himself. Gives us time to get ready for it. And he glanced at the chairs against the wall where Glamdrul Feynt and Bormas Tyle huddled together, exchanging occasional whispered words. The perfect picture of conspirators, Shavian thought, shaking his head at them warningly.

The three of them had only the bare outline of a plot as yet. It would require three deaths: that of the general, that of Gendra Mitiar, and that of Lees Obol. One, two, three. Like a starting chant for a race. One to get steady, two to get ready, three to go.

Since Glamdrul Feynt was to end up as Lord Marshal of the

Towers, he would dispose of Gendra Mitiar. Bormas Tyle wanted to be General of the Armies, which meant Jondrigar was his meat. Since Glamdrul and Bormas had charge of the elixir, nothing should be easier for them than a little selective adultera- tion. One, two. And then Lees Obol, with Shavian Bossit to take his place as Protector of Man—three votes in the council guaranteed: Bormas, Glamdrul, and his own—and the assembly already primed to vote for him.

Shavian started from agreeable visions of this future and was brought to himself.

"It's decided, then," Gendra Mitiar intoned. "I'll take her to Red Talons."

"That's closest, yes," Tharius Don approved.

"You'll keep her safe?" asked General Jondrigar, his voice heavy and obdurate as iron, oily with suspicion. "You, Mitiar, you'll keep her safe?"

Gendra smiled maliciously. "Of course, General. Of course I will. That's why I'm going."

The smile made Tharius wince, but only for the instant. Of course the old fish was up to something, but it didn't matter. What did she think of Pamra Don? Did she think anything at all? How could she know that Pamra Don was the divine intervenor, the peace bringer, the messenger of God, sent to mitigate violence and death? The messenger sent to Tharius Don to say he had been right in holding his hand, right to delay the strike. It would not be needed. The Thraish could be converted. The cause might be fulfilled without violence.

"It's settled, then," said Gendra Mitiar. "We'll leave in the morning." She cast an enigmatic look at Ezasper Jorn, who had been silent throughout the meeting. He and Koma Nepor had exchanged two or three carefully casual glances, nothing more, though inwardly they were jubilant. The old crock had fallen for it. She thought she was going to gain support for herself. By the time she got back—it would be too late. If she got back at all.

So, the Council of Seven adjourned. Both they and their ancillary personnel rose to move about the room. Shavian Bossit rang a small bell, its sound hanging in the hall like a strand of tinsel, a bright shivering of metal. Through the high doors came screeching carts bearing tea; a dozen soft-footed servitors in

gray livery to tend the tall silver and copper kettles with handles
worked into nelfants and gorbons and other mythical animals,
the charcoal stoves below them emitting a pungent smoke.
Plates of cakes were passed: puncon tarts, nutcakes, sweetbean,
and mince. The council members floated upon an ebullience
that was infectious, every member of it assured that his or her
own ambition was shortly to be fulfilled.

Ezasper would be Protector. Shavian would be Protector.
Gendra would be Protector. Each of them knew it, was certain
of it, glorying both in the absolute sureness of it and in the fact
that no one else knew.

Koma Nepor would be Marshal of the Towers. Glamdrul
Feynt would be Marshal of the Towers. They chatted with one
another, laughing, each glorying in the other's eventual
discomfiture.

The general would use his position to rectify distortions and
lies. He thought of this as he listened to Bormas Tyle, who was
certain he would soon become general. The two of them stood
together in a window aperture with their cakes. General Jondrigar
even made a little jest about the flower chaplet he had worn.
They laughed.

And Tharius Don stood alone, happier than he had been in
fifty years.

From behind the curtain a querulous old voice exclaimed,
"What's everyone laughing about? Tell me the joke. Tell me,"
and several Jondarites went to busy themselves within.

To the assembled council, Lees Obol's command only seemed
amusing, and even the general smiled. How could any one of
them explain his joy? Each, knowing the reason for his own,
thought better to pretend it was inexplicable.

The euphoria passed. Voices died down. The babble gave
way to whispers, winks, nodded heads. Cups were set down on
the waiting trays. Servitors scurried about with napkins to brush
up the crumbs. The carts went screeching away, complaining
into the vaulted silences. Ezasper Jorn hesitated in the doorway
long enough to whisper to the Chief of Research, "As soon as
she's well gone, Koma. As soon as she's well gone." And
they, too, departed in good humor.

Above, in his guest suite, Tharius Don sat down with Pamra

before the fire while Lila waved her hands at the flames and chortled in words he could not understand.

"Let me tell you about the Talkers," he said gently, watching her face to be sure she paid attention.

But she, nodding and making sounds as though she were listening, heard very little that he said. She was far away, in some other world.

· 15 ·

At the end of each month those aboard the *Gift* celebrated
riotously on the extra day. Eenzie the Clown juggled
hard melon and eggs on the main deck, discovering the
eggs in the ears of the boatmen and losing them again down the
backs of their trousers. On this occasion, Porabji brought out a
great crock he had had fulminating in the owner-house and
poured them all mugs of something that was almost wine and
almost something else, cheering as Glizzee, though in a different way. Thrasne himself had taken a generous amount of the
gift Glizzee from the locker and given it to the cook for inclu-
sion in whatever seemed best. They played silly games and sang
children's songs and ended by pouring wine on the new boat
and naming it the *Cheevle*, which, said Eenzie, was the name of
the delicious little fish that thronged the streams of the steppe.
She mimed taking bites out of the new boat, making them all
laugh. They took the canvas cover off the boat and sat in the
hull, wrapped in blankets against the night chill, singing River
chanteys and old hearthside songs. By the middle of the night
they were all weary but wonderfully pleased, and most of them
wandered off to their hammocks or bunks.

Thrasne came to himself atop the owner-house, staring at the
stars, humming tunelessly, almost without thought. Medoor
Babji found him there, came to stand beside him at the railing,
leaning so close her bare arm was against his own and the
warmth of them both made a shell around them.

"Babji," he sang, more than half-drunk. "Ayee, aroo, Babji,
Babji." He smiled at her, putting an arm around her.

She did not answer, only pressed closer to him, knowing

what would happen and willing that it happen. When he put his lips on hers, it was exactly as her body had anticipated. His mouth was sweet, wine smelling, his lips softly insistent. He cupped her bottom in his hands, pressing her close to the surging hardness of him. When he moved toward the *Cheevle*, toward the blankets piled in the bottom of it, she did not resist him. When he laid her down, himself above her, and found a way through their clothing, she did not say no. She cried out, once, at a pain that quickly passed, then all thought ceased.

It was a long time later she opened her eyes to see the stars again. She was cradled on Thrasne's shoulder, his right arm under her and around her, blankets piled atop them like leaves over fallen fruit. No sound on the ship except the water sounds, the creak of timbers, the footsteps of the watch on the forward deck, the rattle of ropes against wood.

"Babji," he said again, not singing, in a voice totally sober and a little disconsolate.

"What?" she said, knowing he had been awake while she slept. "What are you thinking?"

"I was thinking about what you said the other day, Medoor Babji. About the two kinds of people in the world. Those like you and me, who see puncon jam on our bread, and those others who see other things. I have been thinking about that. Those of us who see jam are the most numerous, I know. But does that mean the jam is really there?"

She stared at the silhouette of his face against the night sky. "Does it not, then?"

"I don't know. After a great, long time thinking of it, I could tell myself only that. I don't know."

He brought her closer to him, reached down to arrange the blankets against the night's chill. The wind was cold, his voice was colder yet. "It was Pamra's madness made me think of it. She does not see the world as we do. As you and I see it. As the boatmen see it. As your people see it. And so we call her mad. She will not come into the world I wanted for her, so I call her mad. She will not love me and bear my children, so she's mad. She talks with dreams and consorts with visions, so she's mad. I was thinking of that as I lay here, listening to you sleep."

She did not reply, halfway between sobbing and anger, not

knowing which way to fall. After what had just passed between them, and it was Pamra in his mind still! She took refuge in silence.

He went on, "The Jarb Mendicants could come with their blue smoke to sit beside me and tell me, 'Yes, she's mad.' But what would it mean, Medoor Babji? It would mean only that they see the same dream I see, not that the dream is real. So—so, if I were to share her dream, couldn't that be as real as my own?"

"How?" she asked him, moving from sadness to anger. "Your good, sensible head wouldn't let you do that, Thrasne."

"If the Jarb root gives one vision of reality, perhaps other things give other visions. Glizzee, perhaps."

"Glizzee is a happy-making thing, truly, Thrasne, but I have never heard that visions come of it."

"Then other things," he said thoughtfully. "Other things." He looked down at his free hand, and she saw that he held a jug of the brew old Porabji had made. "Other things."

She moved away from him, less angry now, though he did not seem to care that she went, for he began to lace up the canvas cover of the little boat. In the owner-house she undressed and braided the long crinkles of her hair into larger braids to keep them from tangling while she slept. Perhaps tomorrow she would cry. There was a bleak hollow inside her full of cold wind. Perhaps she would not get up at all.

Eenzie stirred. "Doorie? Where've you been? Up to naughty with the owner, neh?"

"Talking," she said tonelessly, giving nothing away.

"About his madwoman, I'll wager," Eenzie said with a yawn, turning back into sleep. "He has nothing else to talk about."

The morning found many less joyous than on the night before, with Obors-rom leaning over the rail to lose all he had eaten for a day or more.

"It's that brew of old Zynie's," he gasped. "I should have had better sense than to drink it."

"Perhaps," Thrasne suggested, "you should only have had better sense than to try and drink it all." Medoor Babji was passing as he said it. He saw her and looked thoughtfully at her, half remembering he had done something unwise, perhaps unkind. He needed to apologize to her for whatever it had been, if he could only have a moment to remember. She stared through him, as through a window.

"It is never wise to drink too much of old Porabji's brews," she said. "I have had a word with him." She passed Thrasne by, not stopping, and he stared after her in confusion. The night before was not at all clear to him. Part of it, he thought, he might have dreamed. And yet something was owed because of it, he thought. Something needed to be done.

Late that afternoon came wind. It was no small breeze. At first they welcomed it behind them, but the sailors soon began to shake their heads. They reefed the big sail, leaving only a small one at the top of the mast to maintain way. Later the wind fell, but the sailors did not put the sail out again.

"Storm," said one of them to Thrasne. His name was Blange, a laconic, stocky man who looked not unlike Thrasne himself. "Last time I remember the clouds lookin' like that"—he gestured to the horizon, where a low bank of cloud grew taller with each passing hour—"last time we were lucky enough to get behind an island and ride it out. Five days' blow it was, and the ship pretty battered when it was over. I don't like the looks of that."

Certainly if Thrasne had been near Northshore, he would have tried to get behind something. He didn't like the looks of it, either. The sky appeared bruised, livid with purpling cloud, darted with internal lightning so that sections of the cloud wall glowed ominously from time to time, a recurrent pulse of pallid light that was absorbed by the surrounding darkness as though swallowed.

The River surface looked flat and oily in that light, full of strange, jellylike quiverings and skitterings, as though something invisible ran across the surface. Swells began to heave at the *Gift*, lifting and dropping, lifting and dropping.

"What's it likely to do?" Thrasne asked.

"It's likely to give us one hell of a beating," Blange replied.

"Then let's get that little boat off the owner-house roof," Thrasne commanded. "We don't need that banging around."

They lowered the *Cheevle* into the water, running her out some distance from the *Gift* at the end of a stout rope. The two boats began a kind of minuet, bowing and tipping to one another across the glassy water between.

The wall of cloud drew closer even as they worked, still pulsing with intermittent light, muttering now in a growl that seemed almost constant. Obers-rom and the other boatmen were busy tying everything down that could be tied down and stowing everything else in the lockers and holds.

"Best take some of the spare canvas and nail it over the hatches," one of the sailors told Thrasne.

"Surely that's extreme?"

"Owner, if you want to keep your boat and our lives, I'd recommend it. I'm tellin' you everything I know, and I don't know half enough."

Thrasne stared at the wall of cloud. Perhaps the man was one of those doomsayers the River bred from time to time. On the other hand, perhaps he wasn't. Blange wasn't a young man. He had scars on his face and arms—from rope lashes, so he said. His hands were hard. One thing Blint had always said: "You pay a man for more than his strong back, Thrasne. You pay him for his good sense if he's got any."

So. "Tell Obers-rom what you need, Blange. I'm going to see what's going on in the owner-house."

What was going on was a card game among four of the inhabitants and naps for the other two.

"Thrasne," burbled Eenzie the Clown. "Come take my hand. I'm being beaten, but you could fight them off. . . ."

"Yes, Thrasne," Medoor Babji said in a chilly voice. "Take Eenzie's cards and we'll do battle."

He shook his head at her, scarcely noticing her tone. "No time, Medoor Babji. The sailors tell me we are probably going to be hit by a storm. They say a bad storm. Anything you have lying around should be put away." The sound of hammers came through the wall, and old Porabji sat up with a muffled curse.

"What're they doing?" Eenzie asked, for once in a normal tone of voice.

"Nailing canvas over the hatches to keep water out."

"Waves?"

"I don't know. I've never been in a bad storm. Rain, I suppose. Waterspouts, maybe. I've seen those." Thrasne was suddenly deeply depressed. The *Gift* was about to be assaulted and he had no idea how to protect her. "If things get violent, you might rig some straps over the bunks and strap yourself in. Less likely to be hurt that way, I should think." He turned and blundered out, needing to see what Blange was up to. Surely there would be something he could do.

When he emerged from the owner-house door, he was shocked into immobility by the wall of black that confronted him. The *Gift* rocked in a tiny pocket of clear water. Straight above them Potipur bulged toward the west, pushing his mighty belly toward the sunset in a tiny circle of clear sky. Elsewhere was only cloud and the ceaseless mutter of thunder. At the base of the cloud lay a line of agitated white, and Blange pointed this out, his face pale.

"There's the wind," he said. "Those are the wave tops, breaking up. It will be on us soon." He turned away, shouting for men to help him cover the other hatch.

"The ventilation shafts," Thrasne cried suddenly. "We have to cover the ventilation shafts."

"I'll help," said a small voice at his side. Medoor Babji. "Taj Noteen and I will help you. We can do the front shaft." Indeed, she knew well where it was, for she had sat there many an hour during the voyage, watching as Thrasne himself had once watched. Birds. Waves. The floating stuff that the River carried past.

"Get tools from Obers-rom," Thrasne said, hurrying away to the aft shafts, one eye on the rushing cloud.

Obers-rom gave them a hammer, nails—worth quintuple their weight in any nonmetal coin. "Take care," he growled at her. "Don't drop them, Medoor Babji. These are all we have." He sent one of the other men to carry the cleats.

She and Taj Noteen scrambled across the owner-house roof and dropped onto the grating above the shaft. They would have to squat or lie on the grating and lean downward to nail the cleats across the canvas. There was not room for two of them.

"Get back up," she grunted. "You can hand me the cleats as I nail them." She spread the canvas beneath her, holding it down with her body, pressing it against the outside of the square shaft, reaching behind her to take the cleat.

The wind struck. The *Gift* shuddered, began to tip. Medoor Babji cursed, thrust the hammer between her body and the canvas, and held on. Above her, Taj Noteen shouted, but she could not understand what he was saying.

The wind got under the canvas, lifted it. Her hands were clenched tight to it, her eyes shut. Only Taj Noteen saw her lifted on the bellying sail, lifted, flown, over the side and down into the chopping River. The water hit her and she screamed then, opening her eyes, seeing the loom of the *Gift* above her. Under her the canvas bulged like a bubble, air trapped beneath it, floating her. She was moving away from the boat. Away. She screamed again, soundless against the uproar of the sudden rain.

Then something struck the canvas, brushed it, away, brushed it again. The *Cheevle*. It bowed toward her once more, and she grabbed the side, lifted by it as it tilted away from her, pulling herself in. The canvas was tangled around her legs. It followed like a heavy tail, and she rolled onto the cover of the *Cheevle*. The wind stopped, all at once, and glassy calm spread across the waters.

Medoor Babji shouted. There were figures at the rail of the *Gift*, staring at her. Blange shouted at her. "Get under the cover, Babji! Get under it and lace it up. The wind is coming back. There's no time to pull you in. . . ."

She had scarcely time to comprehend what he had said and obey him, hurriedly loosening the lacing at one side of the little boat enough to crawl beneath it. She lay in the bottom of the boat, on the blankets tumbled there, and tugged at the lacing string with all her strength, pulling it tight again only moments before the wind struck once more. It was like being inside a drum, then, as the rain pounded down upon the tight canvas, and she clung to the lacing strings, flung this way and that by the wind, protected from battering only by those tumbled blankets and the wet canvas that had almost killed her, then saved her from drowning.

There were sounds of thunder, muttering, growling, sharp cracks like the sudden breaking of great tree limbs. After one such crack her ears told her the *Cheevle* was moving, racing, driven by the wind. She imagined the *Gift* also driven, wondering briefly if one of them preceded the other or whether the wind sent them on this journey side by side. After a time the violent rocking stopped. The rain continued to fall in a frenzy of sound. Lulled by the noise, by the dark, by her fear and the pain of her bruises, she fell asleep, still clinging to the lacing strings of the cover as though they held her hope of life.

Aboard the *Gift*, darkness fell like a curtain, rain-filled and horrid. Wind buffeted them. The old boat creaked and complained, tilting wildly on the waves. They had seen Medoor Babji crawl beneath the cover of the *Cheevle*. They had no time to worry about her after that. In breaks in the storm they managed to cover the forward ventilation shaft. The hammer and nails were caught between the shaft and the forward wall of the owner-house. Except for Thrasne, and for the steersmen, struggling mightily to keep them headed into the waves and wind under only a scrap of sail, the others went into the owner-house and cowered there, waiting for something to happen. Thrasne lashed himself to the rail and peered into blackness, seeing nothing, nothing at all, rain mixed with tears running down his face. He could feel the pain in the *Gift*, and he was awash with guilt for having brought her on this voyage.

After an endless time, the wind abated. The rain still fell in a solid curtain of wet. Men went below and came back to say there were leaks—none of them large, but still, water was seeping into the holds. They set up a bailing line, using scoops to clear the water, chinking the seep holes with bits of rope dipped in frag sap. Night wore on. The rain softened to a mere downpour, then to a spatter of wind-flung drops. Far to the west the clouds parted to show Abricor, just off full, descending beneath the River. In the east, the sky lightened to amber, then to rose.

Thrasne untied the knots that held him to the railing, coiled the rope in his hands, and staggered up to the steering deck to relieve the men there and give orders for repairs. He was half through with it, Obers-rom busy in the hold, Blange and a crew restacking the cargo to make room for caulking, when he chanced to look over the railing to the place the *Cheevle* swam along in their wake.

Should have swum. The rope that had tied it lay frayed on the deck, broken in the storm. Of the *Cheevle* itself, or of Medoor Babji, there was no sign.

• 17 •

To most of the crew on the *Gift*, it seemed that Thrasne owner had gone mad. He was determined to search for the *Cheevle*. No matter what they said, he would not hear them. "She'll be downtide," he said, again and again. "We have to look for her downtide."

Taj Noteen had his own reasons for wanting the *Cheevle* found. He did not want to go to Queen Fibji and tell her the chosen heir had been lost upon the river, lost with no attempt made to find her. Still, looking about him at the measureless expanse of heaving water, searching seemed ridiculous and was made to seem more ridiculous still by the advice of the sailors, those men who had plied the island chains throughout much of their lives.

"Thrasne owner," they begged. "Making great circles here in the midst of the water will do no good! The *Cheevle* was blown as we were blown. The tide moved it as it moved us. If it is not near us now, and if it cannot be seen from the top of the mast, anything we do may merely take us farther from it."

Thrasne would not hear it. Why it meant so much to him, he did not bother to figure out. Why his eyes filled at the thought of Medoor Babji alone, possibly injured upon the deep, he did not wonder. Why his gut ached at the idea of her lost, he did not put into words. He spoke often of finding the *Cheevle*. What he really longed to find was Medoor Babji herself, though he never said her name to himself. The name he had attached for so long to this feeling was Pamra. He had not brought himself to replacing the name, though her image had been replaced by another in his imaginings. In his sexual fantasies he would have

113

whispered Pamra's name, though the woman in his mind would
have been dark and fringe-haired, fire-eyed and silk-skinned as
only Medoor Babji was. If he had realized this, he would have
accounted this as being unfaithful to his dreams, his hopes, his
vows, and therefore he did not admit to any change. If someone
had asked him he would have said he loved Pamra Don as he
always had, as Suspirra, as herself.

"She is as a member of the crew," he wrote in his journal, in
yet another of those many books he had filled over the years
with *Thrasne's Thoughts*. "We would not abandon a crew
member until all hope was lost; so we may not abandon her."
As he wrote this, he was conscious that it was not quite the
truth, but he could find no other words that satisfied him. "It
may be," he continued, "as the sailors say, that it is already
hopeless."

And yet he would not cease searching for the *Cheevle*.

They spent some days tacking, circling, up and down, back
and forth, the sailors trying to keep some record of the way they
had gone, shaking their heads and snarling at one another from
time to time. During the storm several of the great water casks
had been broken. Thrasne set the carpenter to repairing the
casks, a job that did not take them long, but he either did not
notice or did not see the implications of the fact that the casks
were now empty. In this he was quite alone. The crew and the
Noor saw well enough that the remaining water would not last
them long. One could drink the brackish River water for a short
time, a day or two, perhaps, the sailors said. Longer than that
and people drinking the water doubled in cramps and fits and
died.

On the evening of the fifth or sixth day of this aimless
searching—during which every available pair of eyes had been
stationed at the rail or on the steering deck or even aloft, at the
top of the mast, the watchman having been hauled up there in a
kind of swing—Taj Noteen made his way to the place Thrasne
brooded atop the owner-house.

"Thrasne owner," he said. "Would you dishonor Medoor
Babji?"

Thrasne turned on him, lips drawn back in a snarl. Then,
seeing the quiet entreaty on the man's face, he subsided, won-

dering what ploy this was. "I would not," he growled. "As you well know. Medoor Babji is my . . . friend." He heard himself saying this, liked the sound of it, and repeated it firmly. "My friend."

"Then if you would honor your friendship, you should do as Medoor Babji would wish, Thrasne owner."

"I would presume she would wish to be found," he growled, becoming angry.

"Any of us would," agreed Taj Noteen. "Unless we were on a mission to which we would willingly sacrifice our lives. In that case, we might feel our mission more important than being found." He sweated as he said this, and his mouth closed in a hurt, bitter line, for he revered Queen Fibji, as did most of the Noor. Blame for the loss of the Queen's daughter would fall on the leader of the group. Who else could be asked to bear it?

"So you say," Thrasne argued. "You, who lead this group. Perhaps those who follow you feel differently. Perhaps to them the mission is not more important than their lives."

"We go at the Queen's command," Noteen said softly. "You have been told this."

"I have been told. Yes." It meant nothing to him.

"Medoor Babji is the Queen's daughter, her chosen heir. Medoor Babji is the real leader of this expedition, boatman. I speak with her voice when I tell you to give up this fruitless search."

"How can you?" Thrasne cried. "You know her! How can you?"

"Because there are ten thousand Medoor Babjis among the Noor," he replied, gesturing wide to include all that world of suffering humanity. "Ten thousand to be killed by Jondarites and taken slave in the mines. Ten thousand daughters to weep, ten thousand sons to die. We do not go to Southshore out of mere curiosity, Thrasne. We go because we must. The Noor are being slaughtered, day by day, week by week. Medoor Babji knows this! How do we honor her death if we perish of thirst here upon this endless water and the mission comes to nothing? Then she will have *died* for nothing! Would you dishonor her, Thrasne owner?"

Thrasne did not give up easily. Still, Noteen's words burned in his head. He went below to his airless little cubby and anguished to himself, thinking that everything he cared for was always reft from him, surprised at the thought, for it was only then he admitted to himself that he cared for Medoor Babji. Realizing it made his grief the worse, and he spent the night attempting to assign that grief some cause and function or to find some reasons in his own life for his being punished in this way. It was no good. He could not really believe in such punishment, though the priests and Awakeners taught it as a matter of course. It was nothing in his own life which controlled the lives of Pamra or Medoor Babji. They, too, were creatures who moved of their own will. He could only touch their lives a little, share their lives a little, if they would give him leave.

And Medoor Babji had given him leave where Pamra had not. The thought fled, like a silver minnow through his mind, elusive and yet fascinating.

Still, when morning came, he gave in to Taj Noteen's entreaties. The sailors turned the *Gift* toward the south, praying they would find water before many days had passed.

Despite his decision, Thrasne kept at the rail every hour of the light, or had himself hoisted to the top of the mast, or stood on the steering deck peering into the quivering glow of sun upon the waves for endless hours. He would resign himself to the need of the Noor to go south, he could not resign himself to the fact that she was gone. Something within him cried continuously that he would see the *Cheevle* dancing in the sun, beyond the next wave.

I remember when Blint first brought me aboard the *Gift*, sometimes at night I would wake from a dream of being lost upon the River. I was only twelve or thirteen, I suppose. Not a man yet, or anything near it. Perhaps they were a child's dreams, just as children dream of falling or flying but grown-ups seldom do. At least, I suppose that is true. I used to dream of falling all the time but don't anymore. I don't dream of being lost on the River anymore, either, but sometimes I dream of swimming—as though I were one of the strangeys. . . .

From Thrasne's book

Medoor Babji woke to the slup-slup-slup of wavelets on the side of the boat, to the heat of the sun on the canvas above her. The air was stifling. She lay in a puddle of wet blankets, cozied into them like a swig-bug into water weed. It took her some minutes to extricate herself and untangle the lacing strings from fingers that were stiff and sticklike. "Blight," she cursed at herself, attempting cheer. "My fingers have the blight."

Her head came out of the *Cheevle*, bleary eyes staring around at the sparking wavelets on all sides, taking some notice of the clear amber of the sky and the high, seeking scream of some water bird before realizing, almost without surprise, that the *Gift* was gone. It was as though part of herself had been prepared for this eventuality—aware of it, perhaps, when the rope snapped, even during the fury of the storm—even as some other, less controlled persona prepared for panic.

117

"Now, now," she encouraged herself, quelling a scream that had balled itself tight just below her breastbone and was pushing upward, seeking air. "It may not be the *Gift*'s gone. Maybe I'm gone. Separated, at any event. Oh, Doorie, now what?" Her insides were all melting liquid, full of confusion and outright fear, but the sound of her own voice brought a measure of control.

The persona in charge postponed answer of this question, postponed thought while she unlaced half the drum-tight covering of the *Cheevle* and folded it over the intact half. She wrung out the blankets as best she might and laid them over the loose canvas, seeing steam rise from them almost immediately. Her clothing followed. There was water in the bottom of the boat, though not much, and she sought the bailing scoops the sailors had carved, still tight on their brackets beneath the tiny bow deck. She postponed thought still further while bailing the boat dry, and further yet by turning and returning the blankets and clothing so that all were equally exposed to the drying rays of the sun.

And when all this was done, when she had dressed herself and taken a small drink of water from the River, brackish but potable—so Thrasne had told her, though one should drink very little at a time and not for long—there was no change in the circumstance at all. The *Cheevle* still bobbed on the wavelets, alone on the River, with no rock, no island, no floating flotsam in view.

"And no food," she murmured to herself. "And no really good water." The taste of the River on her tongue was mucky, a little salty. It had done little to reduce her thirst.

The mast lay in the bottom of the boat. She had slept between it and the sharp rib corners all night. Now she considered it with a kind of fatalistic resignation. She had paid some attention when the sailors had demonstrated how the mast was to be stepped. It had, as she recalled, taken two of them to get it up. Still. If she had the wind, she might go somewhere. If she went on bobbing here, like some little wooden toy, lost in immensity by a careless child, she might float forever.

The mast was heavy. After using her strength to no purpose for a time, she stopped fooling with the thing and thought it through. She took the lines loose from the canvas cover, maneuvered the butt of the mast into position against its slanting block, then attached a line halfway up the mast, running it under and over two of the lacing hooks and using a third to take up the slack. She heaved, sweated, cursed, saw the mast rise a little. She tied it off and recovered, panting, then tried again. By alternately heaving and cursing at this primitive pulley arrangement, she managed to get the mast almost upright, at which point it slid into its slot with a crash that made her fear for the bottom of the boat. She felt around it gingerly, praying to find no water. There was water. Was it left over from bailing or from a new leak? She had no idea and spent several anxious moments measuring it with eyes and hands to see whether it got any higher.

When she had convinced herself—deluded herself, her other persona kept insisting—that the hull was sound, she restored the lacing to the cover and relaced half of it, folded the now dry blankets under this shelter, remembered to drop in the wedges that held the mast erect, and set about trying to recall what Blange had said about sail.

"If you cannot remember what you are told," Queen Fibji had told her more than once, "you must use trial and error. The thing to keep in mind about trial and error is that some errors are quite final. Therefore, it might be wise to listen carefully to the instructions of those who have experienced what they are trying to tell you about."

"People are always telling me things," Medoor Babji had complained. She had been about twelve at the time, coming as inevitably into rebellion as a flame-bird chick into its plumes. "They don't even ask me what I think."

The Queen had nodded, brow wrinkled a little at this. They were in the Queen's own tent, and her serving women were redoing the Queen's hair as well as Medoor Babji's. It was a long process, though infrequent. Each strand was carefully combed out, washed and rinsed, one by one, then rewound and decorated at the bottom with a bead of bone or faience. The serving women chatted between themselves, politely, pretending that the Queen and Medoor were not present, thus allowing the mother and daughter the same freedom.

"Ah," Queen Fibji had said. "Well, let us suppose you have broken your leg. Chamfas Muneen is sent for. Chamfas says to you, 'Hold fast, this is going to hurt,' and then sets your leg and binds it up. Do you want Chamfas to ask you what you think before doing it?"

"Chamfas is a bonesetter!"

"So?"

"So of course he won't ask me what I think! I don't know anything about bonesetting."

"Well, let us suppose it is Aunty Borab. Suppose she tells you to eat your breakfast."

"Yes, that's what I mean. She doesn't ask me if I want breakfast. She just tells me."

"And what is Aunty Borab?"

"She's just an old woman."

"Ah, no, Medoor Babji. There you are wrong. Aunty Borab is a life liver. She is a survivor. She is a power holder and a health giver. She is no less expert at what she does than is Chamfas Muneen. But you call her an old woman and disregard what she says."

"She's bossy!"

"So is Chamfas, when he knows what is best for you. So am I when I seek to save my people hurt. And so is Borab when she knows it is best for you to eat your breakfast."

The Queen's expression had been mild, but there had been obsidian in her eyes. Hard, black, and questioning. *Is this one to be my heir, or shall I choose some other?* After a pause, she continued. "Instead of thinking of older folk as bossy persons with whom you must contend for control, Medoor Babji, think first what they are trying to tell you, or save you. Indeed, they may only be attempting to assert the privilege of age, but it does no harm to listen, even to agree. They will die before you, and you will have time to do it your way."

Medoor Babji had not wanted Queen Fibji to choose some other heir, so she had begun to save the rebellion for other targets and pay attention to Aunty Borab.

Now she wished she had paid as much attention to Blange and the other sailors.

"My fault," she said, putting the rising sun on her right hand

and bowing her head in the direction she assumed was north, toward the Noor lands, toward the Queen. "I called them common sailors in my mind. I should have called them expert boat handlers and learned from them." She closed her eyes in meditation. One had to meditate on mistakes when they were discovered. Otherwise, the opportunity to learn from them might pass one by. Another of the Queen's axioms that Medoor had adopted as her own.

When the meditation was over, she had remembered a few things. Other details came to her as she worked. There was a line to haul the triangular sail on its boom up and down the mast. There were lines to move the trailing end of it right or left. In the morning, they kept the wind behind them. That she remembered, for Thrasne had said it over and over. "Morning wind to take us out, evening wind to bring us back." After a time she got the hang of it, even remembering to steer a bit east of south. Then there was nothing to do but sit hot under the sun, watching a far bank of cloud in the west retreat below the horizon and disappear while other clouds formed out of nothing, fled away into shreds, and vanished. Around her the River heaved and pulsed, clucking against the boat's side. She grew half-blind from sun glimmer. She thought she saw things, strange winged figures larger than people, riding upon the waves. She blinked, and they were gone.

When the sun was directly overhead, something huge moved beside the boat. She felt the planks quiver and shift, not a natural, water-driven movement. Fish broke the surface of the water, leaping high to escape whatever was below. Two of them fell into the boat, flapping there with high-pitched squeals. Medoor Babji was not squeamish. She grasped them by their tails and banged them against the side of the boat. Her folding knife was in her sleeve pocket with her other essentials. She gutted the fish and filleted them, laying most of the strips of yellow flesh on the canvas to dry in the sun, eating the others slow mouthful by slow mouthful, grateful both for the sweet flesh and for the water in it.

"Strangey below," she told herself. What else could be that size? Some monster of the mid-River? Had the provision of the fish been accidental? Somehow she didn't think so. What was it

Thrasne had said? Sometimes strangeys picked up boatmen who had fallen overboard and returned them to their boats. Perhaps they fed stranded River wanderers as well.

By midafternoon she knew one thing more. Sometimes strangeys took small boats where they wanted them to go. In the lull after the morning wind had failed, Medoor Babji had attempted to set the sail as she remembered the sail on the *Gift* being set in the afternoons. She had accomplished this more or less and was headed westward once more when the boat shuddered, the sail flapped, and she found herself moving in a slightly different direction. Perhaps a bit more west of south than she had intended.

"When things are moving inexorably in a given direction," Queen Fibji had told her, "only foolish men attempt to move against the flow. And yet, those men who give themselves over entirely to the movement may also be foolish. The wise man works his way to an edge, if he can, and waits for opportunity to get ashore. From there he can observe what is happening without personal involvement."

Having no other occupation, Medoor Babji meditated upon this saying of the Queen's. She had some time in which to do it. At sundown she ate some of the sun-dried fish. It was well after dark when the movement of the boat changed from one of being towed to a mere floating once again. Against the stars she saw the bulk of hills crowned with trees. The tidal current washed her onto a shelving beach, whether of sand or rock she could not tell, and all motion ceased. She crept into the blankets beneath the canvas cover and fell asleep.

Morning came with a twitter of birds, a bellow of lizards. By the shore stilt-lizards walked, their narrow heads darting into the shallows to bring up bugs and fishes, stopping now and then to utter their customary cry, "Ha-ha, ha-ha," without inflection. Stilt-lizard meat was edible, Medoor Babji told herself, coming out of sleep all at once, fully conscious of being somewhere new, different, unknown. This place could not be too foreign, she thought, if there were stilt-lizards. Edible. Yes. Hunger pinched her stomach and brought a flood of saliva into her mouth. She sat up in the boat, unwrapping herself. The lizards fled at the sudden motion, then returned to stalk the shore once more, meantime keeping a wary eye on her.

The boat was halfway up a narrow beach, less sandy than stony, cut by a streamlet that bubbled down a shallow channel into a little bay. Contorted protrusions of black rock jutted from the beach and from the smooth surface of the bay, culminating in two writhing shapes, like a mighty arm and hand at each side of the entrance, reaching toward one another, braceleted with colonies of birds. Outside that embrace the River swept by, empty and endless.

Now the immediate danger was past. Now there was food and good water. Now that persona who had wished to cry for some time could cry.

It was some time before she realized what she was crying about, where the grief came from, boiling up from some deep well within her. It was not being lost, not being fearful for her life. It was being separated from Thrasne, lost from him, fearful for his life. And with that realization, she dried her tears, laughing at herself. The *Gift* was a strong, heavy boat, one that had plied the World River for generations. She thought of Thrasne fussing over it, repairing it at every opportunity, and of his crew of experienced men. Why had she assumed at once that he had met with some disaster? She was far more likely to have perished in the tiny *Cheevle*, and yet she lived. And if she lived, she could find the *Gift* again, somewhere, if not on Southshore or mid-River, then on Northshore when it returned.

"If the strangeys allow it," she told herself with some asperity, trying to give herself something else to think about. It was a cheerless thought, yet it had the same strengthening force as one of Queen Fibji's lectures. "Settle," the Queen had said to her often. "Settle, daughter. Consider calmly what you will do. Cry when it is done with, when you have the luxury of time."

"How did you get to know absolutely everything?" Medoor had asked, somewhat bitterly.

There had been a long silence, then a humorless laugh. Medoor had looked up at her mother, startled, almost frightened. She had not heard that laugh before.

"I'll tell you a secret," the Queen had said with a faraway, angry look on her face. "I don't know. Much of the time I

don't know anything. However, my not knowing will not help
my people, so I must know. And I do. It is easier to correct a
mistake than to be caught doing nothing. It is easier to beg
forgiveness for a mistake than to beg permission to act. People
will forgive you, child, but they will not risk allowing action.
Go to a council and say, 'Let me do this thing.' They will think
of ten thousand good reasons you should not. It could be wrong.
Or it could be not quite right. Or it could be right, but of a
strange rightness they are unfamiliar with. Oh, daughter, but
they will talk and talk, but they will not say, 'Do it.' That is
why I am Queen and they are my followers. Because they
cannot risk anything nor take part in others doing so. They are
herdbeasts, daughter. And yet I love them. When I speak to you
of trial and error, Babji, whose experience do you think I am
speaking of? . . .''

"So," Medoor Babji told herself. "If the Queen can prevail
in such a way, so her daughter can also prevail."

The resolution did not help her much in deciding what to do
next. Securing food seemed most logical, and this decision was
helped by a cramp of hunger that bent her in two. Fish was well
and good, but it left one empty between meals.

It was important she not lose the *Cheevle*. She tugged it
farther up the beach and tied it firmly to a tree. A tidal bulge
might come by; the presence of beaches argued for that proba-
bility. As she faced the bay, the sun was rising on her right
hand, so the bay faced northward. Could this land be Southshore?
Had the strangeys brought her to her journey's end? The beach
extended on either hand as far as she could see, riven with
tormented rock outcroppings here and there but interrupted by
no headland, curving slightly outward at its western extremity to
vanish in the River haze. She had come ashore in the only
protected place within sight, though the haze prevented her from
being sure she was on the only land in the vicinity.

The forest was made up almost entirely of one variety of tree,
one unfamiliar to her, a short, thick-trunked tree, rather twisted
in habit, with two or three main branches, also short and stout,
with many graceful twigs bearing lacy clusters of pale green
leaves that seemed almost pruned, so gracefully they barely
overlapped one another, allowing each leaf its measure of sun.

Some of these trees carried large, waxy blooms of magenta and azure blue, fringed with silver. Others bore seed heads, drying, almost ready to open. Among these strange trees were other, more familiar ones. She found a puncon tree—a larger one than she had ever seen on Northshore—with fruit almost ripe. Not far from the fruit tree was a small grove of fragwood, and beyond that, inland, stood a gawky, feathery tree that looked and smelled almost like the thorn trees of the steppes. The leaf was more divided than in the trees she knew, and the fruit was larger. The scent pulled her halfway up the tree, stretched along a branch as she fumbled for ripe ones among the cluster, finding them sweeter than she was used to and more welcome for that. She ate a few bites, filling a sleeve pocket with more. She would stuff herself later, if she didn't get sick or die in the meantime.

Returning to the boat, she robbed it of enough line to make snares. By noon there were three stilt-lizards caught, killed, gutted, and drying in the smoke of a small fire. There were patches of white on many of the rocks, River salt dried by the sun, and she sprinkled this on the lizard meat. She had bought River salt in the markets of half a hundred towns but had never seen it in its natural state before. There had been no unpleasant result from eating the thorn tree fruit, so she ate a bit more, chasing it down with roast leg of lizard. The water in the streamlet was chill and pure. She felt less inclined to weep. "Full stomachs," Aunty Borab had been fond of saying, "make calm judgments." Or the reverse, sometimes. "Hunger makes haste."

It was time, she felt, for a slightly longer exploration. The boat could always be found so long as she kept the River within sight or hearing and went out with it on the one hand and returned with it on the other. The boat was safe enough. She piled brush over and around the lizard carcasses to let them dry a while longer in the smoke of the smothered fire, then strode off into the forest as far as she could without losing sight of the River through the trees, walking westward at a good pace, taking note of what she saw but making no effort to examine any aspect of the landscape in detail. There were more and more of the lacy-leafed trees interrupted by occasional groves of other kinds, some fruit bearing. She gathered the ripe fruit, filling her sleeve pockets as instinctively as a bird might gather seed. The Noor had been gatherers for generations. They did not pass bounty by.

Occasional outcroppings of the black stone broke the flatness of the land, peculiarly fluid-looking piles of it, as though it had been poured and then hardened. Medoor Babji found herself staring at it, trying to fathom what it made her think of, and realized it was like sugar candy poured out upon the slab, before it was worked and pulled. There were places on the steppes of the Noor, places near the Teeth of the North, where similar glossy stone was found. The wise men among her people said it came from the center of the earth, out of fiery vents, with great noise and plumes of ash. If so here, it had been long ago. Green lay over all, blanketing and softening.

There were many tiny streams. Once or twice she stopped, thinking she had heard something moving off in the woods among the recurrent bird noise. Once she looked shoreward between two groves to see a winged figure standing upon a rocky point, ready to dive into the sea. She blinked, and it was gone. It had not looked real, even at first, she told herself. Sun dazzle and weariness and being alone caused people to see things. The Noor were well aware of that. "Steppe visions," they called them. Well, these would be "River visions." When the sun had fallen before her, she turned to put it at her back, moving closer to the shore for the return trip.

Her mind was set on the outline of the boat, the stack of leafy branches she had placed over the fire. So it was she almost passed her campsite by, not recognizing it. The boat was shattered, great holes bashed through the planking as though by some heavy missile, a great spear, perhaps, thrust and withdrawn, thrust and withdrawn again. The fire was scattered into gray ash. The stilt-lizard meat was gone. All around the site and in the stream lay small blobs of guano, white and reeking.

Their footprints crosshatched the shoreline, coming out of nothing. Fliers. They had ruined her boat. They had stolen her meat. They had fouled her campsite and the stream. Two of them, she thought, who had walked side by side to do their hateful damage.

Worse, they had laid a trap for her. She put out her hand to coil some of the rope. She had almost touched it when a familiar glisten on the rough twist caught her eye. She put her hands behind her and bent forward, peering. A Tear of Viranel. Oh, hadn't the Noor learned long and long ago to watch for that glisten as they walked the steppes? The Tears could not kill them, but they made nasty sores where they touched, sores that were painful for a long time and took weeks to heal. Tears would grow anywhere, sometimes here, sometimes there. The Noor spread wood ashes on any patches they found, but the danger was always there. Medoor cursed, briefly, suddenly aware of danger from an active intelligence, out there, somewhere. They hadn't seen her except at a distance. They didn't know she was a Noor.

There were other Tears at the site. Not many she could find in the failing light. The destroyers had not bothered to rip the canvas cover away from the boat; the blankets were untouched. She took them. The light was too poor to do more than that. Tomorrow she would return to see what else could be salvaged. She stepped carefully away from the place, watching where she put her feet, scraping them again and again through the dry sand to remove any Tear that might have clung to her shoes.

Then she was back among the trees, looking up through the boughs into an empty, amber sky. They had spied on her, without doubt, seeing her easily on that barren beach. Now perhaps she could return the favor. Medoor Babji's lips parted in a snarl, an expression her mother would have recognized. When darkness came, she was well hidden in a copse of thick foliage, well wrapped against the night's chill, reasonably well fed on the fruit she had gathered during the day, and perhaps unreasonably set upon vengeance.

Inside her, shut away, someone grieved anew for Thrasne, for the near-kin, for all old, familiar, and much loved things. She had no way to repair the boat. Without it—without it her whole life might well be lived upon this shore. She shuddered with tears that she would not allow herself to shed, summoning anger instead.

In the earliest light of morning she went to the beach and salvaged all the rope she could lay hands on as well as all the

canvas. They had been fairly clever in placing the Tears where
she might have been expected to put her hands. She dragged her
salvage through the ashes of her fire again and again, meantime
protecting her hands with canvas strips cut from the boat cover.
She would not cut the sail. Not yet. Morning and calm showed
only four planks of the boat actually splintered. Perhaps, somehow, she would think of a way to restore them.

Heavily laden with her salvage, she went back into the woods
and sought a cave, thrusting a long stick into every opening she
found until she located a bottle-shaped hole in one of the
black-rock outcroppings. The neck was almost too narrow for
her to wriggle through, but inside it opened out into a comfortable shape, smooth-walled. Here she stored the blankets, the
rope, the canvas, her snares. The opening was hidden behind
freshly cut branches. She brought out the snares to set them
among the rocks where a streamlet rattled out of the forest onto
the beach, hiding them with branches cut from the nearest tree.
It trembled oddly when she cut it, but Medoor Babji had no
time to pay attention to that. She picked fruit once more, filling
her sleeve pockets. Then she went back to the shore to keep
watch.

From a horizontal branch halfway up the largest tree in a
small grove of frag trees, she could see the wrecked boat, the
scattered ashes of her fire.

It was after noon when they came, spiraling down to land at
the edge of the sand, their feet just above the waterline, as
though fearful of it. They stalked into the campsite, examining
each step of the way with nodding heads, peering eyes. One
was of an unfamiliar type, taller and more slender than the
other, better-groomed, with a shine to his feathers. The other
was fusty and scurfy, feathers awry, and yet of the two, this one
appeared the stronger and more vital.

"It came back," croaked the taller one in harsh but understandable human language.

The other answered, making sounds Medoor Babji could not
understand.

"Speak in meat talk," the first croaked again. "I don't
understand your flier talk."

"*Horgha sloos,* something-something," the second said in a

hideous, screeching tone. Then, in recognizable speech, "Meat-talk soils my mouth."

"Then let your mouth be filthy," commanded the first. Though the shorter being croaked its speech, as though words were seldom used, the taller creature's words were clear and understandable. From her perch above them, Medoor Babji named it a Talker, unaware it was the name the whole class of creatures had chosen for themselves. It went on, "At least I can understand meat talk. You barbarians from the wild lands talk like savages."

The shorter flier deposited a blob of shit and held its wings at a threatening angle. "Fliers not savages. Fliers important. We keeping meat animals in our care. Your highmost Talker commanded. We do. You, Slooshasill, nothing but Talons servant, do nothing, blat, blat, blat. Share meat. Dirty yourself."

"Stop your words," screamed the Talker in a rage. "All that is unimportant. Do not speak of what is true on Northshore. We are not on Northshore. Thraish cannot fly over water, but storm can blow where Thraish cannot fly. Storm brought wind; wind brought us here. Now is only one importance. Food to keep us alive. Living or not living. Human meant much food, but human is gone."

"Maybe got Tears on it. Maybe wandered off." The flier opened its wings. For some reason, Medoor Babji thought it might be a female. Something in the way it moved, like a crouching barnyard fowl.

"No. Rope is gone. Cloth is gone. Ashes are spread around. Human took those things. Human saw and avoided Tears."

The other cocked its head, took quick steps toward the waterside, then darted sideways with a hideous, serpentine stretch of the neck to snatch an unwary stilt-lizard that had poked its head from among the rocks. Medoor Babji watched in horrid fascination as the flier tossed the lizard up, caught it, tossed it again, each time cutting it as it struggled and shrieked, gulping it down at last while it still wriggled feebly, all its bones broken.

"Not enough of those, Esspill," said the tall flier in a bleak tone. "Not enough to keep us alive long."

"Enough for me," replied the other one. "Enough for unimportant Esspill. Savage Esspill. Not enough for Slooshasill, important Slooshasill, Fourth Degree, that one can eat fish.''

The Talker darted his beak at the shorter bird, bloodying its head just above the beak. Dust rose around them as they fought, screamed, beat at one another with their wings. Then was silence. The dust settled. Medoor Babji could see them crouched across from each other, panting. The taller one had had the worst of it. Hungry, her mind said to her in Aunty Borab's voice. That one's half-starved.

"Only filth eat fish," the one called Slooshasill said at last. "Only ground crawlers eat them."

"Then catch lizards for yourself!"

"I am Talker." In her hiding place, Medoor Babji's mouth twisted in amusement. She had named the creature correctly. "You are flier. You are supposed to catch them. Fliers are supposed to bring food for Talkers. Females are to serve males!"

"Males," the flier screamed in scorn. "At mating time, Esspill will serve males. Talkers not males. And Slooshasill not even Talker now. Slooshasill nothing."

They still crouched. "When we get back to Northshore, Slooshasill will again be Talker. You will be punished, then, Esspill."

"How get there? Cannot fly over water."

"Did," said the other in a hopeless tone. "Did fly."

"Didn't. Wind carried. Couldn't stop. Wind brought. Wind will have to take back again. Can't fly over water."

A long silence. At last the Talker asked, in a tone that could only be the Thraish equivalent of a whine, "What we do now, Esspill?"

"What you do, don't know. What I do is get more Tears. Then find human. Put Tears on. Eat it. I be strong then. Fly back. Fear or not." It was an empty threat. Even to Medoor Babji, unused to the sound of flier talk, it came across as mere bluster. The wings came down in a hard buffet, throwing sand into a quickly falling cloud. Medoor dodged behind the trunk of the tree, afraid to be seen. When she came out again, both pairs of wings were above her, above the land, one in the lead, the other following. She watched them as they circled low above the forest, low above the beach, searching. Never, not even for a moment, did they fly out over the open water.

It seemed unwise, she felt, to stay in the vicinity of the boat, though she did not want to risk losing it. She climbed higher in the tree and took a sighting. It was likely this small bay was unique. The bay lay midway on a line between two tallish hills, one crowned with a monstrous frag tree grove. There seemed to be no other hills within sight.

She came down the tree in a chastened mood, her desire for vengeance chastened by reality. Esspill, the flier, was as large as she. Lighter, perhaps, but with talons and a sharp, hooked beak. Likely those talons could hold Tears without danger to Esspill herself. Herself. Medoor Babji would have been sure of it even without the verification of their speech.

But then what was the one called Slooshasill? A male? Not according to the other one. Not male or female. A kind of neuter thing. A Talker.

Who would have thought the fliers could talk? Queen Fibji had never spoken of any such thing. Of course, there were few fliers seen upon the steppes, but still it was odd that none among the Noor had known. If, in fact, they had not known.

And now? What?

She could hide indefinitely. She was confident of that. She had fruit to eat and would eat fish, which the flier creatures would not. Even if Esspill caught every stilt-lizard on the place, which wasn't likely, Medoor Babji could be sure of food. But it would have to be a covert, sneaky kind of existence.

Or, she could fight. Reason said that the odds against her would be reduced if she waited a while. That tall Talker creature was half-starved. The flier wouldn't feed it, and it didn't seem able to catch food for itself. Given only a little time, it would be dead or too weak to threaten her. So, patience was called for.

Still, it would be a difficult, nervous business, surviving with an eye in the sky looking for her. She went back to her cave, stopping at the snares on the way. Two stilt-lizards, not bad. She would smoke them. . . .

She wouldn't smoke them. Medoor Babji cursed. Smoke would bring the damn feather mops on her in a moment. Smoke could be seen at great distances on any clear day or moonlit night. She would have to salt and sun-dry the meat. She could eat raw fish with resignation, perhaps even with a modicum of pleasure, but she could not face the idea of raw stilt-lizard. Hot bile stirred at the back of her throat. She needed a smoke oven. Perhaps one of the caves. . . .

Smoke. She thought about that. It might be worth the effort, just to get the creatures away from here. Otherwise they would be haunting her. She thought about it for an hour and then decided upon it. She would begin today. There was no reason to wait.

One blanket and some food made a small pack. She headed east through the forest, moving as rapidly as possible while still keeping a fairly good watch on the land around her. When darkness came, she stopped on the beach to stack a large pile of wood with a smaller one next to it and then returned to the forest to build a small, smokeless fire of driftwood under cover of a stone outcropping. She cooked a lizard over it, putting the fire out at once when she had eaten.

At early light, she lit the smaller pile of wood, connecting it to the larger one with a line of thin, dried sticks and shavings. Over the larger woodstack she laid leaves and grasses. By the time it caught and smoked, she should be some miles away to the east.

An hour later she climbed a tree and peered back the way she had come. A pillar of smoke rose straight into the windless sky, where two black dots swung and circled toward it. She allowed herself a brief moment of self-congratulation, then climbed down to walk east once more.

After the third smoke on the third morning, she went deeper into the woods and turned back the way she had come. If the fliers were not cleverer than she thought they were, they would go on east, looking for her there. The line of smokes had led them in that direction. There would be no smoke on the following morning, but they might think she had seen them and was hiding from them. If they kept on moving in that direction, she might be free of them for a very long time.

She slept in the woods for the two nights it took her to return, each time awakened by stirrings and rustlings as though something or someone wandered in the leafy spaces. She was not foolish enough to call out. Her campsites were well hidden. She saw no evidence that anyone had wandered nearby when she woke. Still, it made a small itch of apprehension at the back of her mind.

When she returned to the boat, she unstepped the mast, laying it among fallen logs in the forest, half covering it with branches. The hull she drew deep into the woods, tugging and hauling with much smothered cursing in between. It left a clear and unmistakable trail, one she took great pains to eradicate. She raked away all the ashes of her earlier fire, gathered up the bits of charcoal, and built another fire half a mile down the beach, scattering it when it had burned out. If the fliers had not paid particular attention to the landmarks, they might assume that was the place the boat had been. She scattered some broken wood in that place and drew a heavy timber down the beach into the River. Now it looked as though she or someone had returned, had made some hasty repairs, perhaps, and then pulled the boat out into the water.

"Where it promptly sank, drowning me," she said with a hopeless look at the carcass of the *Cheevle*. Two of the holes were small. They could be patched with wood whittled to size and pounded in, caulked with—well, caulked with something or other. Frag pitch. She knew where there were frag trees, and gathering the pitch was merely a matter of cutting the bark and collecting the hardening sap when it gathered in the scar, then melting it in—in something.

The remaining two holes, however, were sizable.

"When faced with a number of tasks," Queen Fibji had said, "so many that the mind balks at getting them done, pick one or two small ones and begin. When those are done, move on. Never consider all that must be done, for to do so is quite immobilizing. . . ."

She began. Repairing the two small holes took five days, from dawn to dusk. She had caulked the wood with fresh frag sap, learning that it did quite well if applied in many thin coats and allowed to dry between. Using melted resin would have been quicker. It would also have been impossible. She had nothing she could use for a vessel and could find nothing that would serve. There were no gourds or hard-shelled nuts. Clay could be made into pots, of course, but that would have taken still longer.

While working, however, she had decided how to mend the larger holes. She would cut flat pieces of wood, glue them to the outside of the boat with frag sap, then cover the entire outside of the boat with the canvas boat cover.

It took five days more to complete the repairs. She dragged the hull back to the beach and into the water, where she managed to get the canvas under and around it, lacing the rope across the boat to catch the hooks on the opposite side. The mast was up, raised the same way she had raised it when on the River, with panting and grunts and a good deal of helpless cursing. She looked at the thing where it floated, shaking her head. It had a deck of rope, almost a net, where the lines laced across to hold the canvas. She would have to worm her legs between the ropes to sit at the rudder. She would have to wriggle herself beneath them to lie down at night. If there were another storm, she would probably sink.

In all that time, she had not seen the fliers. In all that time, she had almost forgotten them.

In the morning she could forget them completely, for she would be on the River once more, where they could not follow. Westward. To the end of this land, if it had an end. Then south. And if it had no end, then northward once more. Back to Northshore. She had a plentiful supply of dried fruit stored in canvas sacks, an almost equal supply of sun-dried lizard meat. The last two days she had spent digging edible roots, which lay in well-washed succulence among the other provisions. She had raveled some rope to make a fishing line and carved some fragwood hooks. Even if the strangeys had forsaken her, she should be able to manage. She would not be out of sight of land unless she came to the end of this land and turned north or south once more.

So she built her small, smokeless fire under cover of the rocks, ate fresh fruits and roots, freshly roasted meat, curled into sleep in satisfied exhaustion. There would be plenty of time to rest on the River.

During the night there was a tidal surge which washed the

canvas-girdled *Cheevle* half back onto the shore. Medoor Babji, wanting an early start, was on the beach when the sun had barely risen, struggling to get the boat back into the water. Its canvas bottom did not wish to slide on the rough sand, and she swore at it fruitlessly, knowing she would need rollers to get it moving, which meant another day before she could leave.

The screech that came from behind turned her around, bent her backward over the *Cheevle* as though to protect it, before she even saw the fusty, raddled form of the flier stalking toward her over the sand. It carried a leaf-wrapped bundle in one set of rudimentary wing fingers. Without asking or being told, Medoor Babji knew they were Tears.

"So, human," said Esspill. "You tried to trick us." It cawed laughter. "You did trick stupid Talker. He went that way, long ago. Looking for you."

"You weren't tricked?" she asked from a dry throat, the words croaked almost in the flier's own harsh tone.

Esspill shook her head, a mockery of human gesture. "Oh, no. Was no meat in those fires. No bones. No reason for them."

"You're very smart," she gasped. "Smarter than I thought."

"Oh, fliers are smart. Smarter than Talkers think. Talkers think . . . think they are only smart ones. All words. No faith."

"Faith?" She edged to one side, trying to get the boat between her and the flier.

"Stand still," it commanded. "Don't try to run. Tears won't hurt much. After that, humans don't feel." It clacked its jaw several times, salivating onto its own feet, doing a little skipping dance to wipe the feet dry.

"Faith?" asked Medoor Babji again, thinking furiously. "What do you mean, faith?"

"No faith in Promise of Potipur. Potipur says breed, grow, have plenty. Talkers say not breed, not grow, live on filth. Now Thraish have herdbeasts again. Soon have many. Then all humans will die. No more filth. No more *horgha sloos*."

"But if you breed, your numbers will grow, and you'll eat all your animals and go hungry again."

"Promise of Potipur," it said stubbornly. "Promise. You hold still now. For Tears."

"Tears don't work on the Noor," she cried. "They don't work on blackskins."

The flier stopped, beak agape. "Noor. You are Noor?"

"I am, yes. Medoor Babji. One of the Noor."

"No. Dark from sun. Humans turn dark from sun."

"I am not dark from the sun, Esspill. I was born dark. Look at my hair. The Tears won't work on the Noor. It won't grow inside us."

"Try," the flier snarled. "Try anyhow."

She edged away again, feeling in her sleeve pocket for her knife. "I'll fight," she threatened. "I may kill you."

"Fight!" it commanded. "Do that!"

Wings out, claw fingers stretched wide, talons lifted, beak fully extended, Esspill launched herself at Medoor, who dived in a long, flat dive into the River. It was instinct, not reason. It was the best thing she could have done. She came up in the water, clinging to the bowline of the *Cheevle,* began tugging at it, frantically working the boat into the water beside her. On the shore the flier danced up and down, pulling the boat away from her, screaming its rage.

Then it was gargling, its beak wide, eyes bulging. A long wooden shaft protruded from the flier's breast. She turned around, staring. Through the rocky arms that embraced the bay came another boat, no larger than the *Cheevle.* In it sat a man. In it stood a . . . a flier? Not a flier? Something very like, and yet not?

It had a bow in its wing fingers, an arrow nocked, the arrow pointed at the shore where Esspill still staggered to and fro, falling at last in a shower of dark blood onto the sand.

"Hello?" called the person. "We saw your smoke. We've been looking for you for over a week."

"Thraish," cried the other, drumming his keeled breast with his wing fingers to make a hollow thumping. "I have killed a Thraish." Thumpy-thump, delight in that voice. "Look, Burg, I've killed a Thraish!" It turned toward Medoor Babji, bowing. "Happy day, woman. I have saved you."

"We're called the Treeci," he told her, working the sculling oar as they moved down the coast, westward, the *Cheevle* in tow. "Have you heard of us?"

"I have," she admitted. "There are Treeci on a place called Strinder's Isle."

"Oh, there are Treeci on half the islands in the River," he said, making an expression that was very smilelike with a cock of head and flirt of eyes.

"That's possibly an exaggeration," said the human person. He was a stout, elderly man with white hair that blew around his head like fluff.

"Possibly. Or possibly an understatement, so far as that goes. What was that Thraish trying to do to you, eat you?" The Treeci turned to Medoor Babji once more.

"She had Tears of Viranel wrapped up in a leaf. She wanted to put them on me and then eat me. Tears don't work on the Noor, though. Our skins are too dark."

"I've heard that. Had you heard that, Burg?"

"Oh, it's probably written down somewhere. In the archives over on Bustleby. It's probably written down there."

"You know about the Noor?"

"We have histories, young lady," said Burg. "We aren't savages. We're literate, human and Treeci both."

"But where—where did you come from?"

"The same place you did, originally. Probably for the same reason. Trying to get away from the senseless conflict over there." He jerked a thumb to the north. "Long ago. At the time of the Thraish-human wars. They were eating humans then. It's a wonder they haven't eaten them all by now."

Medoor Babji shook her head. "No. No, we have a—they have what my mother calls a detente. An agreement. They eat dead people. Northshore dead people, not Noor dead people."

The Treeci spat. "Carrion eaters," he gasped. "So I have heard, but I find it hard to believe, Medoor Babji."

"Oh, come, Saleff, the Thraish were eating human dead during the wars. You know that."

"Out of desperation, yes, but . . . ."

"I presume they are no less desperate now."

"They could do what we did."

"We've talked about this a thousand times," the human said

irritably. "The ones who could do what you did, *did* what you did. The ones who were left *couldn't* do it. They had offspring who also couldn't do it. The Thraish could no more eat fish and become flightless today than they could become sweet-natured and stop shitting all over their living space. It's called selective breeding, and they've done it."

It was only argument, not even addressed to Medoor Babji, but the words rang inside her, setting up strange reverberations. Why? Something fled across her mind, trailing a scent of mystery and marvel. What? She tried to follow it, but it eluded her. She concentrated. Nothing. At least she would remember the words. *Selective breeding. Those who could do it, did it.* She would think about those words later.

"You know all about them?" Medoor Babji asked. "How do you know all that?"

"Oh, some of us human islanders sneak back to Northshore every now and then. Young ones of us, boys with time on their hands and adventure in their blood. Some of them go and never return, some go and come back, enough to give us an idea what's going on. One of the more recent returnees was a slave for the Thraish for five years."

"And they didn't eat him?"

"Would have, I suppose. He didn't give them a chance." Burg spoke proudly, almost boasting. "My son."

Silence fell, except for the sloshing of the sculling oar. After a time, Medoor Babji asked, "You came to find my smoke?"

"You could have been one of ours," said Burg. "Lost. We use smoke signals. It looked like that, one fire each day for three days. We do that sometimes. Or sometimes three fires all at once."

"Where are we going?"

"Down to Isle Point. West end of the island. You can look across the straits to the chain from there."

"Who lives there?"

"Treeci, mostly. About a dozen humans, too. Most of our folk are down the chain, on Biddle Island, and Jake's."

"How many?"

"A few thousand in this chain. The islands aren't that big. We have to spread out. Otherwise we'd overfish the River, kill off all the edible animals, the way the Thraish did during the hunger.''

"What edible animals?"

"The ones there aren't any more of on Northshore, girlie. Did you ever see an espot? Or a dingle? Little furry things? 'Course not. Thraish ate 'em all. They're extinct on Northshore. From what I understand, you've no mammals left at all on Northshore.''

"That flier, Esspill, she said they had herdbeasts again. I didn't know what she meant.''

The white-haired man pulled in his oar and stared at her, mouth working. "Is that possible?"

"A few might have survived," the Treeci responded. "Somewhere. Perhaps behind the Teeth.''

"If they have herdbeasts again, it's the end of humans on Northshore," the man snarled. "You can depend on it. The Thraish will kill them all.''

Medoor Babji shook her head at him. "I don't think the humans would let them do that," she said. "I think it might be the Thraish who would end up dead.''

"Hush," said the Treeci. "Don't upset yourself, Burg. Northshore is none of our business. Don't we always say that, generation on generation? Northshore isn't our business.''

"How about Southshore?" Medoor Babji asked. "That's what we were looking for.''

"Over there," said Burg laconically, pointing over his shoulder. "That way. About a month's travel or more.''

"It's really there?"

"Was the last time we looked. Bersdof's kids sailed there last year, just for the hell of it.''

"Is it empty, Burg? Is there room there for the Noor?"

"Room for the Noor and anybody else, far's I know. Nothing there but animals and plants. No human grain over there, though. You'd have to plant that.''

"Why? Why is it just sitting there? Why hasn't anyone gone there?" She tried to imagine an empty land, one without Jondarites. It was impossible.

"Well, those of us who fled with the Treeci landed here on the island chain first. Seeing what the Thraish had made of their

world, we took it as kind of a religious thing to behave differently. We don't expand much. Small societies in small places.
Closeness. That's why we haven't gone to Southshore. As for
other people, I don't know. Maybe the place was just waiting
for the Noor.''

The Treeci Saleff interrupted them with a long-drawn-out
hooting call. There was a response in kind from the shore.
''There's Isle Point,'' he said, turning to her with his cocked-
head smile. She looked shoreward to see the water moving
around the end of the island, and a little way westward another
island, the long line of land broken only by this narrow strait. A
village gathered itself beneath the trees, small wooden houses,
curling smoke. A mixed group of humans and Treeci stood on
the shore, old and young.

''Will you be my guest?'' Saleff asked. ''Burg would ask
you, I know, but he has a houseful just now. New grandchild.''

Medoor Babji bowed as best she could in the tilting boat. ''I
would be honored, Saleff.''

''You'll be better off,'' Burg snorted. ''Saleff's mama—Sterf,
her name is—she's a finer cook than my wife is, that's honest.''

''My mother will welcome you. As will my nest sister and
the younger siblings.''

Medoor Babji bowed again. She was already lost. She had
already told them about her need to find the *Gift*. It would seem
rude and ungrateful to mention it again so soon. And yet their
invitation had had an air of complacency about it, as though
there could be no refusal nor any limit to her stay. She cast a
quick look at the horizon. Where was Thrasne? And her people?
She swallowed, smoothed the lines out of her forehead, and set
herself to be pleasant. The boat was rapidly approaching the
shore, and half a dozen people of various kinds were wading out
to meet her.

> Blint told me once there are fliers who can talk, or at least
> that some people say they can. At first this seemed a silly
> thing to believe, but as I got to thinking about it, I wondered
> if it wasn't sillier to believe that talk was something only
> men could do. I've heard the strangeys calling, and the
> sounds they make are so large and complicated they must be

words of some terrible, wonderful kind. But the sounds the fliers make, if those are words, they are short words and hard words. And I wish I'd heard the Treeci talk, those Pamra spoke of, for if they can talk, then surely the fliers can, too, and all we've thought about them for all our lives must be lies.

It would be interesting to talk with fliers, and strangeys. Except their words may not mean what our words mean at all, and it would be worse to misunderstand them than to just have them a mystery.

From Thrasne's book

• 19 •

At Isle Point, the house of Saleff squatted beneath a grove of stout trees with ruddy-amber leaves that filtered golden light into the rooms and onto the many porches where Saleff's kin moved about like orderly ghosts. Medoor Babji was at first amused by and then solicitous of the silence.

"We have a habit of quiet," Saleff's mother, Sterf, told her. "Originally adopted, I'm sure, out of rebellion against the cacophony of the Thraish. Later it became our own, particularly satisfying trait. The children tend to be a bit loud, of course, and must learn to go into the woods or out on a boat if they wish to shout or yodel or whatever it is they do."

There were three children in the house, three young ones, at first alike as puncon fruit in Medoor's eyes, each then acquiring a mysterious individuality that she found difficult to define. Mintel was the serious one, the quietest. Cimmy was graceful, with a lovely voice. Taneff was the most delightful, curious, always present, full of whispered questions, ready to run quick errands, even without being asked. The three soon named her Cindianda, which meant in their language, they said, "little dark human person." Medoor Babji thought they might be fibbing to her, that the name might mean something very disrespectful, though Sterf assured her not.

"How old are they?" she asked, watching them cross the clearing with amazement. They moved like darting dancers, lithe as windblown grass.

"Oh, just fifteen," Sterf said, a little wrinkle coming between the large orbs of her eyes. It was one of the things that made Treeci so like humans, the way their faces wrinkled around the eyes. If one looked only at the eyes, not at the flat, flexible horn of their beaks, they could have been humans in disguise, got up for some festival or other. "Just fifteen." There was something vaguely disquieting in her tone, and Medoor Babji thought back to everything Pamra had told her about the Treeci. Hadn't there been something? She shook her head, unable to remember. During that time Pamra Don and Medoor Babji had known one another—a misnomer of sorts, Medoor felt, since she did not feel she knew Pamra Don at all—Medoor had been so busy wondering what it was about Pamra that held Thrasne in such thrall she had paid too little attention to what Pamra had said.

"Trial and error," she murmured to herself, being contrite. When Queen Fibji learned how many times Medoor Babji had remembered that particular lesson on this trip, she would no doubt be greatly gratified.

Also in the house was the mother of the young ones, Arbsen, who was also Sterf's daughter and Saleff's nest sister. Of them all, Arbsen was the most silent, the most withdrawn. Some days she sat on one of the porches, her eyes following the children, broodingly intent. Other days went by during which Medoor Babji did not see her at all. She seemed to spend a great deal of time shut up in her own room at the top of the house, carving things. They were not Thrasne kinds of things, not definable images, but rather strange, winding shapes which seemed to lead from the current and ordinary into realms of difference, strangeness. Several of these articles decorated the walls of the house, and seeing them, Medoor Babji thought of Jarb Houses, wondering if the Treeci had such things. "Though I don't suppose Treeci ever go mad," she commented.

"Of course we do," said Saleff, amused. "We are in all respects civilized."

"You mean primitives don't go mad?"

"I mean they don't consider it madness. They would probably consider it being possessed by the gods, or in thrall to ghosts. Something of that kind."

"How do you know all this? You've never seen a primitive."

It came out as more of a challenge than she had intended, but Saleff did not take offense. "The humans have books, Medoor

Babji. There is a printing press on Shabber's Island. There are
archives on Bustleby. There are men on Jake's Island who
spend all their time collecting information and writing things
down. During the hunger—that is, the period before and during
the Thraish-human wars after the weehar were all gone—the
humans who came here brought many things with them. Books.
Musical instruments. Equipment for laboratories where they
make medicines. It was part of the reason they came, to pre-
serve their knowledge. The humans called what was happening
on Northshore a 'new dark age.' You understand that? We have
learned from men, but we have also taught them. It has been an
equitable exchange.''

Medoor Babji had that flash of elusive thought again, as
though someone had just told her the answer to a long-asked
question, but it was gone before she could grasp it, leaving her
shaking her head in frustration.

She walked in the groves with the children. ''Cindianda,''
Taneff begged, ''tell us stories of Northshore.''

''What do you want to know?''

''Tell us of the Noor. Tell us of the great Queen.''

So, she invented, spinning incredible tales into the afternoon.
Taneff was insatiable. Whenever she stopped, Taneff wanted
more, more and more stories, and she began to look forward to
these sessions under the trees during which she could let her
imagination spin without fault. Nothing hung upon her stories
but the day's amusement, and she relished that.

Each morning when she woke, she resolved to get the boat
repaired and set out in search of Thrasne. Each evening, she
resolved it anew. Still, the days went by in placid grace, full of
quiet entertainment.

One morning she rose early, conscience stricken or dream
driven, determined to go to the shore and examine the
Cheevle. She was amazed to find it had been almost entirely
repaired. Only one of the planks remained to be replaced. Saleff
had said nothing to her of repairing her boat, and she felt
shamed that so much had been done without her help or thanks.
She looked up to find him beside her, head cocked in that
smiling position.

"Soon," he said. "Some of the young people will want to go journeying soon, and they can go with you to find your friends."

"When?" she begged, suddenly aware of how many days had passed.

He pointed skyward. "After Conjunction. Not now. The tides will be treacherous for a time. When Conjunction passes, they will fall into a manageable state."

She examined the moons, surprised she had not noticed how near to Conjunction they were. It would be weeks before she could go. "I'll never find him," she said hopelessly. "Never."

"Oh, we think you will. We've sent word by island messenger to all the settlements, east, west, south. The word is spreading among the island chains. Even the strangeys know we're looking for it. The *Gift of Potipur* will be spotted somewhere, don't fear."

She went walking with the children. Cimmy and Mintel ran off into the woods, saying they smelled fruit ripening. Taneff stayed with her, leaping into the path, then out again, whirling about, seizing her by the hand to drag her, protesting, to the top of a pile of rocks.

"Ouch!" She bit the word off. "Damn it, Taneff, that hurt." There was a long graze on her arm where it had been dragged against the black stone. "I'm bleeding."

Taneff stood, looking at her stupidly, saying nothing, shifting from foot to foot, a dark shadow moving behind the eyes, utterly unlike their usual expression. Then the eyes cleared, and Taneff smiled, a little uncertainly. "Sorry. I am sorry, Cindianda. I got carried away with the running and leaping, I guess. Everything in the village is so—so . . ."

"Circumscribed," she offered with a wry laugh. "Orderly."

"Well, yes. Lately it just seems to irritate me." Legs stamping, wings held slightly away from the body, Taneff began to gyrate, a mockery of a dance. "I need to get it out of my system."

Medoor Babji repeated this to Saleff with a laugh. "I'm glad to know it isn't only among the Noor that young people get tired of order."

Saleff received it in silence, with only a few murmured words of apology for Medoor Babji's injury. "Yes. The young people need some excitement," he said at last. "We'll have some dances."

They had one two days later, drumming and a lot of very elegant prancing on a dance floor, all the young mixed in together, leaping and jostling. Among the crowd were half a dozen who were magnificent dancers, the feathers around their eyes flushed a little with the unaccustomed noise.

"Cimmy and Mintel are going to visit some kinfolk," old Burg announced one morning, apropos of nothing. "Next island over. Would you like to go along?"

Medoor Babji allowed that she would. They left early in the morning, Sterf, Burg, Cimmy, and Mintel in a little, light boat with Medoor Babji perched in the stern like an afterthought, trailing her fingers in the water and humming to herself.

"I need to see some of my colleagues over on Jake's," Burg told her. "The Treeci are better with boats than I am, so I hitch a ride whenever anyone is going."

"There are a lot of boats going," she answered him, pointing them out, counting them off. Six boats from Isle Point, all setting out in various directions, all with young ones aboard.

"Bringing home the brides," said Cimmy in a depressed little voice, at which Sterf said something sharp in admonition. Medoor Babji started to ask, but Burg shook his head at her. A taboo subject. Very well, she would not ask.

On Jake's she went with Burg to meet the humans on the island, spent the day, the night, and a greater part of the next day doing so. They were many, garrulous, and eager for new faces and new information. Every word Medoor Babji uttered about Northshore was soaked up by an eager audience, and by afternoon her voice had given out.

Burg gave her puncon brandy and let her sit in a corner of the laboratory while he talked shop with his kinfolk. She dozed, warmly content after a night with almost no sleep.

"Arbsen was here last week," someone was saying to Burg.

"Arbsen? She hardly ever leaves her room, except to walk with Taneff in the woods."

"She was here, Burg. She wanted the blocker hormone."

"That's illegal. Unethical, too."

"It's only illegal for Treeci to use it, not for us to give it."

"Don't be silly. We live with the Treeci; of course we obey the spirit of their laws. Have you told Saleff? Have you told *any* of the Talkers?"

"Not yet. I was waiting for you to come over. You know the family."

"I'll talk to him. What did you tell Arbsen?"

"Just what you said. It's illegal."

In her corner, Medoor Babji stirred uneasily. This was evocative of something she had heard before, something Pamra Don had said. Something.

Burg roused her sometime later, and they walked together to the shore. There was a strange youngster waiting with Sterf, wide-eyed and frightened looking.

"Treemi," Sterf introduced her. "Coming back with us to Isle Point."

"Will Cimmy and Mintel be staying here long?" Medoor Babji asked. "Will I have a chance to see them before I leave?"

The question somehow went unanswered in their bustle to load the boat. She did not ask it again. Taneff met them back at Isle Point. Taneff was carrying flowers for the visitor and was unwontedly silent. He did not even answer Medoor Babji's greeting.

There were other visitors. All the youngsters seemed to be paired off, one local and one visitor, the locals wandering around a good part of the time with the visitors in attendance. Taneff, who had not let Medoor Babji alone in his demand for stories, now seemed almost to avoid her.

"All right, Burg," she asked, seeking him out and peering around to be sure they were alone, human to human. "What's going on?"

He shook his head at her, making a taciturn, pinch-lipped face.

"No, don't give me that. I know it's a taboo subject, but you've got to tell me what's going on or I may transgress. I don't want to do that."

He sighed. "I suppose you're right, Medoor Babji. It's Conjunction, that's all. Conjunction in a year in which some children in the community reach mating age."

"Breeding age?" she asked, suddenly remembering some-

thing Pamra Don had said. "Couldn't they put it off a few
years? Gods, they're only children."

He shook his head. "No, actually, they're at exactly the right
age. Biologically speaking, that is. Or so my friends over at the
lab on Jake's tell me."

"So the visitors are what? What was it Cimmy said, 'brides'?"

"Yes. Cross-island mating, to prevent inbreeding. Do you
know anything about that, Medoor Babji?"

"I know you breed champion seeker bird to champion seeker
bird if you want the traits passed on. I know if you breed too
close for too long, though, sometimes the chicks don't live."

He nodded. "It's the same for all creatures. Inbreeding inten-
sifies characteristics, both desired and undesired. With seeker
birds, you can destroy the faulty ones. The Treeci wouldn't
approve of that, so, Cimmy and Mintel went over to Jake's
Island to meet a couple of the young roosters over there, and
little Treemi came back here to meet Taneff. That's really all
there is to it."

It was not all there was to it. There was a great deal more to
it than that, but someone came to the door of Burg's house, and
the conversation ended.

As she was walking back to Saleff's house, she met Taneff
on the path.

"Hear you've got a new friend," she called, teasing him a
little.

He looked at her, head down, wings slightly cocked. "Friend,"
he said. His eyes were glazed, dull, as though a film lay over
them. The visitor, Treemi, came out of the woods and took him
by the wing, her fingers caressing him as she cast a quick,
warning look at Medoor Babji.

"I've got fan fruit for you, Taneff," she said. "Fan fruit."

"Fan fruit," he said, turning toward her, feet dancing, wings
lifting.

"Fan fruit," she sang, leading him away, half dancing.
Arbsen came out of the wood and followed them, at some
distance, her eyes wild and haggard.

Medoor Babji stood looking after them, more troubled than
she could explain. Of the three children, Taneff had been her
favorite. Taneff, as he was, not this strange, withdrawn creature

who talked in monosyllables. She shook her head, annoyed at herself.

That night she was wakened by voices. She rolled from her mat on the floor and went to the window to close it, only to stop as she recognized the voices coming from the room below her.

"I want you to give it to Taneff." Arbsen's voice, husky with pain, anguish. "Saleff, you've got to."

"Arbsen, you've been eating Glizzee, haven't you."

"What difference if I have? Glizzee is the only thing keeping me sane. That has nothing to do with what I asked you. I asked you to give the hormone to me. For Taneff. He's my child, Saleff. I can't let him die."

"Arbsen. You, of all people, should know the folly of that. Remember Kora? Kora and her son, Vorn. Remember them?"

"Taneff isn't in the least like Vorn. I think Taneff's a Talker. Vorn wasn't."

"No, Vorn wasn't. And Taneff isn't a Talker, either, Arbsen. I've been testing him myself, the last time just yesterday. Do you think I wouldn't do that, carefully, with a member of our own family?"

"You made a mistake," she wept. "I know you did. He's a Talker. I just know it."

"If he were, my dear, I would know it. Can't you resign yourself, Arbsen? Go to Sterf. She'll help you."

"How could she help me! She never had this happen to her. She had a *damn Talker*. She had you!" The sound of wild weeping erupted into the quiet glade. In the houses, lights went on. Silence fell below.

Medoor Babji shut the window, hideously uncomfortable. There were things she felt she should remember, things she wanted to ask Burg on the morning.

And on the morning, she could not. Burg had gone to Jake's for a time, she was told, taking his family with him. He would be back for her after Conjunction. There were only two human families left in Isle Point, neither of them with young people. Despite her affection for Saleff's family, Medoor Babji felt abandoned.

The whole settlement seemed to be under emotional strain. There was a sense of communal anguish which kept her from

asking Saleff any questions. Several times over the succeeding
days, she met Taneff and Treemi in the woods or on the beach
paths. Taneff scarcely seemed to know her. His voice was only
a croak, though the rest of him was becoming glorious, frilled
with feathers, flushed with rose. Always, Arbsen followed them
at a distance. She had grown gaunt, almost skeletal. Almost
every night there were dances somewhere nearby. Medoor Babji
was not invited to attend, but no one could hide the sound of the
drums.

And Arbsen was suddenly much in evidence, a hectic flush
around her beak, very talkative. Both Saleff and Sterf watched
her with a worried grimace, and Medoor Babji wondered if she
should not absent herself from the Treeci house.

Which point was decisively answered by Sterf herself. "Mating time is difficult for us," she said. "Emotionally, you
understand. Some of our loved children are far away, and we
worry whether they are treated well. You are self-effacing and
sensitive, Medoor Babji, but being so tactful is hard on you and
us. Burg's house is empty. Would you mind using it for the
next few days?"

To which Medoor Babji bowed and made appropriate expressions of sympathy and concern, all the while afire with curiosity.

There were drums that night, a fever in the blood. There were
drums the night following. And on the third night, Conjunction
came. Mindful of the laws of hospitality, Medoor Babji kept
herself strictly within the Burg house, whiling the long, sleep-
less hours away by reading books. Burg had more of them than
Queen Babji had, and Queen Babji had a good many. The
drums went on most of the night, trailing away into a sad
emptiness a few hours before dawn.

She woke late in the morning. The village was still silent,
empty as a sucked puncon peel. Away in the woods somewhere,
smoke rose, a vast, purposeful burning. The reek of it made the
hairs on Medoor Babji's neck stand up—smoke, but more than
smoke. Incense, too. And something else which the incense did
not quite cover. There was a feeling of sadness, a smell of
bittersweet horror. She sat on the porch with her book, drinking
endless cups of tea, waiting for something to happen, half-afraid
that something would.

What did happen was that Burg returned, with his family, grim-faced and white. Medoor walked down to meet him at the shore. "Have you seen anyone today, Medoor Babji?"

"Not a soul, Burg. Forgive my trespassing on your home, but Sterf asked me to . . ."

He shook his head. "Of no matter. I told her to send you over if things got tense. Which they have. Worse than I thought."

He turned away to supervise the family—son, son's wife, daughter, grandchild, baby—as the boat was unloaded.

"Turn it over, wash it out, and leave it here," he told his son. "Sterf will want to be taking Treemi home tonight or first thing in the morning. I'll go with her." He said this as though he did not believe it, like a courtesy phrase, said out of habit, not out of conviction.

He trudged up to his house, pausing on the porch to feel the pot Medoor Babji had left there, pouring himself a cup when he found it still warm. She held her tongue, not wanting to distress him more than he obviously already was.

"Arbsen stole the stuff," he said at last, looking over her shoulder into the woods. "The stuff we give young Talkers to get them through mating season without dying."

"I—I don't understand." And yet, she did. She remembered things Pamra had said. About Neff. Holy Neff. Her vision, the one that spoke to her all the time. Burg went on, confirming her recollection.

"Male Treeci—male Thraish, the whole species—they die after they mate. The breeding cycle triggers a kind of death hormone. Among the Thraish, the Talkers have learned to make an antidote from their own blood. They locate young Talkers before the breeding season, sequester them, give them the antidote, and it inhibits the breeding cycle." He rubbed his forehead, rubbed tears from the corners of his eyes.

"When we first came here the technique had been lost or something. When young Talkers were born, they just died, along with all the rest of the males. A rare tragedy. Only about one in a thousand males is a Talker. Still, it was always a pity. Talkers don't lose their intelligence, you know, not like the others. The ordinary males—they go into it in a kind of anesthetized ecstasy. Not Talkers. Whatever it is that makes them different also makes them victims. So, we created an antidote in the labs, to save the Talkers. Ones like Saleff. It doesn't inhibit the breeding cycle as the Thraish medication did. It just inhibits the death hormone.''

"Then they can all live?" Medoor Babji said. "Taneff can live! That's what Arbsen wanted from Saleff.''

"No. No, they can't. We tried that, out of compassion, a long time ago. It was a horrible mistake. But Arbsen was so crazy with grief, she stole the stuff. Now I have to find out what she did with it. . . .''

"Why, she gave it to Taneff," said Medoor Babji. "What else would she do?''

"Oh, sweet girl, I pray you're wrong," he said, the tears now running down his face in a steady stream. "I know you're right, but I pray you're wrong.''

At the fall of evening, Treeci began to trickle back into the village, silent as shadows. Somewhere far away a bell began to ring, measured stroke after measured stroke. No one needed to say it was a mourning bell. The sound alone did that.

Saleff came to the house. "Return to us, Medoor Babji. We need the distraction of your presence." He was carefully not looking at Burg.

Burg would not allow the evasion. "Arbsen stole the hormone, Saleff. Took it from the lab when she was over there a few weeks ago." Burg was blunt, demanding a response.

Saleff didn't reply.

"Is Treemi all right?"

"We haven't found her," the other said in a bleak, shattered voice. "Tomorrow we will begin to look.''

"Is Arbsen around?"

"Not Arbsen, no. Nor Taneff.''

"Why wait until morning, Saleff? He has had them a full day. They could still be alive. If we look tonight, we may save Treemi's life. Otherwise you'll have blood guilt to pay her family, which will mean another life. You want to risk Cimmy, too? Or Mintel?''

The other looked up, an expression of despair on the strange, withdrawn face. "If there is any chance she is alive, we will look tonight.''

They searched by torchlight, moving outward from the village, all the Treeci and all the human occupants, all but the youngest children.

They found Treemi first. Alive, but barely. Body bloodied, sexual parts ravaged and mutilated. Burg gathered the body into strong arms and carried it back toward the village, Sterf close behind him, weeping.

Later, down a long, leaf-strewn gully, they found Arbsen. Her body was broken, as though she had been buffeted with heavy clubs, but her eyes opened when they spoke to her.

"Arbsen, why?" Saleff murmured in a heartbroken voice. "Why? You knew. You knew."

"I didn't believe it," she whispered, blood running from the corner of her mouth. "He is my child. He loves me."

"Oh, Arbsen, they only love if they die in the loving. If they live, it isn't love." He leaned across her, weeping, not seeing her eyes, glazed and staring forever at the darkness.

It was dawn when they found Taneff at last, a golden dawn, gloriously alive. They heard him first, crowing at the sunrise. They saw him then, tumescent, flushed red as blood, eyes orbed with triumph, dancing upon a small elevation above the forest floor. Around him the trees were shredded; beneath his feet the earth was a ruin.

Medoor Babji was among the first to see him, all disbelieving. It could not be Taneff. She called his name in her disbelief, careless of her safety. When he turned toward her, she saw that it was he. Taneff as she had never seen him. He saw her, knew her, spoke her name with a kind of brute inevitability.

"Come," he called. "Come!"

He danced on the mound, beckoning.

She stopped, horrified at the sight of him. There was blood on his talons, blood on the wing fingers, which twitched and snapped.

"Why?" she cried, unable to contain it. "Why did you kill Arbsen? Why did you kill your mother?"

"Told me to stop," he crowed at her. "Told me to stop. The young one said stop! Nobody tells Taneff to stop!"

He leaped high, rushed down the slope at her without warning. He attacked her, wings out, fingers clutching, sex organ

bulging and throbbing. He did not see the torch she held; she
had forgotten she held it; her Noor-trained reflexes did the rest.
It was not Taneff who blazed as he fought. It was horror.

Then there were men and Treeci all around. Someone had a
spear. There was a long, howling struggle, and a body at the
end of it. No one she knew. No one she had ever known.

"Why?" she sobbed on Saleff's breast. "Why?"

The Talker stroked her as though she had been one of the
Treeci young. "Because they are meant to die, Medoor Babji.
They are meant to die."

He took her back to the house where Treemi lay, barely
breathing, Burg working over her. They built a pyre on the
shore for the other two, and somehow the night and the day
following passed.

A few days later, Burg showed her the *Cheevle*, mended, as
sound as when it had been built. "Word has come," he told
her. "We can lead you to the *Gift*. You will find it east of here,
nearby a great island where our people do not go, but where the
strangeys have brought your people."

"Will someone go with me?" she asked, feeling suddenly
very lonely at the thought of leaving them.

"Cimmy and Mintel are taking a boat out. They wish to be
gone for a time. It is hard—hard for nest mates to lose one of
their number at the time of mating. It is harder still to lose one
as they lost Taneff."

"He was mad," she said sadly. "Mad, Burg. The whole
experience broke his mind."

"Is that what you think?" He laughed harshly. "Oh, Medoor
Babji, you are far from the mark. No, no. Listen, I will tell you
a little story. Something men have pieced together from tales
told by the Treeci and excavations made long ago, before we
left Northshore.

"Evidently in the long-ago, the males did not die when they
bred. The male Thraish, that is; there were no Treeci then. They
lived. As you saw Taneff, they lived. After the first mating their
blood boiled with the desire for power. They took females,
more than they could possibly need, held them as slaves; they
took territory and held that. And they fought. You saw. That is

how they fought, competing with one another. Male against male. Tribe against tribe.

"In their violence, they didn't care whom they killed. In or out of season, they raped and mutilated. They killed infants. They killed females. Because the Thraish can lay large clutches of eggs, they managed to hang on for a long time, but in the end so many females died that those tribes could no longer survive.

"I have visions of them sometimes, the last few of those prehistoric Thraish, fighting one another in the skies of Northshore, already dead."

"But the Thraish are not extinct," she objected. "What you are telling me is only a story."

"No. It's the truth. Among all those wild, violent tribes there were some few, even then, in which the death hormone functioned. The males mated and died. There were no wars. Among these tribes was no rape, no slavery, no abuse of the young. And those groups survived. Such is their history. It is what we call a survival characteristic."

After a time of silence, she asked, "Treemi? What of her?"

"She will recover. She has blessedly forgotten what happened. She will even have young this season. There will be no blood price. Arbsen is dead. There can be no retribution."

Medoor Babji nodded, overcome by sadness. Everything he had said was a heavy weight in her head, on her heart. She did not think she could bear the burden of it. There were lessons here she had not been taught by Queen Fibji, words she needed, instruction, comfort. And there was something more, fleeting like a silver minnow in her mind, something she herself could tell the Queen.

"Burg, you told me Southshore lies a month over the River. Do you swear it?"

He was startled. "Why, I will swear it if you ask, Medoor Babji. Why do you ask?"

"Because I do not want to spend more time away from my own kin. Because we were sent to find if Southshore is there, and if you will swear to me that you have seen it, with your own eyes, then I can go back and say so to the Queen."

"I swear it, Medoor Babji. It is a great land. Empty, so far as we know, of any people, human or Thraish or Treeci. There are beasts there and familiar trees. I swear it. I have seen it with my own eyes.''

She surprised him by kissing him, then. It surprised her, as well. She was afire to reach Thrasne and the others. They would turn back now, racing home, home to the Noor. Something within her told her that only speed could prevent some hideous thing from happening. She remembered things Queen Fibji had said concerning the survival of the Noor, the lusty young warriors, the difficulty of holding them in check. She thought of the strutting Jondarites, their plumes nodding on their helms, as the plumes had nodded on Taneff's head when he'd plunged into the spears. She thought of the mud graves of the warriors, and she longed to be home with every fiber of herself.

• 20 •

It was thirty days after the great storm, according to the journal of Fez Dooraz, that those on the *Gift of Potipur* saw the new island.

Though they could see no end to the land, yet they assumed it was an island, for it loomed up west of them like the prow of a great ship with the water flowing on either side. Behind that mighty rock prow the land fell away west into lowlands and forests, with hills and mountains behind, seemingly limited to north and south but with no end to it they could see to the west, a long, narrow land where they had expected no land at all. Far off to the east a cloud hung over the water, and the sailors said this meant there was land there, as well. "An island chain," they said. "It has been rumored there are island chains in mid-River."

"Do we go ashore?" Obers-rom asked Thrasne. "Is it possible this is Southshore?"

"Southshore or not, it is certainly a great land. And we have no choice if we are to get water." Thrasne felt a bit doubtful, but with their need for water and with all the crew and the Noor hanging over the side, looking at the place, how could they go on by? They needed something to divert themselves from the thought of Medoor Babji. Even Eenzie the Clown was depressed, and Thrasne could not explain the feelings he had had since the storm. Now that she was gone, he realized who she had been. Not merely a queen's daughter—"merely," he mocked himself. More than that. To him, at least.

They lowered a man over the side to swim a line to the land. When the light line was made fast, ropes were hauled in, tying them fast to trees ashore, and then the winch tugged the *Gift* in almost to the land's edge. The island fell sharply at this point, and the mooring was deep enough for the *Gift* to come very close. They built a small raft of empty kegs and planks to get back and forth, the sailors muttering meantime about the loss of the *Cheevle*.

Thrasne left a three-man watch aboard and went ashore with all the rest. He was heartily sick of the *Gift* himself, though the emotion made him feel guilty. The longest he could recall having traveled before without coming to land was a week or two, and that had been when sickness had struck a section of towns near Vobil-dil-go and all the boatmen had been warned away. Years ago, that had been, and then he had had the airy owner-house to live in. Now the little cabin he had squeezed himself out below was cramped and airless. He had considered slinging a hammock among the men a time or two, and would have except for the danger to discipline. It was hard to take orders from a man in his underwear, or so Thrasne had always believed.

At any rate, he was glad to walk on land again. He strolled along the narrow beach, really only a rocky shelf between the River and the cliffs, with a few hardy trees thrust through it. As he walked west, however, the shelf widened, dropped, became a real beach with sand on it, and the cliffs on their right hand also became lower, spilling at last into hillocks edged with dune grass and crowned with low, flat trees. The men of the *Gift* scattered toward the hills, into the woods, searching for water.

The Melancholics had dropped behind to poke among the tide pools at the island's edge, where they were finding brightly colored dye mulluks and flat coin fish. Thus it was only Thrasne at first who saw the carved man, buried to his knees in the sand.

"Ha," Thrasne said, a shocked sound, as though he had been kicked in the stomach. "That looks like old Blint." He stopped short, knowing what he had said was ridiculous and yet filled with a horrible apprehension.

The carved man began to turn toward him, as though he had heard Thrasne speak. As though he had heard his name.

He turned so slowly that Thrasne had time to measure every familiar line of him, the undulating sag of the belly, the little hairy roll of fat at the back of the neck, the wiry ropes of muscle on the legs and arms where old rope scars still showed, the slant of the shoulders. When he was turned full toward him he saw it was Blint, Blint as though carved in dark fragwood, Blint with his mouth opening slowly, so slowly, to give him greeting.

"Thraaasneee," the carved man said.

"Blint?" Thrasne bleated, terror stricken. What was this? His arms trembled, and the world darkened around him, shivering in a haze of red.

A voice in his mind said, "Remember Suspirra, Thrasne. You were not afraid of Suspirra!"

For a time this was only mental noise with no sense to it. After a time his vision cleared, however, and he turned toward the strange figure in astonishment. Yes. He had taken Suspirra from the River, still living—in a way. She, too, had seemed carved. Now Blint—Blint, who had gone into the River that time long, long since, with weights tied to his ankles.

"I put you in the River," Thrasne cried to the motionless figure.

"I know," the carved man said, each word stretching into an infinitely long sound, fading into a silence more profound than had preceded it, as though other sounds upon the island stilled to allow this speech room in which to be heard. "The blight, Thrasne. The strangeys came. Now I am here."

"Where?" Thrasne begged. "Where is here?"

"The Island of All of Us," the carved man replied, his lips twisting upward into the ghost of a smile, the lids of his eyes moving upward also, the face lightening for that instant almost to a fleshy look. "You have come to the Isle of Those Who Are Becoming Otherwise. . . ."

Behind Thrasne the shouts of the searchers stilled. Before them on the long, pale beach there was movement. Lumps and piles that Thrasne had assumed were flotsam or clumps of grass stood up, turned, became men and women. On some, fragments of clothing still hung, as irrelevant as wind-driven leaves clinging on a fence. Though it was possible to tell that some were male, some female, there was nothing sexual about them, as there had been nothing really sexual about Suspirra. In many,

breasts or penises had dwindled into a general shapelessness. Or
shapeliness, Thrasne thought half-hysterically, his artist's eyes
assuring him that the shapes of those least human in appearance
were also the most beautiful. As he thought these things, clinging tight to his sanity, willing himself to show no fear, the
carved people approached him, slowly.

"Is he frightened of us?" one asked, the question seeming to
take up most of the afternoon.

"Does he think we are ghosts?" asked another.

"What are they?" asked Taj Noteen from just behind him,
his voice strained and shaking. "I told all the others to get back
to the boat."

Thrasne responded calmly, betrayed only by the smallest
quiver in his voice. "They are the dead, Taj Noteen. Those
whom the Rivermen have consigned to the River. Blighted then.
And, seemingly, given a new life by the blight, as the workers
in the pits are given life by the Tears of Viranel."

"But these . . . these can talk."

"Talk, yes," said one of the carved people in long, slow
syllables. "And observe. And hear."

"Cannot taste," said one. It was a chant, an intonation,
perhaps an invocation.

"Not smell," said another.

"Not feel," said Blint. "Not much."

Thrasne's immediate terror had begun to subside, and he
looked closely at Blint. There was no fear or horror on that
face. There was none on any face he could see. There was
calm. Expressions that might betoken contentment. A kindly
and very moderate interest, perhaps, though no excitement.
With this analysis, his heart slowed and he swallowed, conscious of a dry throat and scalp tight as a drumhead.

"Are you well, Blint?" he found himself able to ask, almost
conversationally.

"Oh, yes, Thrasne. I am well."

"Are all the River dead here, all of them?"

"Here. Or on some other island."

"How did you get here?"

"The strangeys brought us. They bring us all."

Throughout this last exchange the carved people had turned

away and begun moving slowly back to the positions they had occupied before. There, they faded into the landscape once again, becoming mere manlike hillocks along the sand. Only Blint remained.

"Blint-wife is well." Thrasne bethought himself that Blint might like to know this.

Blint did not seem to care. "I'll leave it in your good hands," he said, each word drawn into a paragraph of meaning. "Thraaaasneeee." Blint's eyes were fixed on some more distant thing. They followed his gaze out across the waters to a swelling beneath the waves, a heaving, as some mighty creature rising from the depths, the great, glassy shells of its rising flowing with a tattered lace of sliding foam.

"The strangeys," said Blint once again, his hands folded before him as though he had been in Temple. Though they spoke to him several more times, he did not answer. At last Taj Noteen tugged Thrasne away, back across the sands to the edge of the forest. By the time they arrived there, Thrasne was shaking as with an ague.

Taj held him, clasped him tightly, until he stopped shivering. Taj was as shaken as Thrasne. Among the dead he had seen were some he thought he knew, one he had known very well indeed.

"Come," said Thrasne at last. "We will explore a little." He knew himself. In a moment his eyes would start to function, his fingers itch for the knife. In a little time, he would start to think. This shock had come only because he had known the old man, known him almost as a father. So, let him move to let the shock pass. "Come." He moved away down a forest path.

They walked. Here and there along the way were others of the dead. Some, evidently the more recent, looked up as they passed. One or two of them spoke. Others did not seem to see them. And some, those who had been longest upon the island, Thrasne thought, were rooted in place like trees, stout trees with two or three stout branches, small tendrils of growth playing about their heads and shoulders and from their fingertips.

Thrasne stopped before an ancient tree, twisted and gnarled by a century's growth. "The leaves are the same," he said, pointing first at the tree, then at one of the dead a small distance away. "The leaves. And see! It blooms." At the tips of the twigs were blossoms like waxen crowns, magenta and sea blue, with golden centers.

"We bloom," corrected a voice from behind them. "And the seeds blow out upon the River and sink down. And grow there into a kind of water weed. Which grows, and after a time takes fins and swims. To become the blight. Which seeks a body to house it. And brings it to life again. And comes to the islands. To grow. To bloom. . . ."

She who spoke had been a woman once. Now she fluttered with leaves, and her feet were deeply planted in the soil.

"And you," Thrasne whispered, needing to know. "Are you well?"

"Oh, yes. I am well."

"There is no pain?"

"No pain."

"Memories?"

"Memories?"

"Your name? Who you were?"

"I am," the tree-woman replied. "I am, now. It is enough." She did not speak again.

"This tree does not grow on Northshore," said Thrasne. "You'd think somewhere, in the forests there. Some of them . . ."

"The strangeys probably don't take them there," said Taj Noteen. "Probably they bring them only here, or on other islands."

"Why? How?"

"You will have to ask the strangeys, Thrasne," he said. "Those, swimming there in the deeps, with the foam around their faces."

For they did swim there, south of the island, shining mounds lifting great, eyed fringes, sliding through the waters like mighty ships of flesh, calling to one another in their terrible voices, deep and echoing as caves.

"Come," Taj Noteen urged him. "Come back to the *Gift*, Thrasne. It will seem less strange tomorrow." And in truth, he hoped it would, for his soul cowered in terror within him.

*   *   *

None of them felt they could leave on the day that followed, or the day after that. Thrasne did not find Blint again, though Taj Noteen found the woman he had once known, spoke to her, and returned to the *Gift* dazed and uncomprehending. On the third day, they wished to leave, tried to set sail, and were prevented from moving. Around them the strangeys moved, pushing the boat back against the shore each time they tried to move away. They had refilled all the water casks. Here and there among the strange trees on the island were some familiar fruiting kinds, and they had gathered all the fruits that were ripe. There was nothing more they could do, but the strangeys would not allow them to leave. It was time, Thrasne felt, to ask some questions.

What Thrasne wanted to know he could not ask from the crowded deck of the *Gift*, with all the crew clustered about thinking him crazy. He did not want to talk to the strangeys at a stone's throw, with old Porabji's cynical eye upon him. He wanted—oh, he wanted to be close to them. Close as their own skins or fins or whatever parts and attributes they had. He wanted to *see* them!

"Pull the raft around to the Riverside," he ordered. "And rig some kind of oarlocks on it."

It was not a graceful craft. Still, it was sturdy enough, an could maneuver it with the long oars in the high oarlo standing to them as he plied them to and fro.

Once he knew well enough what he was doing with the he thought to sneak off at dawn, when the strangeys usu surfaced. He set his mind to wake himself early, a skill n boatmen had, and rose in the mist before the sun. As he slip over the rail, he did not see Eenzie the Clown standing in owner-house door watching him, wrapped tight in a great w robe over which her hair spilled in a midnight river of si strands. As he left, she came to the railing to watch the heave away, clumsy as a basket.

It was dead slack tide with the moons lying at either hori Only a light wind blew into Thrasne's face from the south, laden with scents strange to him. "There is more land there," Thrasne breathed, assured of it for the first time. "I smell it!"

He sniffed deeply, recognizing components of the odor as

resinous, humusy, fecund smells. Swamps and forests. On the island the closer trees were only dark shadows against the mist behind them, a ground fog that rose only slightly above their tops to leave the taller trees outlined against the dawn. This retreating sequence of river mist, shore trees, mist again, taller trees, and yet again mist rising from some valley and the tallest trees on the hills behind it lent an appearance of great distance to the island, as though it had stretched away from him in the night, becoming a place in dream in which no distance could be measured. The far, hilltop trees were an open lacework against the opal sky, motionless in the morning light, with only an occasional flutter of wings among them to let one know they were not painted there, or carved.

He sculled through the rising fogs into the deep channel on the south side of the island. Behind him on the *Gift* the watchman raised his voice in a plaintive call, like a lonely bird. Moving through the shore mist, the dead men and women walked like an orchard come up from scattered seed. Though most of them stood or walked alone, there were a few twos and threes of them who seemed to stay together. As though they had been friends or kin in life? Thrasne wondered, then gave up wondering as the River surged about him, belling upward in huge arcs of shining water.

Upon that swelling wave were winged things, smaller than strangeys, peering at him from myriad eyes. Then they were gone.

"Perhaps they are strangey children," said Thrasne in a conversational tone to himself. "And here are the adults."

They were all around him, their long, eye-decked fringes suspended above the raft, peering at it through the mists, monsters from dream.

"I need to talk with you," Thrasne called. "I want to ask some questions."

A rearrangement took place among the fringes. Eyes were replaced by others. Water swirled, and from the top of a belled wave a comber of lace slid toward him, foaming around the boat. "Yes," said a terrible strangey voice. "We will talk."

"You are preventing our leaving the island," he called. "If we have offended you in some way, we wish to make reparation. We cannot stay here. We must go on. Southward."

"No," the strangey boomed, diving under the water to leave Thrasne bobbing above it, then emerging a little distance off. "Your other one is coming to you."

"Other one?"

"The one you lost. The one you have yet to find. Babji."

"Coming here?" His heart swelled within him, suddenly joyous, leaping like a flame-bird chick from the nest. "Here? Medoor Babji?"

"The Treeci are bringing her."

This baffled him. It could not be the Treeci of Strinder's Isle. Some other Treeci. Before him the strangeys sank from sight, except for one.

"Do you have other questions?" it asked.

"Yes." He licked dry lips. "A long time ago, it was almost twenty years ago. A woman drowned herself off the piers at Baris. She was pregnant."

There was no sound but the River sound, yet Thrasne had a feeling of colloquy, a vibration of the water beneath the boat, a great voice asking and answering in tones beneath his ability to hear them. "Yes," said the strangey voice at last. "Her name was Imajh."

"I don't know what her name was. I called her Suspirra. I thought she was only wood, you know. But she wasn't. She was alive."

"She was alive in a way," assented the voice. "If you had not taken her from the River too soon, we would have brought her here and she would have been alive here, in a way. As the others are."

Thrasne slumped. "I killed her?"

Swirl of water. Sound as of what? Not laughter. No. Amusement. Something like amusement, but of so huge a kind that one could not call it that. Thrasne tried to identify the tone as the strangey spoke. It seemed important to know what the strangey felt as it answered. "She was already dead, boatman. What she was given after that was the blessed time. Perhaps she used it better for her where she was than if she had come here."

Thrasne, remembering, was not sure. "She had a child. Suspirra did."

"Yes. Our child. We want our child returned."

Thrasne had meant Pamra. After a moment he realized it was Lila they spoke of. "Why do you say Lila is your child, strangey? I meant her other child, Pamra Don."

"Lila is our child because she carries our seed. We know of Pamra Don. . . ." The voice trailed away in a sadness too deep to bear, the anguish beating at Thrasne's flesh like hammers.

Thrasne cried out against it. "Don't. Oh, don't. Strangey! Don't you have another name I may call you for courtesy's sake?"

Again that indefinable emotion, the trembling of the water. And then, "The name you call us does well enough. We are strangers, strangers to you and to this place. Aliens. Explorers. Though we were already here when your people came, you will remain here when we go. When our examination—our crusade— is done."

Strangers! Aliens? And yet, why not? If humans had come to this place, why not others, others with their own labyrinthine ways of thought, their own arcane judgments? It should have made no difference, yet it made all the difference. He tried to remember the questions he had wanted answers to. They did not seem so important now. The tone they had used in referring to Pamra Don closed that subject away. He did not want to hear Pamra's name spoken in that voice. There remained only one mystery, and stubbornly he asked about it.

"Why do you bring the blighted ones to these islands?"

Again that gigantic emotion that Thrasne could not identify. A troubling. A monstrous disturbance that had both laughter and tears in it. "Blight is your word, Thrasne. We call it rather 'extension.' It seems a good thing. The human people do not live long; their ends come suddenly. They . . . look beyond too much. Or they refuse to look beyond at all. This gives them time. . . ."

"The blight—you brought it?"

"We created it. Our gift. Just for you."

Again that vastness, rolling around him. He could feel it without understanding it at all. He bent forward, trying to protect the core of himself from whatever it was. He did not understand anything they had said. The words they used were insufficient to explain what they had meant. The vast, rolling emotion came closer, overwhelming him, but he could not apprehend the content of the wave in which he drowned. It passed. He lay gasping on the raft, unsure he was alive.

They spoke again, sadly.

"Bring us our child, boatman. In payment for receiving your lost one back."

Then the water flattened, all at once, as though oil had been poured upon it. There was no reaching swell, no tattered carpets of foam. Only silence, the flap of the sail, and from the distant *Gift*, muted by the mist, the sound of excited voices.

He steered toward it by sound. The cook banging on a pan. Taj Noteen's voice raised. Obers-rom, giving an order. The clatter of wood and the loose flap of the sail. The sound of laughter, cries of joy. Then he saw it, saw the little boat with the *Cheevle* tied at its stern. He called out, in a great, hoarse voice, and saw Eenzie and Medoor Babji waiting at the rail.

"Have you finished with the strangeys? Come aboard, have your breakfast, then let us sail for home!"

He gaped at her, staring into her face, unbelieving. There was a lively intelligence there, a self-interested concern. She reached down and lifted him upward with a strong arm, and his skin woke at the feel of her own against it. He was aware of nothing but this as he took her hand and let her lead him toward the cooking smells, thinking only of what was at that moment and not at all, in that moment, of the strangeys or of Pamra. He had come to a place within himself where he could no longer bear to go back or to stay where he was, unchanging, and yet he hesitated to go forward. With that mighty, enigmatic emotion of the strangeys still washing through him, he hung upon the moment, poised, unmoving within himself, aware of a stillness within himself and at the core of all the liquid shifting of the River's surface, all the windblown agitation of the island, becoming part of it for a time, rather than choose—anything.

Two days later, after Medoor Babji had walked upon the Island of the Dead until she had seen what they had seen, they set sail for home.

• 21 •

No matter what I start out thinking about, I end up remembering what the strangeys said, and what they said seemed to me to be about sadness. The sadness of men— mankind, I guess you'd say. It's that we never have time to be what we know we should be, or could be. And it's not because of the time itself, the gods know we waste enough of it not doing anything at all, but because of what we are. And we don't have time, no matter how old we get, to be anything else. So they've brought this gift, so they called it, to let us be something else for a while. Something that *knows,* but doesn't care so much. It's caring so much that keeps us from being what we could be. Caring so much. About the wrong things, maybe. But still, if we didn't what would we be?

                                                    From Thrasne's book

Word was sent to Sliffisunda that Pamra Don would be delivered up to the Thraish. In the Red Talons, Ilze danced his victory, a wild, frantic prancing upon the rocky height, then sat down upon a shelf of stone to wait, his eyes like polished pebbles, scanning the horizon for the first glimpse of those who would come from the Chancery. Though the message had said clearly that Gendra Mitiar would accompany the girl, Ilze cared nothing for that. It was Pamra Don he would see shortly; Pamra Don he would get into his own hands at last. He thought of her as he had used to think of her: tied to the stake, his whip falling across her shoulders as his caress, her voice rising up in screaming prayers to the empty sky. His body shook, twitched, spasmed with this thought, and the fliers on the rocks around him cast looks at one another, wondering what ailed him.

Sliffisunda was content to wait. There was no hurry about this business. His fliers told him the crusade went on, more massively than before, with great clots of people moving west and north. Wherever they moved, the pits were full, so he cared not whether they moved or not. In a hidden valley of the steppes known only to fliers, the herdbeasts were growing with each day that passed. Already the expedition to steal other young bulls had been planned. More than an expedition, almost an invasion, with enough surprise and numbers to succeed no matter what the humans did. It might prove expedient to stop this crusade; or again, it might not. It was a thing worthy of much screamed discussion, many loud sessions on the Stones of Disputation. Sliffisunda wiped his beak on the post of his feeding trough and was content.

And on the plains, moving southward and a little east, Pamra Don was content as well. "A journey of a week or two," she had been told. "To the Red Talons. To meet the Talkers." There were Jondarites and Chancery people escorting her. Once she felt a fleeting sadness that Tharius Don was not among them. There was scarcely room even for that emotion. She rode the weehar ox the general had given her, refusing to ride in the wagon pulled by Noor slaves. She abjured Gendra Mitiar with great passion to free these men as Lees Obol would require of her. Gendra listened, raked her face, ground her teeth, and said she would consider the matter. In truth, she found Pamra Don amusing in the same way Jhilt had been amusing during the early days of her captivity. So naive. So childishly convinced that her feelings mattered to anyone besides herself. So interestingly ripe to be disabused of that notion.

One day the escort paused on a low hill to let a procession of crusaders pass in the valley, banners, a wagon, a gorgeously robed figure in the wagon. Pamra looked down at it in wonder, not recognizing Peasimy Flot. Peasimy had decided to join Pamra Don at Split River, but he did not even see her riding in her bright armor in company with the Jondarites.

And as for the rest, it was merely travel. Creak of wheels.

Plod of feet. Crack of whip. Wind in the grass. Murmur of voices. Fires at night gleaming like lanterns in the dark. Walking out into the grasses to pee, staring up at the moons which seemed to stare back in wonder, or threat, or admonition, depending upon one's point of view.

The slave Jhilt, walking each day away in a soft chinkle of chains. The Jondarites striding along, their plumes nodding over their impassive faces, their hands upon the butts of their spears, resting at night beside the fire, polishing their fishskin armor with oil. The captain himself, on orders from Jondrigar, polishing the armor of Pamra Don. Gendra Mitiar seeing this with amusement, but not interfering. Time for that. Time for everything.

In fact, Gendra Mitiar felt herself growing strangely weary from the journey, victim of an unaccustomed lassitude. She went to her strongbox and unlocked it with the key she carried around her neck to get at her reserve supply of elixir. Though it was a full season sooner than she had planned to take more of the stuff, she dosed herself liberally with the thick, brownish ichor, at which Jhilt smiled behind her hands and jangled her chains. On those chains, among a hundred other dangling charms and coins, hung a duplicate key to the strongbox. It had taken Jhilt over a year to file it to fit, but once it was done, it had taken only a minute to open the box, months ago, and taste the acrid stuff. When they set out upon this journey, it had taken only another minute to substitute for the elixir a vial of half-burned and diluted puncon jam. Who knew better than Jhilt that Gendra's aged mouth knew no savor, her aged nose knew no scent? "Have some jam, old one," she tittered to herself to the soft chankle-chankle of the chains. "Live a little."

Though she had sometimes forgotten it during her captivity, here on the steppes Jhilteen Nobiji remembered she was Noor. If the Noor could not have justice, they would have vengeance. The key to the strongbox was not the only key that hung upon her chains, and her presence with this troop outside the barrier of the Teeth was one she had hoped for over many years.

There were twelve days like this before they sighted the Talons, looming redstone obelisks, contorted towers that broke the line of the steppes amid a dark forest. This outcropping of redstone ran all the way from Northshore to the Teeth of the North, somewheres mere edges along the land, elsewhere squat cliffs lowering over the plain. Here the stone had been eaten by the wind and rain, chewed into monuments as full of holes as a worm-gnawed pod, and here the Talkers maintained one of their four strongholds. Black Talons, so they said, for strength; Gray Talons for wisdom; Blue Talons for vengeance; Red Talons for blood. Sliffisunda had come from Gray to Red, and the significance of that had not escaped him. "From thought to action," he cawed to himself when the human train was sighted. "So, now we will have something interesting, perhaps some satisfaction."

The Jondarites made camp some distance from the foot of the Talons, yet close enough that the Talkers might come to them without exertion. The tents were set in a circle; the Jondarites took crossbows from their cases and placed quarrels for them ready at hand, the heavy, square-headed bolts most efficacious against fliers. Though there had been little opportunity to use weapons against the Thraish in some hundreds of years, the stories of the last Thraish-human conflicts were well remembered among the soldiers of the Chancery, and the general had told them to be ready for any eventuality.

When all these preparations had been completed, Gendra Mitiar sent a messenger to the foot of the Talons with a letter for Sliffisunda. He might come, she said, to their camp. To question Pamra Don. And to discuss certain matters with her, Gendra Mitiar.

Sliffisunda did not come, himself. He sent a Fourth Degree underling and the human, Ilze. It amused him to do this, setting the humans one against the other. He did it sometimes with slaves or craftsmen, making one's safety dependent upon betrayal of the other. So, now, he thought Ilze might work against Gendra Mitiar to obtain the person of Pamra Don.

But she, remembering Ilze in the Accusatory, was disinclined to pay him attention.

"I must speak with the Talker," she said. "I don't know what he was thinking of, sending you." She sniffed, raking her face, staring at him as though he had been some kind of bug. Her teeth ground, and he tensed in every nerve, expecting pain.

That sound had accompanied pain before, and he wanted to
scream at her.

"Sliffisunda wants to see her," he grated.

"Fine," Gendra said. "Let him come to see her. Talk with
her. Question her, if he likes. I need to talk with him, too, and
I'll not be hauled up there like some sack of laundry."

Taking a quick look at the alert Jondarites, Ilze retreated,
quelled for this time. He had not laid eyes on Pamra Don. For
all he knew, she was not even with the group. She, however,
spying through a slit in the tent side, had seen him very well;
seen him and disregarded him as an irrelevancy. He would hurt
her if he could, but he would not be allowed. The Chancery folk
would not allow it. Her great-great-grandfather, Tharius Don,
would not allow it. She explained this to Neff and her mother
and Delia as all of them nodded and smiled.

Back at the Talons Ilze's failure was reported to Sliffisunda,
who cawed laughter. "I did not think he would do any good!"
The Fourth Degree Talker who had reported on Ilze kept his
beak shut, wisely. Sliffisunda shuffled back and forth on his
perch, darting his head from side to side. "Well, I will go talk
to this old human. Tomorrow, perhaps. Or next day."

He let two days pass before going to the camp. Gendra, who
had studied the fliers for some time, was not concerned about
the delay. The lassitude that had bothered her on the journey
had not yet abated, and she remained in her tent, ministered to
by Jhilt. Pamra, meantime, preached to the Jondarites. They,
remembering how their general had responded to her, varied in
their response from polite to enthusiastic.

And at last Sliffisunda arrived. The Talkers had lately taken
to regalia, a tendency borrowed from humans, and Sliffisunda
wore a badge of degree slung about his neck as well as various
sparkling ornaments on his legs, feet, and wing fingers. Warned
of his coming, Gendra had Pamra brought out of her tent, fully
accoutred in her Jondarite armor, and set in a chair beside the
fire with Jondarites at either side. If the old rooster wanted this
one, Gendra thought, he would have to give something signifi-
cant in return, though nothing of this appeared in her face or
voice as she first greeted the Talker.

"I am honored," she said. "We grant the request of Sliffisunda to talk with—even question—the woman, Pamra Don."

"She was to have been sent to us," the Talker cawed, depositing shit on Gendra's words.

Gendra's fingers twitched toward her face, then stilled, knotted. So, it was to be a battle of insults. "One pays little attention to what Talkers demand," she replied in a bored voice. "Unless one is given reason to listen."

Sliffisunda almost crouched in surprise. So, the humans could engage in Talkerly disputation! Almost always the humans were like spoiled eggs, stinking soft. This one was not. He turned away from her, showing his side—not quite a fatal insult, though close. "What reason would humans understand?" he cawed.

"More subtle reasons than a Talker could ascertain, perhaps," she replied, turning her shoulder toward him to signal the Jondarites. "The Thraish have not been noted for good sense."

He stretched his wings wide and threatened her. She gestured again at the Jondarites. He looked up to see a dozen crossbows centered on his chest. He laughed and subsided. "So. So, Gendra Mitiar. What have you to say?"

"I have to say your interest and mine are the same, Sliffisunda. Do you speak for the Talkers?"

"I speak to Talkers," he boasted. "And they listen."

"Ah," she murmured. So, he could not commit the Talkers to anything, but he could argue a case. If she succeeded in acquiring an alliance with him, she would buy an advocate, not a potentiary. Still, what matter? Those in the assembly would accept a Talker's interest as representative of the Thraish. They would not know the difference.

She turned full face toward him and said, "I have a case to put to you, Uplifted One. . . ."

She spoke of her desire for the post of Protector of Man. She spoke of her intentions, once that post was hers.

"There is no reason the Thraish cannot increase in numbers. Human numbers can be increased to feed them. The Noor are no good to you because the color of their skins will not allow the Tears of Viranel to grow properly within them. Let us eradicate the Noor. Let us replace them with settlers from Northshore.''

Behind the tent flap, Jhilt quivered in shock. This she had not heard before.

"How will you convince the Chancery to do this?" Sliffisunda asked, interested despite himself. Even though none of this would be needed when the herdbeasts multiplied, it was still an interesting concept.

"If your numbers are increased, the amount of elixir can be increased. More humans can receive it. Those whose votes are needed in the Chancery assembly will be promised elixir. A simple thing, Sliffisunda.''

"How will you wipe out Noor?''

"War.'' She shrugged. "General Jondrigar needs opportunity for war.''

"Not enough Jondarites.'' This was said as mere comment, not as objection.

"True.'' Again she shrugged. "We will need to conscript men from Northshore as well. Any man, I should think, who has not fathered a child in a few years.''

Who will then not be available to support children he has fathered, Sliffisunda thought, while keeping silent. The Thraish understood nestlings. Even Talkers understood nestlings. When the parent was lost, the nestlings were lost. Many would die if this woman came to power. The pits would be full. And if that went on for a long time, the Thraish could expand in advance of the day he had planned. The woman was ambitious, but not wise. He could use her, despite her disputatious nature.

"Let us talk,'' he said, smiling inside himself.

On the day following, Sliffisunda arrived to question Pamra. This was a simple feint or, as the fliers put it, *hadmaba*, a threatening posture designed to bluff rather than injure. Sliffisunda wanted to support Gendra Mitiar; he did not want her to think he did it willingly or for his own purposes. So, let her think he was really interested in this pale, thin woman with the blazing eyes with the child on her lap.

"Tell me of your crusade,'' he said, expecting nothing more than ranting or evasions.

"You do an evil thing,'' she said in a level tone, fixing him with her eyes. "All you fliers." The child fixed him with her eyes, strangely.

He hunched his shoulders, staring at her, ignoring her young. "What evil is that?"

"It is for you the workers are raised up," she said. "I did not know that until I came to the Chancery, until my great-great-grandfather Tharius Don told me. I thought it was for the work they did, as we were taught. I thought it was Potipur's will. I had been taught that. It was false."

"It is Potipur's will," Sliffisunda replied, amused. "Potipur has promised the Thraish plenty. The bodies of your dead are the plenty he promised."

"A true god would make no such promise. A true god would not do evil. Therefore, Potipur is not a true god, he is merely your god, a Thraish god. Not a god of man."

"Does man have a god?" Considering the trouble the priests and Towers had been to to suppress all humanish religions, it was amazing that she had come up with this. Despite himself, he was intrigued.

"If the Thraish have a god, then men, also, have a god. My voices tell me that if there is not One, over us all, then there are several, for each race of creatures."

"Or none?" he asked. "Have you thought of that?"

She shook her head at him. "My voices say there is. A god. Of humans and Treeci, for we are like."

Sliffisunda shat, offended, turning his back on her. She did not seem to notice but merely stared at him as though he were some barnyard fowl. He screamed at her, wings wide, and she merely blinked. "Foul Treeci. Offal. Fish eaters."

"The Treeci are wise and benevolent creatures," she said. "As man can be if not brutalized by wickedness. Raising up the workers is a wicked thing to do, Sliffisunda. We know their pain and do nothing. Thereby we condone it. Thereby we are made brutes. Not by the workers themselves, but by the Thraish, who require they be raised. So my voices say."

Gendra, sitting on the other side of the fire, blinked in amazement. She had not heard more than five words from Pamra Don during the entire trip. Now this! What had gotten into the woman?

"Heretic!" Sliffisunda cawed. "Unbeliever in Potipur."

"If Potipur is only a Thraish god, why should I believe in him?" she asked. "If the weehar had a god, would it be the god of the Thraish?"

Theology dictated that the weehar could have no god except the Thraish god, but Sliffisunda had his own doubts about that. He recalled the quasi-racial memories of the fliers' last hunt, as he taught them to nestlings. Certainly the weehar had not seemed to rejoice in Potipur. Perhaps the weehar did not rejoice because they were being punished. But for what? What sins could a weehar commit? The sin of offal eating? The sin of debasement? The sin of doubt in Potipur's care for the Thraish? The sin of failing to breed? The sin of failing to give honor? How could the weehar or thrassil commit any of these? More likely the weehar were only things, needing no god at all. As the humans were things. Sliffisunda shook his head. The woman didn't talk like a thing, which was troubling. Abruptly he rose, stalked to the edge of the encampment, and raised himself into the air. Too troubling. Too much talk.

Behind him, Pamra watched him go, a little wrinkle between her eyes. It was hard, so hard. She could not reach him. She looked around for Neff, for her mother. They would have to help her with this one. She could not feel her way into his heart, not at all. They stood remote, their effulgence dimmed in the light of the day, hard to see. She listened for their voices and was not rewarded. Nothing. Tears crept into her eyes, and she shook them away angrily. If they did not speak to her, it was because they didn't need to. She could not expect them to be with her every minute. Perhaps they had other things to do, other people to guide as well.

Sliffisunda arrived at the Talons in a foul mood. He stalked into his aerie, snatching a mouthful of food as he passed the trough, ripping an arm from the twitching meat and cracking it for the marrow. It had no savor. The human, Ilze, was waiting outside. Sliffisunda could smell him, that sweetish, human stink which only the Tears of Viranel softened and ameliorated into something almost satisfying. Almost. Sliffisunda drooled, thinking of weehar.

A human god? To believe in a human god, that would be a

sin. But if weehar believed in a god at all, what god would it be? Sliffisunda made a noise like a snarl in his throat. Under the Thraish, the weehar had ended. Under the humans, they had multiplied. Which god would the weehar accept? And that could be the sin for which they were punished—except that the punishment had come first.

Ignoring the crouching human on his porch, Sliffisunda launched himself toward the Stones of Disputation. This was not a matter he cared to think about by himself.

Behind him, Ilze pounded his knee with his fist, livid with frustration. Where was Pamra Don? Why hadn't this Talker brought him Pamra Don?

In the camp, Gendra Mitiar watched Pamra Don, her eyes narrowed. She had noticed for the first time that Pamra Don ate almost nothing. The woman seemed built of skin tightly drawn over her bones, like a stilt-lizard, all angles, with eyes like great glowing orbs in her face.

"Doesn't she ever eat?" she asked the Jondarite captain.

"Very little," he admitted. "A little bread in the morning. She seems to like Jarb root, and one of the men sought it for her during the journey."

"You'd better detail him to find more," she said. "The woman may not last a week if she doesn't eat something."

"I can force her if you like," the captain suggested. It was sometimes necessary to force-feed captives, particularly Noor captives, who often tried to starve themselves when their families had been killed before their eyes.

Gendra shook her head. "No. I need her cooperative with the Thraish. If she will eat Jarb root, see she gets it. At least enough of it to keep her alive." She looked up, drawn by a distant cacophony. "What's that?"

"The Talkers on the top of the Talons, Dame Marshal. They do that sometimes, late into the night—sometimes all night long."

"What are they doing?"

"Arguing, so I've been told. Only the high-mucky-muck ones like the one who was here. Sixth Degree ones. They have the highest pillars all to themselves. The less important ones, they meet lower down. Some nights there will be three or four bunches of them, all going at it. Not always this loud, though. Sliffisunda must have a bone in his craw!'' The captain laughed, unawed.

Gendra's eyes narrowed once more. So. Sliffisunda had talked to Pamra Don, and then some great argument followed among the Thraish. Perhaps Gendra's case was even now being argued. She smiled. Good. Very good.

As she rose from her chair and moved toward the tent, she stumbled, a sudden dizziness flooding over her.

"Jhilt,'' she gasped, feeling the slave's hands fasten around her arms and shoulders.

"The Dame Marshal has been sitting too long near the fire,'' the slave soothed, hiding a smile behind her hand. "It makes one dizzy.''

"You get dizzy, sitting by the fire?'' Gendra said childishly. "You do?''

"Of course. Everyone does.'' Jhilt half-carried the woman into her tent and eased her onto the bed. "Everyone does.'' Especially, Jhilt said to herself, when one is some hundreds of years old and is no longer getting any elixir. The woman on the bed looked like a corpse, like something in the pits, gray, furrowed skin gaped over yellow teeth, like a skull. "Everyone does,'' she soothed, wondering how long it would take. Jhilt had a small supply of Tears in a vial hanging on her chains. She had toyed with the idea of using the Tears before rather than after Gendra's death. She amused herself by thinking of this now, weighing the idea for merit.

"No,'' she sighed at last. "The captain would know what I had done. If she merely dies, he will not know.''

Perhaps she could use the Tears on someone else. That Laugher, perhaps. That would be amusing, too.

The disputation on the stones went on until almost dawn, not merely acrimonious, which most disputations were, but becoming increasingly enraging as the night wore on. Blood was drawn several times before the argument broke up, and only Sliffisunda's quickness in parrying attacks kept him from being among the injured. It was clear the Talkers would not accept the idea of a human god or any weehar god. Only the Thraish had a god, and the god of the Thraish was the god of all. The Thraish were the chosen of Potipur, who set aside all other creatures for the service of the Thraish. So the Talkers believed.

Sliffisunda, bruised and tired, was not so sure. The other Talkers of the Sixth Degree had not heard Pamra Don. He did not like to think what might have happened if they had heard Pamra Don. It might be better if none of them heard her, ever. Better if Sliffisunda had not heard her himself. He settled upon his perch, head resting upon his shoulder. In the afternoon, he would talk with the human, Ilze. In the evening, he would go to the camp of the humans again and make an agreement with Gendra Mitiar. It did not matter what agreement with her was made. The woman stank of death. She would not live long enough to worry him.

"What will you do with Pamra Don?" he asked Ilze.

Ilze's mouth dropped open. He salivated. The stench of him rose into Sliffisunda's nostrils, sickeningly sweet. "Teach her," he said at last, a low, gargling sound. "Teach her she cannot do this to me."

"Where?" Sliffisunda asked. "Where will you do this?"

"Here. In the Talons. Anywhere. It doesn't matter."

"Before those from the Chancery?" Sliffisunda was watching him closely. If, as Sliffisunda thought likely, all those in the crusade had been contaminated by Pamra Don's ideas, then some mere private vengeance against the woman would not suffice. Her followers would have to be convinced that Pamra Don was wrong. "Would you punish her before those from the Chancery and all her followers?"

Ilze shivered. He wanted to say yes, but his soul shrank from it. He had orders not to touch her. If he punished her in public, they would kill him. He knew that. They would kill him at once. Those from the Chancery would do it. Her followers would do it. And no one would care enough to save him from them. "If you would protect me," he whined, hearing the whine and hating it.

"Ah. Well, suppose you don't do it. Suppose we do it, the Thraish. How should it be done?"

Ilze had only thought of whips, of stakes. "Tie her to a

stake,'' he said, then stopped. The Talkers didn't use whips.
"Eat her?" he offered.

Sliffisunda cawed his displeasure, pecking Ilze sharply on
one side of his head so the blood flowed. "Take into our bodies
the foul flesh of a heretic? Stupid human!''

"Well, do whatever you do, then,'' Ilze sulked, trying to
stanch the blood.

"We have a ceremony,'' Sliffisunda said. "A ceremony."

Night came. Sliffisunda came again. Pamra Don came again,
to the fireside.

"Do your followers believe as you do?" the Talker asked
her, already certain of the answer.

"Yes. Most of them. All of them, in time. All mankind, in
time." It was not the question she had expected, not one of the
questions she was ready for, but the Talker asked nothing else.
He turned and left her, going to Gendra Mitiar to carry on a
lengthy, soft-voiced conversation which Pamra could not hear.

Jhilt could hear it.

"You wish to be Protector of Man?''

Gendra Mitiar nodded. Her voice was very husky tonight,
and it tired her to talk.

"What can Thraish do to guarantee this?" he purred.

"Wait until Lees Obol dies. I will let you know. Then send a
messenger. Tell the assembly the elixir will be decreased unless
I am elected. In which event it will be increased.''

"And when you are Protector, you will increase the quota of
humans? You will eradicate the Noor for this?''

"You have my word.''

"And in return for this agreement, you will give me the
person of this woman, this Pamra Don?''

"As you like, Uplifted One. She is nothing to me. What do
you want her for?''

"To prove she is a false prophet, Dame Marshal. In ceremony before all her followers at Split River Pass. To show them
Potipur will not be mocked.''

Gendra laughed, thinking of Tharius Don. "How may I assist
you, Uplifted One?''

Jhilt heard all this, her ear tight to the tent flap.

When Sliffisunda had gone, when Gendra Mitiar was asleep, an uneasy sleep in which her heart faltered and her lungs seemed inclined to stop working, Jhilt walked out to the cage of seeker birds that every Jondarite troop carried with it. The message bone was already in her hands.

"A message for Tharius Don," she said, keeping her voice bored and level. "From the Dame Marshal."

The Jondarite keeper made a cursory examination of the seal. It looked like the Dame Marshal's seal, and who else's would it be? The bird came into his hands willingly, accepted the light burden as trained to do, and launched itself upward to turn toward the north without hesitation, strong wings beating across Potipur's scowling face.

Jhilt shivered, thinking of what was in that message.

"You cold?" leered the soldier, opening his cloak in invitation.

She shook her head. "The Dame Marshal needs me," she said, turning back toward the tent. Though, indeed, if the Dame Marshal needed her at all, it would not be for much longer. Queen Fibji should be told of this conspiracy against the Noor. Jhilt had no seeker birds for the Queen; therefore she must find some Noor signal post that would have them. Gendra would not spend time looking for a slave, not now, not as weak as she was and with so much going on. Jhilt fumbled among her chains for the other key, the one that unlocked her jingling manacles. Moments later she moved off across the steppes, silent as the moons.

• 22 •

A yawning servant brought word to Tharius Don in the middle of his sleep time. "The general asks for you at once in the audience hall, Lord Propagator. Most urgently." He waited for some reply, and when Tharius waved him off, he scurried away into the darkness. The midnight bell had only lately struck. Tharius had heard it in his sleep, through the purple dusk that was night in this season.

He wrapped himself in a thick robe with a hood and made his way down the echoing corridors and endless flights of stairs to the audience hall. Muslin curtains hung limp against the closed shutters, like so many wraiths in the torchlight. At the side, where Lees Obol's niche was, the curtains were flung wide, and General Jondrigar stood there, face impassive and his hand upon his knife. Something in his stance recommended caution to Tharius Don, who approached softly, pausing at some distance to ask, "You needed me, General?"

"Dead," Jondrigar replied. "I think. Dead."

"Dead? Who?" Only to understand at once who it was and why this midnight summons. "The Protector?"

The general nodded, standing aside to gesture Tharius forward. In the niche, still overheated by the little porcelain stove which was only now burning itself out, the bed stood with its coverlets thrown back. On the embroidered sheet the body of Lees Obol lay immobile. His eyes were open. One arm was rigidly extended above him, as though petrified, pointing.

"Telling me, go!" Jondrigar said, indicating the hand. "Telling me. As he always did."

182

"Rigor," Tharius murmured. "All dead men get rigor, General. It doesn't mean—"

"Telling me go," the general repeated, his eyes glowing. "Rigor comes long after. He died like this. The message for me."

Tharius moved to the bed, put his hands gently upon the ancient face, the neck, the arms. Rigid. All. Like rigor, yes. Or blight. His face darkened. So. Plots. Perhaps.

"When was he last seen alive?"

"You were here one time."

"Yes. Last evening. Shavian Bossit and I met in the hall for a few moments. I didn't look in on Lees Obol, though Shavian may have done."

"He did. Through the curtains. Jondarite captain reports this to me." Jondrigar took off his helmet and ran a trembling hand across his mane. "Jondarite captain looked in every hour. Served tea late, as Protector wanted. Then, at midnight bell, he looked in again. This is what he found."

We could have a bloodbath here, Tharius thought. Better defuse that. "We have been surprised he has lived this long, General. We all knew he would die very soon. The elixir does not give eternal life. Only more years, not an eternity."

"No one killed him."

It could have been a question, or a statement. Tharius Don chose to interpret it as both.

"No one killed him. Age killed him. As it will all of us."

"But he left a message for me," the general said again. "He told me to go."

Tharius thought it wiser to say nothing. He had no idea what was in the general's mind and chose to take no chance of upsetting him.

"The Noor Queen. She is coming to Split River Pass," the general said suddenly. "I need to go there."

Tharius thought the general's mind had slipped and said soothingly, "There will be a council meeting within hours. You should be here for that."

The general nodded. "Yes. Then I will go to Split River Pass." He turned and made his way out of the hall, unsteadily, as though under some great pressure. Tharius felt a fleeting

pity. Lees Obol had been all Jondrigar's life. What would he do
now?

He put the question away. There were customs to comply
with. "Send someone to Glamdrul Feynt," he said to the
Jondarite captain who hovered against the wall. "Tell him to
look up what funeral arrangements were made the last time a
Protector died, then come tell me what they were. Send someone else for servants. Wash the body and clothe it properly.
Then get the messengers moving. Let them know at the Bureau
of Towers. Tell them to get the word out to the towns. There
will probably be some period of mourning. Find out who's
running things over there while Gendra's gone, and send them
to me. Oh, and find my deputy, Bormas Tyle, and send him to
me as well."

Tharius chewed a thumbnail. Should a seeker bird be sent to
Gendra Mitiar? Suppose Pamra Don was just now having success with the Talkers? Suppose this message interrupted something vital? He shivered. Better let it alone. Send a message
later, if at all.

He turned, catching a glimpse of a scurrying figure out of the
corner of one eye. Nepor? Here? Surely not. Probably a curious
servant, fearful of being caught away from his assigned duties.
Well, they would all have their curiosity satisfied soon enough.

· 23 ·

"**D**one," whispered Koma Nepor, pausing at a shadowed doorway.

"Dead? Ah. How did he look?"

"Who can say, Jorn? I didn't look at him. The Jondarite put the tea kettle down on the table by the curtain as he always does. From my hiding place behind the curtain, I put the blight in the kettle. The old man called for tea; tea he was served. An hour later, off goes the captain, here comes the general. Then here comes Tharius Don, much whispering and sending of this one and that one. I didn't stay to listen."

"What happened to the kettle?"

"The servants are in there now, cleaning up. They'll take the kettle and cups away. The blight's only good for an hour or so. All gone now, I should think. That's what took me so long to develop, finding a strain that wouldn't last."

"No evidence to connect you, then."

"No evidence to connect *us*, Jorn. None. Shall we go to our beds now, so's to hear it properly, wakened from sleep?"

They went off down the twisting corridor, two shadows in the shuttered gloom, whispering, heads bent toward one another like Talkers, plotting on the stones.

"When will you give General Jondrigar the letter?"

"Later. There'll be a meeting to discuss the funeral. After that."

Their forms dwindled into shadowed silence.

Shavian Bossit was wakened from sleep to receive the news. He sent a message at once to Bormas Tyle, awaiting his arrival with some impatience.

"Where've you been?" he demanded when the other arrived. "I sent for you over an hour ago."

"So did my superior," the other replied, glaring at him. "Tharius Don. It seems we have lost a Protector. Are we about to gain another?"

"It's sooner than we'd planned."

"Nonetheless welcome."

"True. But we're hardly ready. Gendra's still alive. So is Jondrigar."

"So they're still alive. For a few weeks, perhaps. Support one of them for the post."

"The general? Ha!"

"Well, Gendra, then. In her absence. Elect Gendra as Protector, which will vacate the position of Marshal of the Towers. Feynt will take over there, as we've planned, and that will give you two votes. Meantime, the general will not last long. I will take his position when he dies. Last, Gendra will fade away, and you will have Feynt's vote, my vote, and your own. Enough, Bossit." Bormas Tyle slid his knife in and out of its holster, a whisper of violence in the room. "A few weeks or months more and we will have succeeded."

"I suppose. Still, something's bothering about all this. The servants are whispering about Obol's death."

"Did you expect them not to?" Bormas snorted. "Servants whisper about everything."

"Just the way he died. As though he'd been frozen. One arm pointed out like a signpost."

"Some deaders do that."

"I suppose," Shavian said again. "Very well. We proceed as planned. The council will meet in the morning, an hour before noon. And what about the funeral?"

"I don't know. Tharius has our old charlatan in the files looking up what happened last time. I can't even remember who the Protector was before Lees Obol."

"His name was Jurniver," Shavian said, abstractedly. "Jurniver Quyme. He lived four hundred and sixty-two years. He came to office in his two hundredth year. He made fifteen Progressions. He died long before I was born. Feynt knows all about him. It'll be in the files."

"Old faker."

"Why do you say that?"

"He pretends to be ancient and crippled whenever anyone wants anything. Watch him, though, when he thinks no one's looking. He moves like a hunting stilt-lizard, quick as lightning."

"It's a game he plays for Gendra's benefit."

"It's a game he plays for his own. Keep it in mind, Bossit, when he's Marshal of the Towers. Feynt's no fool."

"Would we be planning together if he were?" Shavian made an impatient gesture. "Get on with it. I'll have to see what happens at the council meeting. If you can find Feynt, tell him we've talked." And he turned away across his room, groping his way to the shutters and throwing them wide. The sweet breezes of summer dawn immediately raised the muslin curtains, flinging them like perfumed veils into the room, where he struck at them impatiently. Outside in the plaza the trees' leaves had unrolled to their fullest extent, glistening in the amber sun, a bronzy green light that covered everything like water, flowing and changing, rippling along the stones and over the walls in a constant tide. "Riverlight," it was called. "Summer Riverlight," created by the wind and the trees.

The fountain played charmingly, the little bells hung in its jet tumbling and jingling. On the nearest meadows the weehar lowed and the thrassil neighed, gentle sounds. With the wind in this direction, one could scarcely hear the axes, far off in the hills.

At the center of the plaza, near the fountain, Tharius Don and Glamdrul Feynt stood in the midst of a crowd of servants and craftsmen, hands pointing, voices raised. Funeral arrangements, Shavian told himself, yawning. Evidently there was to be a catafalque in the ceremonial square prior to entombment. Respected members of the Chancery were not put into pits on their deaths. It was presumed the Holy Sorters would take them directly from their roofless tombs into Potipur's arms. Shavian yawned again. The truth of which would be easy to ascertain, he thought, if anyone wanted to climb over a tomb wall and look. Since he was reasonably certain of what he would find—considering the number of small birds and vermin that congregated around tombs—Shavian was not tempted to do so.

He rang for his servants. There was time for a bath and a massage before the meeting of the council. He ordered perfumes for his bath and others sprinkled upon his clothing. The chamber of meeting would stink of death.

When they met, the body of Lees Obol had already been removed and there was no smell at all. They sat about impatiently, waiting for Jondrigar to arrive. Jorn and Nepor were side by side, pretending no interest in one another, though usually they were collusive as heretics. Shavian watched this, mildly amused. They were up to something. Across the table, in the secondary row of chairs, Bormas Tyle and Glamdrul Feynt bore similar expressions of disinterest. No doubt if Gendra had been present, she would have looked the same. Shavian adjusted his face to one of polite alertness. Why not break the mold, behave somewhat differently, confuse them all?

Tharius Don brooded, but then he always brooded. He had not sent a message to Gendra. He hoped no one else had, though there was no guarantee someone in the Bureau of Towers had not. Or Bormas Tyle, perhaps. Tharius had no illusions about his deputy's sense of loyalty. Bormas Tyle had none, except to himself.

A clatter of feet in the hall, more than one. The doors at the end of the great chamber were flung wide, and General Jondrigar entered at the head of a company of troops. The others stared. Ezasper Jorn bit off an exclamation, throwing a sideways glance at Nepor. What was this?

Shavian, no less surprised than the others, decided to treat it as a normal occurrence. "We have been waiting for you, Jondrigar. Do you wish to sit down?"

"I'll stand," he boomed. "There is little time to do what must be done. I have received the message Lees Obol meant for me. 'Go,' he said to me, and go I must. He wishes me to finish the work he could not finish. He desires I take upon myself the title of Protector of Man."

There was a stunned silence. Into that silence crept the sound of Bormas Tyle's knife, sliding, sliding in its scabbard. Shavian Bossit swallowed, tried to concentrate, torn between laughter and shock. What had he and Bormas Tyle said only that morning? Support either the general or Gendra for the position of Protector. Soon both would be dead. He swallowed his surprise and found his voice.

"I would support you in that, Jondrigar." He turned to find two faces frozen upon his own, Jorn's and Nepor's. Ah, so they had been up to something. "Tharius, you would support Jondrigar's accession to the title, would you not?"

"I would," said Tharius in a strangely husky voice. It was another sign. A sign from heaven. From the God of man, if one cared to say it that way. From Pamra Don. "I would support General Jondrigar. He knows what is needed to protect mankind."

"I have already begun," the general boomed. "When I returned with Pamra Don from the pass, I sent commands to all the mines that the slaves should be released and taken over the mountains to their homeland."

There were gasps from around the table. Shavian bit his tongue. Tharius looked upon the general with loving, glowing eyes.

"Now I must go to the place Queen Fibji is, to beg her forgiveness. And when that is done, I will return to take up this great office, which Lees Obol intended from my birth." He turned away, strode away, the feet of his troops drumming behind him, the chamber echoing with the sound. Behind him was silence.

"No slaves in the mines?" Bormas breathed at last.

Shavian shook his head warningly. "There is metal in the warehouses. Enough for a very long time. We can bear a hiatus."

"Queen Fibji will have evidence of slavery when her people come home."

"Cross that stream when it splashes us."

Ezasper Jorn and Koma Nepor said nothing. They were frozen with shock.

"Let be," said Tharius Don. "It may be we are entering a new age." Jondrigar had not said anything about the fliers, but if he had truly understood Pamra Don—it would not be long before he moved in that direction as well. First the Noor, then the fliers. First those close by, then those more remote. Tharius Don placed his hand over his eyes, covering the weak tears that gemmed the corners. Almost he could see through those hands, so thin they were, so translucent. He should eat. He should. There were things he had to do. His stomach turned at the thought. No. No, he would eat after everything was done.

And everything would soon be done. After which he could die—die in thankfulness that it had not been necessary to invoke the strike, in gratitude that Pamra Don would be safe in the general's care. . . .

As would the world of man.

• 24 •

Seeker birds had been bred originally by the Noor. On the vastness of the steppes, messages could be sent, as they were from the signal towers of the Chancery, by helio-graph during the day or by reflector lantern at night. Informa-tion was exchanged in these ways on a more or less regular and formal basis among Queen Fibji's guards and outliers. For more spontaneous sharing of information or to carry greetings among near-kin, seeker birds were used, flying back and forth between their two masters, sometimes over enormous distances. Posses-sion of a seeker bird was no longer considered de facto proof that the owner was a Noor or Noor sympathizer, though that had once been the case. Many merchants used them now. Medoor Babji had taken half a dozen Fibji seekers with her when she sailed away on the *Gift*. Every troop of Melancholics had two or three home seekers, imprinted to seek some near-kin on the steppes. And, of course, Fibji's spies had seeker birds.

One of these arrived in the cage late in the afternoon, after the audiences for the day were done. Strenge thrust his little finger into the bone message tube and twirled it around, bring-ing the paper out in a crackling cylinder, frowning as he did so.

"Which one of our people sent that?" the Queen asked, splashing her footbath at him with one toe. The attendant looked reproachfully at the Queen, pumice stone held ready. "That's all right, Jenniver." She smiled. "Give me the towel. You don't need to rub at my horny feet tonight. After half a century walking on them, it's no wonder they're tough as old fish hide."

He put the message he had just received into his sleeve and

took another instead, twirling a finger into the end of it. "This one first, Fibby. It's from Medoor Babji."

"Doorie! Oh, how wonderful. We haven't had word from her in months, months!" The Queen held out her hands, seeing that they trembled a little, to unroll the tight scroll and lay it flat on the little table by her cushions.

"Dear Mother and most honored Queen," she read. "Today the *Gift of Potipur* turns northward. We have found an island chain in center River where men and Treeci live. Many of the men here have seen Southshore with their own eyes. It is there, about a month's sail farther south. There is no question. It is a huge land, empty of men, so these men believe.

"We do not know when or where we will strike land on Northshore, though it will be at least two months, one hundred long days, from now, and probably some distance west of Thou-ne from where we departed. Send a message to me through all the Melancholics of Northshore from Thou-ne at least so far as Vobil-dil-go.

"I have learned that the fliers have found some herdbeasts. They have a plan to raise the herdbeasts on the steppes until there are great herds and then kill all humans. Two fliers were blown to an island in a mighty storm, and I overheard them. I have not told anyone of this but you.

"The Noor must make plans at once to leave for the south. If the Thraish go on with their plans, the plan we have so long depended upon will be only another kind of grave.

"I have found the answer to Grandfather's riddle.

"Your loving and obedient daughter, Medoor Babji.

"P.S. I think I am pregnant."

"Ah," said Strenge, looking perplexed, gulping a little, hardly knowing which part of the message to think of first. "Well, if she only thinks she is pregnant, it happened after she left."

"Rape," snarled the Queen.

"I think not," Strenge said soothingly. "She would not have used those words had it resulted from rape. No. I have had seeker birds from those who were with the troupe in Thou-ne, and they tell me Medoor Babji was fascinated by the boat owner, Thrasne."

"That is not a Noor name!"

"No. And Noor do not own boats. Shh, shh, Fibji. We have children among our near-kin who are not wholly Noor."

The Queen snarled. Strenge petted her and she wept in pain, anger, and frustration.

When she had finished weeping, he said, "And now, Queen of the Noor, you must hear evil news." He took the just received message bone from his sleeve, turning it in his hands for some moments, a sour expression on his face.

"Well?"

"It's from one of our people long enslaved in the Chancery," he replied in a strained, tight voice. "From a sentinel post near the Red Talons. Things are taking a nasty turn, Fibji."

She took the paper and read from it. "Oh, by all the gods. We heard from the scribe that the leader of the crusade was readying for racial persecution. Now some faction in the Chancery plots our extermination in order to settle our lands with paler skins! Have there been any reports of such action against us?"

"We've had no reports, but the Melancholics may not realize what's going on. There's always the chance of more or less random harassment in the cities."

"Get some inquiries out, Strenge. It's unlikely there's been time for the Chancery to act on this, but they may move more swiftly than usual."

"No matter how swiftly or how slowly, Fibby, we must act now, no matter what they do. One message told you a persecution is being built as a fire is laid, with fuel added each place the crusade stops. Another says that now Gendra Mitiar connives at persecution. If her connivance succeeds, our people may find it impossible to gather coin on Northshore. Now comes word from your daughter to say Southshore exists. It is actual, real. It is accessible, too, without such arduous effort as to make it impractical."

"Then why haven't people gone there?"

"Why should they? The journey is very long. There are vast unsettled stretches on Northshore, to say nothing of the steppes. The Towers have long forbidden exploration of the River."

"But she says there are men living there, in mid-River!"

"Who may have been there for countless generations. What I

find more interesting is that she says there are Treeci, but she does not tell us what those are. Another race of creatures, however. That must be what she means!''

"It is unfathomable to me that men would not have settled another land if that land were reachable by any means," she grumbled, still preoccupied with Medoor Babji's possible pregnancy and not thinking of exploration or settlement at all.

"And perhaps they did," he replied. "And perhaps they are there now. And perhaps they did, and perhaps they all died. And perhaps they did, and some other thing happened. And perhaps, just perhaps, the men who are meant to settle that other land are the Noor.''

She bowed her head, whispered, "You're right, Strenge. As you often are. So. Send word to all the Noor. They are to leave for Southshore by the quickest route, every tribe in its own way. Empty the coffers of the Queen. Hire boats where we can. Take them where we cannot. Arrange provisions. And send word, as Medoor Babji has suggested, to all the Melancholics between Thou-ne and Vobil-dil-go. There must be some plan made for the assembly of our people when we reach Southshore. If we do. . . .'' She took a deep breath, drew herself up.

"We will leave in the morning! We will forget our plans to seek any agreement with the Chancery. It was always a vain hope. Since we are very near to Split River already, we will go down along the river to Northshore. Forced march. We Noor can march in three months or four what would take the Northshoremen a year. She bids us hurry. We will hurry.''

She was silent a time, thinking. With all this threat to her people, still she longed to have Medoor Babji beside her at this time. But pregnant?

"Ah. I am to be a grandmama again. My heir is to have a child. Ah, Strenge, what message shall my heart have for my daughter when she returns?''

Tharius Don slept, deep in the sleep of angels, where no trouble was nor anguish. He flew, as with his own wings, alight with holy fire.

Someone shook him by the shoulder.

He opened his eyes, struggling to penetrate the gloom.

"Your Grace.''

"Ah?"

"A message, sir. It came in this afternoon, but with every-thing that was going on, it got mislaid. When I came on duty, I knew it should be brought to you at once. It's from the Dame Marshal."

The young officer looked haggard. He offered the message bone with a shaking hand.

"Open it," Tharius ordered, pulling himself up in the bed. Even when the message was unrolled before him, he had trouble focusing on it. It wasn't Gendra's hand. . . .

The thing wasn't from Gendra. The words within were signed by the Noor slave, Jhilt. They spoke briefly of the Noor, and then they spoke of Pamra Don, who was to be given to the Thraish for some kind of ceremonial degradation at Split River Pass. The Thraish had not been convinced or in anywise changed by Pamra Don. They planned this thing in order to discredit her before all her followers.

When he had read the words over for the fourth or fifth time, Tharius Don dried the weak, futile tears that were flowing unbidden down his face, dripping off his chin.

"So," he said, reaching for the bell at his hand. "So is my pride humbled."

"Bring me food," he said to the yawning servant who came in response to the sound. "Something hot and strengthening. Find my musician, Martien, and ask him to come to me here."

When Martien arrived, breathless, he found Tharius Don wrapped in a blanket, eating with single-minded compulsion. His face was drawn into an expression of concentration and pain.

"I am not staying here for the funeral," Tharius said. "I'm going over the pass, leaving almost immediately. Send the alert for the strike, Martien. Have watchmen posted on the heights. Though I pray it will not be needed, I will carry the green banner. When it falls, the word is to go out."

"When the green banner falls, the word is to go out," Martien repeated, himself in shock. He had heard so often of this day; he had thought it would never come to pass.

"I may have been a great fool," said Tharius Don. "A weak, prideful fool. Medman tried to tell me. . . ."

"Oh, well, Mendicants," Martien said, trying to comfort him.

"Yes. Mendicants. They tell us what we don't want to hear, so we don't hear. Oh, another thing, Martien. Send word through my secret channels to Queen Fibji that Mitiar is conspiring with the Thraish to wipe out the Noor. This slavewoman Jhilt may have already told her, but I won't take that chance. Nothing may come of Gendra's plotting, but the Queen must be warned, if she'll believe me. Tell her also that General Jondrigar is on his way to her. To beg her pardon. She may not believe that, either."

"Queen Fibji?"

"She is somewhere near Split River Pass. She's been journeying toward it for some time now. I don't know why. Perhaps she planned another visit to the Chancery." He fell silent, drinking the last of the soup, half-choking on it, a sickness in his stomach at the unaccustomed food. "Half the world is at Split River Pass. The crusade. The general. Fibji. And soon, according to the message I have received, the Thraish."

He stood up, staggering a little. Martien looked at him with concern and offered a supporting arm, which Tharius shrugged away.

"It's all right, Martien. I've been forcibly recalled to myself. Late in life to be taught a lesson like this, but not too late, perhaps. Go now. I trust you to see to everything."

He watched his trusted friend go out, thinking he would not see him again, remembering the flat harp music, the flame-bird, Kessie.

"I am thankful," he told himself resolutely. "Thankful that if I have misjudged, I will have an opportunity not to betray myself, my cause, and those whose lives have been given to it." It was a kind of litany, though he did not think of it in those terms. When the room had steadied around him a little, he went up the endless stairs to make his preparations, wondering what kind of ceremony it was the Thraish planned at Split River Pass and how he could comfort and heal Pamra Don when it was over.

• 25 •

Watching Medoor Babji and Eenzie the Clown today. They were washing their hair on the deck, flinging water about, dancing in their small clothes like festival whirlers, making all the men stand there with their mouths open. Some of the men lusting, I'm sure, we've been so long from shore. Medoor Babji has sent all her birds away, and it's as though someone took a heavy burden from her, for she laughs, giddy, like a child, and she comes teasing me during the daytime and inviting me up to the owner-house roof after dark. Sometimes I go, too.

I'm careful not to talk about Pamra Don. I did that once, to Babji's hurt, so I'll not do it again. Still, each time there is happiness with Babji, it makes me ache for Pamra. At first I thought it meant I would rather it *was* Pamra, but that isn't so. If it was Pamra, it would be all tears and pain and sadness instead of this joyousness, and I'm not so silly as to wish that for myself. But I can wish it for Pamra herself, and that's where the hurt is.

Times like this, it would be nice to believe in gods somewhere who took care of things. I could pray, "See to Pamra. Give her joy. Take away whatever the pain is that festers in her."

But there isn't a god to do that. I still love her. I feel unfaithful to her, too, in a strange kind of way, as though it's wrong for me to have pleasure or take joy in life. Good sense tells me that's a wrong kind of feeling. Death lies that way, and I'm no death courter.

So, I'll try to put her and all her pain away, somewhere inside in a protected place. I won't throw it away, or forget it, but I can't go on waving it about like a banner, either, to make Medoor Babji cry.

So, I'll keep it. Quietly. Until I don't have to anymore.

From Thrasne's book

To one coming down Split River Pass toward the cupped, alluvial plain at its foot, the buttes seemed to spread fanwise toward the southern horizon, lines and clusters of level-topped, sheer-sided mountains, all that was left of the great mesa that had lain at the foot of the mountains in time immemorial, now chewed by the river into these obdurate leftovers. Higher up, the pass itself wound along towering canyons and through one enormous valley, more than half-filled by the lake called Mountain's Eye, fed at this season by a thousand hurrying streams carrying melted snow from the heights, itself the source of Split River's flowing both north and south. The south-flowing stream was the larger one, in this season capable of violent excess, sometimes tumbling great boulders into its own path, detouring itself east or west at the foot of the pass to flow in any of a hundred ancient channels among the buttes. This year it had ramified into a braid of smaller streams on either side of the vastly swollen main river, and Tharius Don looked down from the pass to see the buttes glittering among tinsel ribbons of water in the late sun.

Tents were thickly scattered among the buttes, an agglomeration and tumult of peoples. Tharius put his glass to his eye and scanned the multitude. To the south, at some distance down the main stream, were the tents of the Noor, a large party of them with more arriving. Near the Noor, the banners of the Jondarite select guard and the tent of the general. Nearest the pass, the crusaders, thickly sown, like fruit fallen beneath a tree. To the east, not far, a party of Jarb Mendicants, their distinctive round tents identifiable even at this distance, surrounded themselves in a haze of smoke. Tharius put the glass away and went on down the pass, toward a Jondarite guardpost.

Near Red Talons there had been two days of argument, stretched out partly by Gendra Mitiar and partly by Sliffisunda, who wanted to be sure there were plenty of witnesses present at

Split River Pass. When his scouts returned to say that a vast multitude of crusaders and Noor and even Mendicants were gathered there, Sliffisunda delayed no longer.

"I will take the woman now," he said.

"You'll take me, too," said Gendra grimly, drawing on her last reserves of strength. "I must return to the Chancery the fastest way." Jhilt's defection had made her think of treachery, and treachery had made her think of the elixir. Though the bottle did not look in any wise different, its effects were not what she had counted on. She had to get back to the Chancery and a new supply, bartered off old Feynt.

"Take me, too, Sliffisunda."

He had consented, not caring greatly, rather more amused by the request than not. He would take her and the Laugher, Ilze. He wanted to watch Ilze during the ceremony with Pamra Don, see what he did. Abnormal human behavior was very interesting to Sliffisunda, and there would not be many more years of humans in which to study it.

"Very well," he said in a calm voice that any flier would have recognized as dangerous, "I will take all three of you. The others may follow after." He did not like the Jondarites with their crossbows this close to the Talons and was glad to hear Gendra order them to return to the Chancery.

Three of the coarse flier-woven baskets were brought. Pamra Don would not give up the child, which Sliffisunda thought odd, but it added little to the load. There was no hurry. Fliers had gone on ahead to prepare, and Sliffisunda himself had ordered what was to follow. There would be an announcement first, to get the attention of the mob. Then the ceremony with the nest. Then the woman from the Chancery would order the mob to disperse. It was all agreed.

Pamra heard only that they were returning to the Chancery. She rejoiced in this. It did no good to talk to these fliers. Neff comforted her by telling her she had not been sent to the fliers, but to man, which she understood. "We're going back now," she said to Lila, jouncing the child on her knee.

"Back where?" Lila asked. "Do you know where, Pamra Don?"

It was the first time the child had called her by name, and

Pamra looked into her face, wondering at this adult, understanding tone. "Why, to the Chancery," she said. "We will see Great-Great-Grandfather again."

The child shook her head, reaching up to pat Pamra's face. "Pamra Don," she said. "You don't listen."

"Where are the Thraish?" Tharius asked the Jondarite officer who was stationed at the guardpost.

"The fliers are mostly on those two buttes over there, Lord Propagator," the man answered, pointing them out. The rocky elevations he indicated were so near the pass that the river washed their feet. They were about forty or fifty feet high, very sheer-walled, their bases carved inward into low, smooth-walled caves by the water's flow. Tharius put the glass to his eye and stared at their slightly sloping tops. There were fliers there, certainly, quite a mob of them on both butte tops, but there were fliers on several of the farther buttes as well, coming and going, all of them staying well away from the edges.

"Did you plan to shoot at them?" he asked the Jondarite, noting the crossbow case on the man's back.

The Jondarite shook his head. "Not unless ordered to, sir, and even then not so long as they stay in the middle of the butte that way. It's too far from here, and we can't get them from below unless they come to the edge. They're too smart for that."

Tharius shook his head, wondering why they always thought of weapons first and talking later. "Do you have any seeker birds for the general?"

The Jondarite saluted and ran off to get one from the cage. Tharius laid paper on his knee and wrote out the message. "To the Protector of Man. The Thraish plan some ceremony to discredit Pamra Don because she defends the Protector of Man. They seem to be gathering on the buttes at the entrance to the pass. Tharius." They sent the bird off, watching it winging down the river toward the Jondarite tents.

"I've sent three messages by that bird already today," the Jondarite said. "That bird knows right where he is."

Tharius reached into his pocket for bread. He had been eating constantly since he left the Chancery, trying to convince himself he had strength enough to do whatever would need doing. "Can you get on top of that thing?" He indicated the nearest butte. If the ceremony was to occur on that height, it might be necessary for them to get close in order to talk with Sliffisunda.

"With grappling ladders, sure. Trouble is, we start to climb it, they'll just move to another one. We don't have enough men here to put a guard on all of them. The general's already sent a message for all troops at Highstone Lees to join him here."

All the troops? Tharius stared at the man in amazement. There had never been a time when all the Jondarites had left Highstone Lees. "What are the fliers up to?"

"I don't know. They've been coming and going all day. Carrying trash. Look like a bunch of birds building a nest."

A nest, Tharius thought. For nestlings. Juveniles. One could be discredited in the eyes of a multitude by being reduced to the status of a juvenile. Would the mob understand that? Or would Sliffisunda explain it to them? He was too shrewd to let them misunderstand it, that was certain.

"Have any of them come in carrying people?"

The Jondarite shook his head. "Not that I've seen."

Tharius sighed. If Pamra Don was not yet here, then he was in time. There could still be negotiations. He gave quick instructions to the Jondarite. "You can see better from here than I'll be able to from below. The minute you see any fliers carrying people—or any people approaching across the valley from the direction of the Red Talons—send me word. I'll leave a man here with half a dozen of my birds."

He took another bite of the bread and started on down the pass, Martien close behind him. Martien was holding the green banner. Somewhere high above them among the encircling peaks there were signal posts and watchers, their eyes on that banner. Since Pamra Don had failed, he would have to send the signal for the strike soon. Better for everyone if he had sent it a year ago. "Weak," he castigated himself. "You're weak, Tharius Don."

"What are you going to do?" Martien asked.

"I don't know. Try to get to whoever's in charge. Sliffisunda, maybe. Gendra, maybe. Or that Laugher, Ilze. The message I got said he was involved."

"How did the general get so far down the river? He couldn't have left more than a few hours before you."

"He's in better shape than I am, Martien. I have to face it. I've been a fool. Starving myself. It felt right, you know. Light. As though I were taking off weights, enabling myself to fly. I saw everything so clearly. The light was limpid. Nothing was complicated. I'd half convinced myself God was talking to me through Pamra Don. All the time it was only pride pretending to be something else. And Pamra Don the same. Familial stupidity, maybe. Well, I sent her into this. Now I have to get her out."

Far down the valley, Queen Fibji heard the reports of her own scouts. They had not expected this great mob of people. They had not expected to find the originator of the anti-Noor doctrine here, either, but Peasimy Flot was said to be present as well.

Though mobs were always dangerous in the Queen's opinion, and Strenge agreed with her, this one on this occasion was doubly, trebly dangerous. No matter what the general had said. She was not sure she believed him. If she believed him, she was not sure he could do what he promised. Too late, she told herself. His pleas for forgiveness had come too late.

"I think we'd better move south, away from this, don't you?" she said to Strenge, breaking into his musing.

"I think it would be wise," he agreed soberly. "I'll call Noor-count and march." He was out of the tent before she could say anything more, and she had to summon her own people with a trembling hand on the bells. "Pack it up," she said. "We're moving within the hour."

She did not want to think about the mob. General Jondrigar had just left her, and she did not wish to think of what they had said to one another, either. She distracted herself by helping with the packing, scandalizing her people thereby.

From the air, the steppe looked like a carpet of ash and dun and grayed green. Pamra Don stared down at it, fascinated despite herself. If she could convince some of the fliers to carry her like this, her crusade could grow that much faster. Less time would be spent in travel. Though perhaps it was not necessary for the crusade to grow any more than it had. She had not spoken to Lees Obol yet, and when she did, perhaps he would believe her all at once as the general had done. Neff flew beside her, turning his shining face toward hers in the high, chill air. "Don't you think so?" she cried. "Neff?"

He didn't answer but merely sailed there, driven on the wind, just out of her reach.

Tharius and his men continued their descent, the plain coming up to meet them as they twisted back and forth along the downward road. When they arrived at the bottom, a breathless runner confronted them with the general's message. "Wait for him here, Lord Propagator. He follows close behind me."

It was an hour before the general arrived at the head of his battalions, during which time the fliers went on clustering at the butte tops and nothing changed.

"Did you see Queen Fibji?" Tharius asked, wondering at the expression on the man's face. It was full of pain.

"I saw her," heavy, without intonation. For a time Tharius thought he would not explain, but then he went on, "She heard me. She said if the God of man forgave me, ever, then so would she and her people. I do not know if the God of man has forgiven me or ever will, Tharius Don."

"I think—I think he probably has," Tharius said, astonished. Whether the God of man had forgiven Jondrigar or not; whether there was any such deity, they could not afford the time to worry about it now. "What is Queen Fibji doing here?"

"It was the shortest route to Northshore from where they were, because of the good roads along Split River. The Queen said they would be leaving very soon. South. While there is time."

"Time?"

"She says the crusaders plan to kill the Noor because the Noor are black. She says the crusaders have betrayed Pamra Don. A devil has come to lead them. So says Queen Fibji. She called upon me, the Protector of Man, to put an end to him."

Oh, clever Queen, Tharius thought half-hysterically. Turning her enemies or former enemies against one another. "What is this devil's name?"

"Peasimy Flot. He calls himself Peasimy Prime. He teaches no breeding, no children, no Noor. He cries, 'Light comes,' and brings only darkness and death. So says Queen Fibji."

"Where is he?"

The general gestured toward the west. "There. She showed me where. His people and wagons have recently arrived. If you will look with your glass, you can see him between those two buttes, high in his wagon, a crown on his head. I have looked at him. When we have talked, I will go kill him."

Tharius laid a hand upon his shoulder. "First we must take care of Pamra Don." He pointed out the buttes, showed the general the message he had received. "Two days ago, Jondrigar. Almost three. They would be here by now, wouldn't you think?"

"If they flew. Perhaps they didn't. Perhaps they sent her back as she came to them, traveling over the steppe with Gendra Mitiar."

Tharius stared at the high buttes. They couldn't have picked a more visible place to do whatever they planned. Accessible only from the air, only by fliers, yet sloped enough to be unconcealed to all except those at the foot of the butte. Even as he stared, the seeker bird arrived.

"Fliers carrying baskets, slow, coming this way."

From the air, the butte tops looked like tables above the colorful carpet of the valleys. Nearest the pass were two where many fliers clustered, and it was to one of these that Gendra and Ilze were carried and tumbled out with no ceremony. Ilze was on his feet at once, shaking his fist and screaming, but Gendra lay where she had rolled, unable to move. Some link within her was broken, she thought dully. Some vital connection. At last she gathered her remaining strength and struggled to her feet. At the very center of the space they stood upon, Sliffisunda crouched among a few weathered boulders, invisible to anyone looking from below, staring across Gendra's shoulder. She turned. Across from her, level with her eyes, was another butte, perhaps a hundred yards away. Fliers clustered on it like flies on puncon jam, getting in each other's way.

They are building a nest, she thought to herself. The stupid fliers are building a nest. She looked down. Thousands of faces stared back at her, white ovals, mouths open. A ripple moved from the base of the butte outward as people turned, staring, faces and faces. A murmur came, like a murmur of waves. She had not expected this many, not this many.

A new emotion came to her, all at once. Dismay. There should not have been this many crusaders. And there should have been only a few Jondarites, but there were Jondarites everywhere. With their bows. Why were there so many Jondarites?

Beside her Ilze stood, still waving his fists at the crouching Talker, screaming at him. "You owe her to me, Sliffisunda. You owe me!"

A flier came screaming low over the crowd below. Gendra could not understand what it said, but the crowd seemed to understand, for the murmur deepened, became a roar.

Tharius crumpled the message and raised his glass. The fliers had reached one of the buttes near the pass and dumped the basket on it. Someone stood up, shaking his fist. "Ilze," Tharius breathed. "The Laugher. They've brought him. There's another one." This time the tumbled figure did not stand up at once; when it did, Tharius could hardly recognize it. Gendra Mitiar? It looked dead, a staggering corpse. An errant wind brought Ilze's shouts to their ears, though they could not see whom he was shouting at.

"You owe her to me, Sliffisunda. She's mine!"

"Where are the Jondarites who were with Gendra?" the general asked. "What has happened to them?"

"I don't know," Tharius answered. "Gendra and Ilze seem to have come willingly. They haven't been hurt."

He tried to think. He had to get a message to Sliffisunda somehow, get him to talk. But where was Sliffisunda? Was he even here? His frantic thought was interrupted by a harsh cawing as a flier came over them from the east, flying low, screaming its message so that all could hear: "Pamra Don is a heretic. Pamra Don denies Potipur. See how the Thraish deal with heretics!" Elsewhere upon the plain other fliers soared, all screaming the same message.

The flier turned and came over once more, still screaming.

The general spoke to his aide. Before Tharius could intervene, men reached for their crossbows and quarrels flew. The flier choked, sideslipped, tumbled from the sky in a crumpled heap. Elsewhere on the plain, other crossbowmen began to shoot and other fliers fell. From the butte came a cry of rage. The Talkers had not expected this. Fliers and Talkers rose from it in a cloud, straight up, offering no further targets.

Oh, gods, Tharius thought. Now they won't listen to any offer of talk.

The roar became a howl. Gendra sank to her knees. The stupid fliers shouldn't have done it. Shouldn't have threatened Pamra Don. It was all going wrong, all wrong. ''Sliffisunda,'' she croaked, trying to warn him. He ignored her, his eyes glowing. ''Don't,'' she croaked. ''You'd better take the woman down to them and let her alone.''

He turned his back on her, shat, walked closer to the edge of the butte, eyes still fixed on the other tabletop.

When they began to descend, Pamra leaned over the basket side, seeing everything from above, a great, scattered carpet of followers, her followers. She took a deep breath and the rapture came, glowing. All her followers, waiting for her.

''Pamra Don,'' said Lila again.

She scarcely heard the child. Above her, wings tilted toward one of the flat-topped mountains. It had a huge nest built on it, a flier nest.

Before she could think about that, they had taken her out of the basket and tied her to something in the nest. What did they think she was? A nestling? The fliers were screaming in rage. They wanted her to look like a nestling, that was it. Wings lifted in a cloud, leaving only one or two of the fliers behind her. She could not see them. She could not see the nearby followers, either, only the distant ones, a wave of faces, turning toward her, thousands of faces.

She smelled smoke. Smelling smoke always made her think of flame-birds. In her arms, Lila grew very still. Still and hard.

Tharius had no more time to think of talking with the Thraish. A laboring pair of fliers appeared high above the butte and dropped onto it, burdened by the load they carried. "Tell your men not to shoot," Tharius cried. "That's Pamra Don."

Too late. The bowmen were already shooting, but it had no effect. The edges of the butte effectively blocked the bolts, which rattled harmlessly on the rocks. Tharius focused his glass upon the butte top. There was a huge pile of twigs and branches there, an untidy cupped mass, as all Thraish nests were. His stomach heaved, and he vomited violently, Martien holding his shoulders. "Stop them," he croaked. "We've got to stop them!" Suddenly he knew what they were about to do.

There was no time. There was scarcely time to feel horror. The distant figure was tied upright in the nest and it was set alight, all in a moment. A moment. They could scarcely see her through the smoke. "She's carrying the baby," Tharius cried, as horrified at this as at the distant puff of smoke. Flames rose up, almost invisible in the sunlight. Word spread among the crusaders, and they turned toward the butte, seeing the fliers circling above it, the flames, the struggling form there disclosed, then hidden by blowing smoke. A cry rose up, a great shout. One of the bowmen made a lucky shot, and a Talker tumbled from the sky. The fliers rose, screaming, then darted downward, claws extended, only to fall victim to the cloud of bolts. Some fell into the plain still alive and were beaten to death by crusaders as the shout rose, louder and louder.

Ilze watched, his eyes bulging, his body twitching. "Oh, yes," he said. "Oh, yes."

"Don't," Gendra begged. "We've made a mistake, Uplifted One. It won't happen as you expected it to. Put out the fire. . . ."

The first flames touched Pamra Don. Neff, she thought. She tried to look over her shoulder to see his face, but she couldn't. He was there, she felt his blazing glory. Before her on the rimrock were her mother and Delia, but Neff was behind her. He was hurting her. "Neff," she cried. The flames were all around her, and she cried his name again, the word rising up in an agonized howl to fill a silence that had fallen over all that multitude, rising and rising from a throat that could not stop it nor end it nor consider what it was doing, on and on and on into a silence that seemed to resound with it still when it had ended.

"Get grappling ladders onto that butte," the general shouted, not seeing that Jondarites had already done so and were scaling the sheer wall, being attacked by furious fliers, thrown down, replaced by others, with the smoke still blowing. The first man reached the top, was pitched off by buffeting wings, was replaced by two more who flailed with their hatchets at the fliers guarding the fire. Other men poured up the ladders after them. The wind stilled for a moment, falling into an enormous, awful silence. Into this silence the scream insinuated itself as though dropping from the heights of the sky itself to fill all the world. It had all agony in it, all pain, all loneliness. Pamra's voice. One endless scream. Then again the silence.

And after the silence a roar of fury which moved across the multitudes like a mighty wave, from the base of the butte to the farthest edges of the encampment. Fliers had landed here and there to strut and crow before crowds of unarmed crusaders. They were clubbed to the earth, clubbed into the earth, pounded into bloody soil and scraps of feathers.

"You should not have done it," Gendra muttered, falling to the stone. She had no more strength. Nothing mattered now. She knew what would happen next. It was inevitable. From beside her, Sliffisunda watched, amazed and wild-eyed. This was not the way it should have gone. The humans should have cowered before this. On the Stones of Disputation it had been decided, they would be frightened, they would be abased, obedient. But they were not. They screamed. They howled. Sliffisunda felt a strange, unfamiliar emotion. Terror.

"Hostages," he screamed to three fliers near him in the sky. "Take these two humans. We may need hostages."

Obedient, as frightened as Sliffisunda himself, they dropped straight down and took off again, Ilze struggling in their claws, Gendra Mitiar hanging limp, unconscious. They tilted, spun, flew toward the Red Talons. Behind them, bolts filled the air and other, less wary fliers fell from the sky.

*   *   *

Tharius Don found himself running, not remembering when he had started running, only that he was. The general pounded along beside him, both of them headed for the butte that was about a quarter mile away, close to the main river. Without the glass, they could not see its top. They panted their way to its bottom, leaned against the stone, puffing. A Jondarite came down the ladder.

"The woman?" the general asked. "Pamra Don?"

"I think she's dead, General."

"You think?"

"Something there. Strange. The men won't go near it."

They were climbing the ladder then, swaying. Tharius had never liked heights. He didn't think he could climb this ladder, but he was being pulled over the rimrock before he could determine whether it was possible or not. A smoking pyre was before him, a great heap of glowing wood. In the center what remained of Pamra Don, black, contorted, its teeth showing between charred lips, held upright by a partially burned stake.

And in its arms a sphere of softly moving light which pulsed. And pulsed. And breathed.

And broke.

Something came out of it. Winged. Or perhaps finned. Or both. Whatever it was spoke to Tharius Don. "Poor Tharius. She was the last of your line." Then it was gone, falling or flying from the edge of the rock to the river below, entering it with scarcely a splash, moving in it as though born to it, south, southward, away toward the River that encircled the world.

"Lila?" breathed Tharius Don. "Lila?"

The general did not seem to have seen. He leaned from the rimrock to shout in a stentorian voice, "The fliers have burned Pamra Don."

From far off came a treble shout. "The Mother of Truth has been killed. War against the fliers. Night comes, night comes, night comes!"

Tharius looked across the plain to the place Martien waited. He made a chopping gesture, made it again, and again and again. Four times. The far green speck that was his banner dropped and then rose, four times. So. Let it begin. Let it all begin. Let it all come to a bloody end. Let the damn Thraish die as they deserved. He began to weep.

Below he could see Jondarites fighting against a party of crusaders. "Why?" he demanded of the general.

"Someone has said it was Jondarites who killed Pamra Don," he growled. "Perhaps the devil with the crown has set his people against the Jondarites. I go to lead my armies. See, he flees!"

The cart that Peasimy Flot had traveled in was moving away, pulled by a dozen running men. Voices were calling out, wanting to know who it was who had killed Pamra Don. "Jondarites," said some, attacking the nearest ones and falling in their blood. "Fliers," said others, marching off toward the Red Talons, clubs and bows in their hands. And still others said, "Chancery. Those of the Chancery."

"The Noor," cried some, looking around for dark faces. "The blackfaces." Tharius stared out over the valley. The Noor were moving rapidly south, visible now only as a trail of dust upon the horizon, too far away to become victims of this general holocaust. Below him a thousand battles were being waged, generalized slaughter was going on, and Jondrigar moved ponderously down the ladder to get his troops around him.

Tharius sat down where he was, staring at the blackened corpse of Pamra Don. The pyre still smoked.

The Jarb Mendicants left their encampment and began to move onto the battlefield, their pipes smoking, the haze around them thickening. Slowly, slowly, as the Mendicants covered the field, the fighting stopped. Shouting stopped. Cries of fury stopped. Sobbing and cries of pain and grief came after. Beside Tharius Don the ladder quivered, and Chiles Medman climbed onto the stone to regard him with calm, awful eyes.

"She was mad," Tharius said, his eyes red-lined with weeping. "Mad, and I did not see it."

"Was she?" asked Chiles Medman, glancing at the blackened corpse, shuddering, turning his eyes away.

"Of course! Look at the slaughter down there. All madness. Madness."

"Oh, that is probably true, Tharius Don."

"Let it end."

"I do not think it will end, no. Peering through the smoke, I see what is to be." He stood at Tharius's side, taking the oracular stance: hands held out, facing the weeping multitude, head thrown back, the pipe between his teeth so the smoke rose before his eyes. He called in a trumpet voice, "Millions will die in her name. The steppes will be soaked in blood. I see a future in which women are herded into one set of cities, men into another. I see endless processions, mindlessly stamping puddles of light. I see age, coming inexorably, with no youth to soften it, no children to bless it. I see Peasimy Prime immolating himself at last when death draws near, in order to assure for himself the immortality promised by Pamra Don."

"Millions?" Tharius faltered. "What would be left?"

"I see a dozen, a hundred interventions, heresies, rebellions, all of which might succeed, any of which might fail. Still, the Jarb Houses will try, and try. And in the end die or flee, as all else dies or flees. Then there will be remnants, scratching in the ashes, ready to begin again." He lowered his hands, took the pipe from his mouth, put his hand on Tharius's shoulder as though in comfort.

"Madness!"

"Not to Peasimy Flot," he said calmly. "Not to the fanatics who follow him. They do not see this world at all, but only their hope of the next. He has crossbowmen, did you know that? Men he has hired. They have instructions to shoot any Jarb Mendicant who comes anywhere near. He has named us the ultimate heretics. Us, and the Noor, and the Jondarites, for he has heard that General Jondrigar has been named the Protector of Man. Peasimy says no, the general is not Protector. He, Peasimy, is the Protector."

"No hope." Tharius clutched at himself, as though he had been stabbed.

Chiles Medman laughed bitterly. "Oh, there is always hope. Even now the Noor are marching toward the Rivershore. Every boat able to float will soon be headed south with Noor aboard. I do not know why, but they are a saner race than most. There is a riddle there. With the great numbers they have lost to slavery and war, one would think quite otherwise, and yet because of some chance they seem inclined, particularly in recent genera-

tions, toward peace and good sense. Medoor Babji has begged a
boon of her mother, the Queen, so the smoke tells me. Because
of the love she bears for a certain Northshoreman, the Noor
have said they will take certain—peaceful—others, as well.
That proud, persecuted people will take others as well. It is
remarkable.''

"Ah."

"So I suggest you go with them, Tharius Don. There is a
future for you, too. It is not long, but I see it in the smoke."

"Kessie," he murmured.

"Kessie as well. She is in Thou-ne, where you sent her,
where all of this might be said to have begun. Send word for her
to meet you in Vobil-dil-go."

"Your sources of information are better than mine, Medman.
But this did not begin in Thou-ne. It began in Baris, long and
long ago."

"Well, if you must talk of ultimate beginnings, it began long
before that."

"Why? Why? Medman, I read the books in the palace, again
and again. They are old books. If they tell the truth, our history
is full of this. We humans have done this again and again. In
the face of truth we choose madness! Over and over. We choose
madmen as leaders, clever players who will tell us pretty lies.
We repudiate those who promise us honesty and cleave to those
who promise us myths. Never the truth, always the Candy Tree.
Like flame-birds, we do not feel the flames even while they
burn us, as we hatch our like to make the same mistakes in their
time. And I, I who sought to do everything in my power to
achieve life and peace, I have fallen into the trap. Why? Why?''

"Ask the strangeys, Tharius Don. Perhaps they know. I
don't." Chiles Medman stretched wearily, his nostrils flaring at
the stench of the fires. Among the dead and dying moved the
Mendicants, hazing the valley with smoke. On the far green
horizon, Peasimy Flot's cart gleamed in the sun, its bright
banners fluttering as the men drawing it ran at top speed away
from the battle. "Do not let that one get hold of you," said
Chiles in a conversational tone. "Power has come to him, and
he will drive it as a child drives a hobby. He has it between his
legs, and he will make it take him where he will."

"The general will catch him," Tharius said wearily. "He cannot run forever."

"So reason says, and yet that is not what I see," said Medman, putting his pipe away as he started down the slope. "Vobil-dil-go, Tharius. Now. Do not return behind the Teeth. There is nothing there for you."

And indeed, there was little enough left behind the Teeth for anyone. The Jondarites had flowed from Highstone Lees like water; after them the servants, for who would stay if there were no Jondarites to enforce discipline? Split River Pass ran like a river with soldiers and slaves and servants and all, out and away. Tharius Don was gone; Gendra Mitiar gone; the general gone; Lees Obol dead, and none caring that he lay all alone on the catafalque in the ceremonial square.

Shavian Bossit wandered through the empty rooms, wondering where everyone had gone, down the long, echoing corridors to the winter quarters, through those to the deeper caverns of the files. "Feynt!" he called, hearing his own voice shattering the silences. "Feynt!"

There was no answer. Glamdrul Feynt and Bormas Tyle were together in a deep, hidden room of the place, unaware of their abandonment, plotting. In another room, distant from the first, Ezasper Jorn and Koma Nepor were doing likewise. They knew nothing of the slaughter beyond the pass, nothing of the strike that had begun, nothing of the war that had started while they whispered, all unwitting, in the dark cellars of the Chancery.

"Jorn!" cried Shavian Bossit. "Nepor!"

There was no answer, and he struggled up the endless stairs to a high terrace, where he stepped into the light once more. In the ceremonial square a herd of weehar milled about the unguarded catafalque. Around them lay the scattered bodies of dead herders, and over the bawling animals fliers struck and struck again.

"Stop that!" he howled, unthinking that there were no Jondarites to enforce his commands. "Stop that!"

He scarcely felt the claws that seized him from behind and lifted him into the high, chill air. Sliffisunda had told the raiding party to bring bull calves, but also, if they had an opportunity, to bring hostages.

In the deepest corridors below the Chancery, those on whom Koma Nepor had tested his improved strain of the blight began to stir. Bodies began to twitch, to move, to stand up and look curiously about themselves. The incubation period was over. Now they moved, seeking others to touch, to infect, to make as themselves. In all of the Chancery, there were only four live persons remaining. All else had been taken, or had fled.

· 26 ·

When Tharius Don stood upon the height where Pamra Don had been burned, it was the fifth day of the week. He raised and dropped his arm as a signal four times. Four days later, on the ninth day, that which had been long planned would take place. With that gesture, the signal so long awaited had been sent.

From a ledge high upon the Teeth of the North the birds went out near dusk, a flurry of them, like windblown flakes of white, twirling for the moment on their own wingtips with a murmur of air in feathers, a light rustling as of satin, a sound so innocent, so quiet, that no apprehension could attach to it. They were only birds, silver in the light of late afternoon, a little cloud of wings breaking into dots of fleeing light which beat away and away, some along the precipices east and west, others southward, still others in long diagonals away from the wall of mountains.

After the first flurry came a second and a third, glittering spirals, fleeing jots of amber and rose as the sun dropped still lower, and finally a fourth cloud of wings, blood red in the last of the light, darkening to ominous purple as they fled into the waiting dark.

There were thousands of birds, gathered over the years for this purpose alone. Each bird sought a separate person in a separate place. Each bird carried the same message. "On the ninth day, let the strike begin."

Below the ledge from which the birds went out was another on which a signal tower stood, and from here went winking lights like spears cast into the dusk, to be answered by other gleamings in the distance east and west, and then by others farther still, twinkling stars in the dark void of earth's night.

215

There were many thousands of towers transmitting the lights, ranks and files of them marking the edges of areas and zones, of townships and rivers, manned by newly volunteered zealots for the cause or by rebel Awakeners or by Rivermen, and it was to these the word came.

"On the ninth day, let the strike begin."

In far-off places, villages remote from the River, and to the townships themselves, the birds came bearing the same words. "On the ninth day, let the strike begin."

To the nearer places first, to the farther places only after days had passed, still the word ran like fever in the veins of Northshore, corrupting the blood of the world into a fatal hemorrhage.

In Zephyr, the husband of her who had been Blint-wife went to his bird cote at dawn. It was the morning of the ninth day. He read the message almost with disbelief. So long, so long planned. So long in the coming. And so suddenly was it *now*. This coming night. He went down the stairs, the message in his hands. "Murga?"

She was bustling about in the kitchen, making a cheerful clack with her tongue as she fed stewed fruit and grain to the grandchildren. "Murga."

She appeared at the door, wiping her hands. "Raffen? What is it? Are you ill?"

He realized his voice had betrayed him, edged with half excitement, half fear; like a knife, it had cut into her contentment. "The word has come."

She shivered. She had had to know, as all the Rivermen knew, and yet she had kept it closed away in the back of her mind somewhere, along with other unwanted and dangerous lumber. "When?"

"Tonight."

"So soon!"

"Once the word came, it had to be soon. Immediate. We could not expect to keep it quiet long after the word was given. Too many birds. Too many messages."

"So." She wiped her hands again, as though by wiping them she might wipe away the need for acting, for responding. "What am I to do?"

"You are to stay here, in the house. I'll need the children as

messengers for a time, then they must come in and stay close. I
will spread the word now. We will spy out the pits during the
day to see how many men will be needed.''

"The River?''

"Yes. The barge is ready. The stone sacks are ready. We
have men to man the lines.''

"I worry,'' she said, tears in the corners of her eyes. "I
worry the barge may break loose. You may end up west of here.
You could not return to me. How would I find you?''

He laughed, a quick, unamused bark of laughter. "Silly
woman. Such a silly Murga. After tonight, dear one, it will not
matter east or west. When we have done with the Servants of
Abricor, do you not think we will have done with their gods?
And then do you not think we may walk where we choose? East
or west?''

That night he came with others to the pits, well after dark, to
pile the bony remnants and twitching corpses into barrows,
careful not to touch them with naked skin lest there be some
infection from the Tears of Viranel. The barrows creaked down
through the town and were emptied into the barge, and there the
heavy sacks of stone were tied to the bodies while the barge
made its laborious way out into the River, sweeps creaking and
men cursing at the unaccustomed labor. The line that connected
them to shore reeled out, span after span, and at last Raffen
gave the word they had waited for. The bodies went overboard,
into the massive currents of the ever-moving River, and the
Rivermen turned to the winch to take up the line and bring the
barge back to the place it had left.

When morning came, there was nothing different, nothing
remarkable, nothing to show that the world had changed. Except that the worker pits were empty.

In Xoxxy-Do, where there were no piers and great rocks
encumbered the Riverside, a great pit had been prepared, dug
by Rivermen over the decades, deeper and deeper with each
succeeding year, the stones taken from it piled above it on
teetering platforms of poised logs, the earth piled behind the
stones. "A quarry,'' they had called it, taking from it small
quantities of carefully crafted blocks, chosen, so it was said, for

their veining and color. There the Rivermen came to the quarry late, bringing with them the harvest of the worker pits of towns both east and west, their wagon wheels creaking in the dark and lanterns gleaming. It was early morning when the last of the bodies was laid in the great stone hollow, almost day, with the green line of false dawn sketched flatly on the eastern plains. Then the engineers moved certain logs that braced certain others in place, and the mountain of piled rubble fell, the accumulation of years fallen into the place from which it had been taken.

If the Rivermen were to try to dig it up, it would take a generation. The Servants of Abricor could not unearth the bodies in a thousand years.

In the towns of Azil and Thrun and Cheeping Wells, the Rivermen carried the corpses to the ends of the long piers, weighted them well, and tossed them out into the River's deep currents.

In Crisomon a great pyre had been built, and in that township every man, woman, and child danced around the pyre as the bodies of the workers were burned to ashes. In Crisomon, conversion to the cause had been total and unanimous.

Elsewhere that was not so. In some townships the Awakeners were vigilant or wakeful and came out of the Towers to defend the pits. In a few places the Awakeners prevailed, but in most the Rivermen won and the corpses of Awakeners were merely added to other corpses which had to be disposed of before dawn.

Dawn.

Worker pits empty when the sun rose. In B'for, just east of Thou-ne, an Awakener returned in some haste to the Tower to speak with the Superior, who was in company with the lady Kesseret, said to be Superior of a Tower farther east who had come to B'for on urgent business and was receiving Lord Deign's hospitality before going on.

The Awakener was panting so much it was hard to discern the message that the pit was empty.

The Superior was silent, but the lady Kesseret seemed to understand what had been said.

"Then you will not need to go to the fields today," she said calmly. There were great wrinkles around her eyes and lips, and her voice was thready. "Rejoice."

"But, but," the young Awakener stuttered, "but, what shall I do?"

"Go to the chapel and pray," she suggested.

"What should I pray for?"

"Enlightenment. Patience. Resignation."

Were these not what she herself had prayed for? She searched Deign's face for signs of shock. None. Both of them had been ready for this. Now it had happened, and she must plan to leave B'for to travel westward to Thou-ne. In a few days or weeks, if they were permitted to live that long. She would not fail to be in that place where Tharius Don would come for her or send her word.

In a few towns the word had not arrived in time, or there had been no Rivermen to receive it. In a few towns there had been no strike, no disturbance at all. The Servants of Abricor fed as usual in the bone pits, looking up with surprise to see their fellows from neighboring townships circling high above, dropping down to sit with them in long, dusty lines upon the pit edges, talking of this thing.

"No workers in our town," the fliers said. "No workers."

"Sometimes there are no workers," they told one another. "Sometimes it happens."

"Not often," they agreed. "Not so many places all at once."

It was almost noon of the day after the strike before they sent some among them off to tell the Talkers at the Talons.

"How long?" the Rivermen asked one another. "How long will it take before they do something?"

"Pile the fish upon the wharves and wait," they said to each other. "Each day, fresh fish, there for the eating."

It took only another day before Servants descended upon the towns, snatching at children or smaller adults. In Baris one among them distracted a group of townsmen while others made off with a living, pleading victim. In some towns, the Rivermen were ready for this; ready with crossbows and stone-tipped bolts, ready with nooses and obsidian clubs. In other towns the victims screamed into unheeding air, were flown away to be dosed with Tears and left in some pit or other until ready for eating.

The Servants had never considered human anger. In the wake of these seizings, anger rose like a veil of smoke around the towns, palpable as wind. Even they who had not been Rivermen, who had revered the Awakeners, even they could feel nothing but anger as they saw their children hoisted aloft, blood dripping from sharp talons as the screaming prey were carried away. Towns in which the first victims were easily taken proved to be impregnable on the second try. Doors and windows were closed. Farmers were not working in their fields. Children were not playing in the streets. Where groups moved, armed men moved with them.

On the wharves the fishermen, guarded by bowmen, drew in their nets and piled the bounty of the River upon the wharves.

On the third day after the strike, Servants attacked some of the towns, tearing at shutters with their talons and beaks, screaming rage at the inhabitants, making short flights to the Riverside to attack the fishermen and to drop tiny blobs of stinking shit upon the fish piled there. The bowmen were practiced by now and used their bolts to advantage. The fliers, in their rage, scarcely noticed how their numbers were being reduced.

In Zephyr, Murga and Raffen sat in their kitchen, listening to a fury of wings outside, like the sound of a great, windy storm. The children cowered beside them, both frightened and excited by this frenzy. "When will it be over?" they asked, not sure whether they wanted the excitement to end.

"Soon," said Raffen. "They will weaken soon." He sighed. Thus far, not a single one of the fliers had taken any of the fish from the shore. Though many of the Rivermen were not unhappy about this, Raffen believed in the purity of the original cause. He had not wanted the flier folk to die. "They will weaken soon," he repeated, hoping they would grow weak enough to succumb at last to reality and eat what was offered them.

In most Towers, Superiors ordered their Awakeners to stay within. Even those most dedicated to the worship of Potipur, and to the virtual immortality that worship might have gained them, learned that discretion was needed. Blinking lights told them of Awakeners in neighboring towns beaten to death by mobs of outraged citizens. Seeker birds arrived to tell them of Awakeners burned in their Towers because they had seemed to favor the Servants of Abricor. These messages had been planned by Tharius Don and long arranged for, designed to be sent a day after the strike to prevent the Awakeners from interfering with what was going on.

And in the Talons was a fury such as Northshore had not seen in a thousand years. Upon the Stones of Disputation the Talkers sat in their tattered feathers, screaming at one another of fault and blame and guilt and shame, while below them in the aeries the last of the Talkers' meat struggled mindlessly in the troughs. Sliffisunda brooded alone in his own place, considering the likelihood of survival, his mind sharpened by the knowledge that there had indeed been a heresy afoot.

"Promise of Potipur," the surviving fliers cried, dropping from the sky like knives of black fire upon the Stones of Disputation while the Talkers scurried for cover. "Promise of Potipur!" From his concealed room, Sliffisunda heard them, heard the shrieks of pain and rage as those like himself were slaughtered by the angry flocks, his mind working relentlessly as he determined to go on living whether any other of the Thraish lived or not. He would wait until dark. He would fly into the north, to the Chancery, to that place he had flown once before, against his own will, where the herds of thrassil and weehar still grazed on the grasses of Potipur's Promise. Enough to feed himself, he thought. For years. The hot, lovely blood of thrassil. In the north.

He forgot that others of the Thraish had already been sent to hunt among the herds beyond the Teeth.

On the great moors of the Noor, Peasimy Flot learned of the conflagration to the south. Some among his entourage could read the flicking lights. There was even one who was sought out by a seeker bird. The days brought increasing information, until even Peasimy could not but be aware of what was happening.

"Light comes?" he asked, almost whimpering in his hatred for whoever had done this without him. "Light comes?" He had sworn vengeance upon those who had burned Pamra Don, and now those who had burned Pamra Don were dead or dying without any action by Peasimy Flot. Without his hand in their guts, his knife in their throats. He had fled—though, he told himself, he had done so only to consolidate his strength—but still they died. How dared they?

"Who did it?" he asked at last, while they conferred and tried to come up with an answer. "Who killed them?"

"Someone in the Chancery," they said. "It had to be someone in the Chancery."

"Heretics," he hissed. "All those in the Chancery. We go to war!" For it had been near the Chancery that Pamra Don had died. And near the Chancery that the great assembly had seen him flee away. And from the Chancery that some troop of soldiers had been seeking him ever since. He would make sure there were no witnesses to that defection left to speak of it.

"War," he said again, telling his close advisers to make that message manifest among the multitude.

During the night some among the followers faded away to the south, but enough others were still there when the sun rose, polishing their axes and making ready new bolts for their bows, to make a great army.

Not far to the east, General Jondrigar pursued Peasimy Flot, eager to chastise him for his insults to the Noor.

After about a week, and in only a few towns, a flier or two descended upon the wharves to gorge themselves on the fish piled there. They did not return for another meal. Scarcely had they time to arise from their feasting before the talons of other, more traditional Thraish hurled them from the sky. Then there was screaming and feasting of flier upon flier, with much buffeting of wings and thrusting of beaks. For the most part the Rivermen were faithful to the instructions of Tharius Don, taking no action against the fliers unless they themselves were attacked— they or other humans in the towns. In some, however, it was an excuse for general slaughter, and more of the fliers died.

"When?" asked the children. "We don't hear anything anymore."

"Now, I think," said Raffen the Riverman. "Let us go out."

The streets were littered with bits of broken shutter, with blown feathers, with the wind-tossed refuse that accumulates in every town unless swept away daily by those whose business it is to keep the streets. People wandered here and there, peering around them as though to see whether there might not be just one Awakener among them, just one group of workers. There were none. The Tower stood in its park. No one had looked inside it yet, but it gave the appearance of a place that was tenantless. Empty. Like a shell when the nut has been eaten away.

A bustling man came to Raffen for advice. There were dead in the town to be disposed of, and Raffen went away with him to instruct the townsfolk how this should be done in the future.

Murga and the children went on wandering the streets. On the highest point of the town, the Temple still stood, its high dome gleaming white with paint. From inside came the sound of hammers.

"What are they doing?" Murga asked a passerby.

"Taking the moon faces off the wall," came the answer. "They are setting up an image of the Light Bearer instead."

Murga took the children by the hands and led them to the Temple to see what was going on. The Temple floor was littered with shattered stone before the wall where the masons' hammers were at work, but the image that stood at the top of the stairs was one Blint-wife had known well. She was carved in ivory stone, her arms curved around a child. It was a copy of the statue in Thou-ne.

"Thrasne's woman!" Murga whispered to herself. "That's Thrasne's woman!"

The serene face gleamed down at her, unmoved, unmoving, just as it had always seemed aboard the *Gift*.

"Well, at least she's got her baby," said Murga, unawed by this elevation to divinity. "At least that."

• 27 •

The *Gift* had returned to Northshore, thanks to the skill of the sailors, three towns east of Thou-ne. Those who had sailed in her gathered at the rail, watching the familiar shoreline grow closer, each of them aware that something was wrong, was missing, without knowing precisely what until Medoor Babji said, "There aren't any fliers!"

It was true. There were no wings aloft except for the little birds. There were no great, tattered shapes floating above the Talons.

There were great heaps of fresh-caught fish on the piers, which no one seemed to be eating or selling. Within an hour of their arrival, they had been told why and how, and Thrasne had gone to the Temple to see the wall where the moon faces had been. A stone carver was there, working on a large figure. When Thrasne asked what it was to be, he said it was to be the Light Bearer. A woman, with a child in her arms. It did not look at all like Suspirra, but then the carver was not very talented. Or so Thrasne thought, wondering what Pamra would think of this image. He said something of this to the carver, twitting him only a little, saying the image was not really like unto her.

"Well, as to that"—the man spat rock dust at him—"likely she will be carved in a hundred fashions or more. What was left of her after they burned her, so I'm told, didn't leave much for us to model from."

Thrasne had him by the throat before the poor man knew what he had set off, and it was only when two people came up from the Temple floor, pulling at him and screaming in his ear,

224

that he let the carver go. They told him then what they knew, which was not much and already overlaid with myths.

"She rose," one woman whispered. "Like the flame-bird, burning, into the very heavens, singing like an angel."

Thrasne stumbled out of the place.

There was a hurt place inside him, one he could cover with his outspread hand, a hot burning as though he were being consumed from within. He burned as Pamra Don had burned. The fiery spot widened, spread, reached the limits of his body, and then erupted through his skin in a fleeing cloud of spiritual flame, vaguely man-shaped, the heat of it an emotional blast which fled away as a hot wind flees. He could feel it as a presence departing, an actuality with motivations of its own, now vanishing from his understanding. In that momentary excruciation he felt he had emitted an angel which now expanded to fill all the universe, becoming more tenuous with every breath until all connection with Thrasne was teased away into nothing.

He flexed his hand across the place the angel had left, somewhere near his stomach or heart, an interior place that had nothing to do with thought but only with the tumbling of liquors and the rumbling of guts, the living heart-belly of his being. Where the fire had burned was a vacancy. A hole. He poked a finger at himself, half expecting it to penetrate into that emptiness, but he encountered only solid muscle and the hard bones of his ribs. Whatever the emptiness might be, it was not physical, and there was no pain associated with it. The angel had taken the pain with it when it departed.

"Pamra Don," he said, testing himself for a response. There was none. Perhaps a twinge of bittersweet sadness, like dawn mist blown across one's face, carrying the scent of wet herbs, evocative of nothing but itself. "Pamra Don?"

And then again he tried, "Suspirra?"

To find her gone as well.

So, what was it that had fled? A ghost? A fiery spirit? A succubus who had lived beneath his heart?

Or was it some soul-child of his own, self-created, dreamed, hoped-for, stillborn in this world but released into some wider universe?

Whatever it might have been, it would not be. "I can do nothing," he said to himself in wonder. "There is nothing I can do for Pamra Don."

Except perhaps, his hands said of themselves, twitching for his knife or a chisel as he remembered what the carver was making in the Temple. Except perhaps. Whatever she was, whatever she had become, Thrasne could show her as she had been.

"I knew her, after all," he said to himself wonderingly. "I knew her."

· 28 ·

The days of the strike had fallen into memory. In Vobil-dil-go, order had been restored. The heights of the Talons on the eastern skyline were empty of wings. The Tower was empty of Awakeners. Only Haranjus Pandel had occupied a room there when he had come with the lady Kesseret and the widow Flot from Thou-ne. He came down to the town occasionally to greet this one and that one, well accepted by all. To the north, it was said, great armies moved, but at the Riverside there was a precarious calm, like that at the eye of a storm before the great winds come again.

On a stone above the River, Queen Fibji drew her feet beneath her and sat thus, cross-legged, looking across all that mighty water to the place she hoped to arrive with her people in a little time. Below her the Noor and some Northshoremen toiled among the boats, carrying endless bales and barrels into the holds. She approved this, searching among the busy forms for the tall bulky one her daughter had just mentioned. Thrasne. Boatman. Not a Noor and, to hear Medoor Babji tell it, in love with someone else to boot. And yet, her daughter's choice.

"How long before we leave?" she asked for the tenth time.

"Three hours," answered Medoor Babji. "Perhaps four."

"And how many boats?"

"A dozen have gone that we know of. Fifteen are readying to go. There will be more. There are Noor in every town, buying boats, hiring boats. There will be hundreds, thousands."

"If we get away before they kill us all."

"We will. The battles are all on the steppes, behind us where the Jondarites are fighting the crusaders. The towns are not involved."

227

"Not yet!"

"Oh, I agree, great Queen. They will be. But they are not, yet."

"How will we find one another, when we get there?"

"Those who leave from towns west of Vobil-dil-go are to march east when they arrive at Southshore. Those who leave from towns east of Vobil-dil-go are to march west. When we arrive on Southshore, we will build a great tower upon the shore. We will light beacons on the top of it at night. We will leave messages in cairns upon the beaches. We will send runners. We will find one another, great Queen."

"And the islands of the River . . ."

"Are full of friendly folk, human and Treeci. And the strangeys of the depths are not to be feared."

"And Southshore waits."

What they said to one another was a litany. A ritual. They had repeated it a hundred times. Perhaps the Queen would say it a hundred times more on the boat, convincing herself.

"Does that man know you're pregnant?"

Medoor Babji looked at her swollen belly and laughed. "It would be very hard for him not to know."

"What does he say about that?"

"Thrasne says very little about anything. I have told him it is his. He got a strangely bemused expression on his face. It seems to me he smiles a great deal more recently, though he still goes into those odd abstractions and stares at the water. I know then that he is thinking of Pamra Don."

The Queen had resolved not to remonstrate, and now she shut her teeth firmly upon her tongue. Her whole self writhed at this self-imposed silence, and she sought a subject that was not—or would not seem to be—related. She would talk about . . . about something global.

"Medoor Babji, since you are my heir, let me share my mind with you as my father once shared his mind with me. Since I received your message, I have spent much time in thought. Perhaps my thoughts will interest you.

"When I was very young, I often wondered what I was for. The boys, most of them, seemed to know. They were to be warriors. The girls were to bear children. But my father told me

I was to be Queen, and we did not have a queen then, so I could not see what one was. Whatever it might be, I was quite sure it was something wonderful and eternal. Then, when I was about seven or eight—with some it happens earlier, I suppose; there may be some with whom it never happens—the understanding came all at once, in one hot burst, that Queen or no, I would not always be, that someday I would die and stop being. I screamed and wept. I thought I knew something no one else knew, but my father comforted me. He told me it was the first accomplishment of mankind, to know our own mortality, a thing the beasts and fishes never know.

"So, it seemed my father knew all about it. At that age, grown people seem to know everything about everything—you accused me of that once, I remember.

"Well, when it was time to sleep, back then when I was a child, I would lie on my blankets and go drifting into a certain world. I remember little of it now, except that there was music everywhere, and fountains of pearl, and beasts one could ride, and funny little furry things that talked. . . .

"So, one day I said to my father that I wished he would get me a—what was it I called them? a foozil or some such—get me a foozil. And he asked me what a foozil was, and I explained that it was one of the furry, talking animals, and he told me I had made it all up. Imaginary, he said.

"Well. I had not known that the world I drifted in before sleep was only my own. I had thought it was a world everyone knew of. I thought we shared it, other people and I. It was the first time I knew that we all have separate worlds, Medoor Babji. No one else knew of my foozil. No one else had seen my fountains of pearl, or my wondrous beasts. How sad for them, I thought. Until I realized that they, each of them, had a world of his own.

"And I was shut out of them, daughter! Oh, the tragedy and wonder of that! The wonder of knowing that my own universe, much of it unexplored, bright or dim, shadowed or sunlit, full of every possible expression of dream and imagination—that the universe I have inside me was *not shared*. But more tragic, to know that all around me were a hundred thousand others, also dim or bright, full of dream, none of which I could ever see or know. The tragedy of knowing I would never know! Do you understand what I mean, Medoor Babji?''

Medoor nodded, thinking perhaps she did, perhaps she did not. Her mother did not wait for a response.

"I was a child. I didn't realize how limited our lives really are. I decided to learn all about the worlds of others. I asked them to tell me stories of their worlds, and they gave me words, daughter. Do you know how limited words are? People try to describe their worlds to you, but their words are like a map drawn with a burned stick beside a campfire. At best they let you in a little; at worst they hide the way entirely. I found that people go through life giving each other these little maps and little passwords. We explore one another, and gradually the maps accumulate, the passwords become more numerous. The more we are alike, the more we share, the more we understand. So, we Noor can see further inside one another than most. We can share each other's worlds better than most. But we can never really see it all. . . .

"So, you have a world inside you, child of my heart, which I can see a little. And the one you love, this Thrasne, he has a world as well, and it is utterly strange to me, to all the Noor. You ask me to love him for your sake. And I have not even a little map drawn with a burned stick to find my way to that.'' She smiled at Medoor Babji, shaking her head ruefully, receiving an equally rueful smile in return.

"So, I must do what we all do. I will take it on faith. His world is real because you tell me so. I cannot perceive it. I can only assume it. I will love him for your sake, Doorie.''

Medoor Babji took her hand and held it tightly. There were tears on the Queen's cheeks as she went on.

"Perhaps you will ask him to show me what he can of his world. Perhaps he will give me a map. From his map, I will travel in his strange world of water and boats if I can.''

"Oh, great Queen . . .''

"Call me 'Mother,' child. There may be no Queen of the Noor where we are going. There may be no throne for you to ascend.''

"I think he is afraid of you, Queen Fibji.''

"Well, so, and I am afraid of him as well. We must do what

we can about that. I will give him passwords to walk in my world, and he must give me passwords to walk in his, so we can pass each other by without disruption. There are many passwords, child. 'Be careful,' or 'Forgive me,' or 'I love you,' or 'Take care of my child.' ''

"What do I do if he still loves Pamra the Prophetess? Or believes he does? Or remembers doing so?"

"You have told me he is an artist, and she was beautiful. I never saw her, but I have seen the image of her in the Temple here. He may always love that image of her. But it will not matter. Pretend it is God he loves, or his art. It is much the same thing."

"And you will give me your blessing?"

"You have had my blessing since I conceived you, Dorrie. It is not something one can take back. But if you want it renewed, so be it. Have your Thrasne, child. To whatever extent you can. Take whatever password he gives you, and be grateful."

The Queen brushed at her trousers and threw back the long tassels of her hair. "It is time we were done with this serious talk. All day has been full of weeps and moans. I cried this morning, thinking of all those who would not come with us to this River. How many there were who would not follow me! How many there were who stayed, to revenge themselves upon those who had persecuted us. How many there were who chose that, rather than this. . . .''

"The River is frightening," Medoor admitted. "I was frightened by it."

"They were not frightened of the River," Queen Fibji contradicted. "They were frightened of going where there would not be any enemies to fight. These were the young men with battle in their blood. They thumped their spears on the ground and leapt high in a battle dance and sent their spokesmen to me to explain. They spoke of honor. Of glory. I tried to tell them what I have told you, but it meant nothing to them. I told them of my father. I told them the riddle he had given me as a child. 'Of what good are dead warriors?' I asked them. It did no good. They stayed behind. They did not see my world, child. They would not see my world. . . .''

She gazed out over the water, not seeing Medoor Babji's eyes fixed on her, wide and terrible.

And she, Medoor, within herself but without speaking, said to her mother, "Mother. I found the answer to your father's riddle. I sent a message to tell you. . . ."

She imagined that the Queen was silent for a moment, thinking. "Of course you did. And you told me you were pregnant. And that Southshore awaited. And those things drove the other from my mind. So. You have the answer. Will you tell it me?"

"It is the answer to your riddle of long and long ago. The riddle your father set you. 'Of what good are dead warriors?' I found the answer to that."

"Where did you find it?"

"I learned it from the Treeci, by chance."

"So? Come, child. Why this hesitation? Tell me!"

Medoor imagined herself delaying, knowing she was right, and yet the answer was a hard and hurtful one. "Warriors are those who desire battle, Mother."

"Yes?" The Queen would be puzzled.

"Warriors are those who desire battle more than peace. Those who seek battle despite peace. Those who thump their spears on the ground and talk of honor. Those who leap high in the battle dance and dream of glory. . . .

"The good of dead warriors, Mother, is that they are dead."

The Queen would stand staring at her for a long time. After that time, tears would begin to run down her cheeks. Medoor saw them clearly. If she told her mother the answer to the riddle, her mother would cry once more and there had been enough tears today. She would not tell her mother the answer. Not today. Perhaps not ever. It was a stony answer, a hard answer.

When all the warriors were dead, when they made no more children like themselves, then others might live in peace. She would not tell the answer, but she would keep it in her heart.

"Let us go down to the River," said the Queen.

They walked together down toward the *Gift*, the ship that was to take them to Southshore.

• 29 •

There were some others who would sail aboard the *Gift* as well: Haranjus Pandel, the widow Flot, and two very old and feeble people, Tharius Don and the lady Kesseret. Tharius had sent word for her to meet him in Vobil-dil-go, and here he had begged passage for them both from Thrasne.

"I have not seen a flier in weeks," the lady said, her voice quavering. "I think the last was a month ago."

"They are probably all dead," answered Tharius, his voice emotionless. He had done grieving for the Thraish. His grief over Pamra Don had been all the grief he had left. "I was wrong, that's all. A few survived for a time, eating stilt-lizards and the lesser birds, until there were no more. Except for a few, they wouldn't eat fish, even to save their lives."

"Medoor Babji told me a strange thing," the lady said. "She said that at the time of the hunger, long and long ago, all the Thraish who could eat fish had done so. They left Northshore then, in fear of their lives. Only those who couldn't do it had remained here on Northshore, and there were very few of them. And all those who lived here on Northshore were descendents of those few who could not. It wasn't your fault, Tharius. It was bred in them. They couldn't. That's all."

"It's no one's fault," he said.

"Medoor Babji told me something else. She says that when the dead are put in the River, they are touched by blight and then taken by the strangeys to the islands. They go on living there, Tharius. They grow slower and slower, rooting themselves like trees, time all quiet around them. I want to go there."

"Why? Why?"

"Because there has never been time for me. Only for the cause. It would be nice to have time for me."

He buried his face in her hair and said nothing. He would grow roots beside her if she liked. He didn't know whether to believe Medoor Babji's tale or not.

"It's a pity Pamra Don could not have been put in the River. What did you do with her body, Tharius?"

"Buried it," he said. "Wrapped it in a robe and buried it beneath a thorn tree. There was nothing but bones. And a kind of child-shaped shell that Lila hatched out of. I think it was Lila."

"Lila?"

He told her of Lila. He had heard more about Lila from Thrasne, though he wasn't sure how much of that he believed, either. "I don't know what it was that went into the River," he said. "The strangeys called her their child. She was something strange."

"They're taking up the plank," she said. "The oars are beginning to sweep."

He looked out across the railing. The River slid between the *Gift* and the shore, and they began to move out onto the waters. All the deck was crowded with Noor amid a sprinkling of other folk. "Half a year," he said. "To Southshore."

"It is unlikely we will see it," she said, contented. "I don't care."

Behind them on the bank, a few standabouts stood watching their slow progress. Most paid little attention. Too much else was happening. There were no workers anymore. The Towers were empty. There were no fliers, not anywhere. All of them had starved to death, it was said, though a good many had been killed when they'd attacked humans, trying to dose them with Tears or carry them off to the Talons. If one wanted excitement, one might think about joining the war going on, back on the steppes. Two Protectors of Man, one true, one false, fighting each other, and who knew which was which? There was even talk that one side wanted to kill off all the Noor. People were taking sides, joining up with one or the other, getting irate about one side or the other in taverns. Some were Peasimites, some Jondarites, and the gods knew where it would all end.

The gods knew; not that anyone meant the old gods. Potipur was finished. His image was scratched right off the Temple walls, and so were Viranel and Abricor. The Mother of Truth stood there now, shining, and people came from far away to make measurements of her so they could carve copies for their own Temples. The man who had carved her had actually known her, so it was said, before she was the Light Bringer. He had written it, right there on the image, for all the doubters to see.

Still, other carvers carved her differently. Sometimes they carved her with a child in her arms, sometimes with a flame-bird chick, for it was told how a flame-bird had hatched in her arms when she was put in the fire. Her soul, some said, which flew straight to the God of man. Something else, others said, which had not looked like a flame-bird at all. She had been burned by Jondarites, some said. By Peasimites, said others. By the fliers, said others yet. But who knew the truth? Priests used to answer questions like that, but they were gone, along with the Awakeners. Who knew where? They unbraided their hair, laid down their staffs, wiped the paint from their faces, and disappeared. Just like anyone else, now.

The gates were gone now. People went east if they felt like it, though some felt very uncomfortable about it. And sure as sure, some oldsters couldn't stand the changes and had to carry their dead west for the Holy Sorters, even though everyone knew there weren't any such things. The Rivermen kept watch, though. There weren't any bodies left lying around to attract fliers, even though no one had seen any fliers for weeks. Sooner or later, everyone ended up in the River.

Or across it. For there was word of a new land there, a far land, a land where the Noor were going—and smart of 'em, too, if the Peasimites were coming. Now and then someone might stop a moment and look in that direction, saying the word over as though it had some magical meaning.

Southshore.

· 30 ·

They were somewhere near the Island of the Dead when the two old people died. First Tharius Don, all at once, with one deep, heaving breath; then Kessie, calling his name once and then not breathing again, as though there were no reason to breathe once the other was gone. Thrasne found Medoor Babji crying over them, the tears lying on her cheeks like jewels, and he kissed them away, comforting her.

"Aiee, Medoor Babji, but those were old, old folk. Tharius Don told me he'd lived hundreds of years. More than you and me put together ever will."

"I know," she wept. "It's just they loved each other, Thrasne."

She would not be comforted, but she did stop crying. The late evening mist hid the waters, and he couldn't see whether the island was really near or not, though he smelled it, or another one like it, and had been doing so all day. There was a peculiar odor about the Island of the Dead, a tree fragrance unlike any other, and he could detect it now, faintly borne on the light wind. The two old people lay on the deck, side by side, and the Noor Queen came out of the owner-house to say some words over them in a high, singsong voice before Obors-rom slid their bodies into the River.

They sank down, out of sight, quickly, as though eager to depart. Medoor Babji clung to Thrasne almost fearfully, and he held her close beside him, bringing her into his bed that night, big belly and all, feeling the babe kicking inside her with a kind of quiet joy and fear all at once. There had still been no words, no real words, between them. They had not talked of Pamra

Don or of Thrasne's feelings. He did not know how she felt about him, really, or how a queen's daughter would be allowed to feel. He was afraid to ask. And yet she lay there beside him, deeply asleep, and he took it to mean something.

In the night he dreamed of Lila.

She had become a creature wholly strange, not human at all and yet, one could have said, not totally unlike. There was something one thought of as a head, with organs of sight and smell and perhaps taste and hearing, this part already fringed at the edges. There were parts that could have been arms and legs on their way to being something else, not flippers or fins, precisely, and yet fulfilling those functions as well as other, unimaginable ones. Her voice, when she spoke, was Lila's voice, a child's chuckling voice using words that set up unfamiliar chains of association in his mind as he heard her demanding to know why Medoor Babji was grieving.

"Medoor Babji was crying because they died, and they loved one another," he explained to her.

"My people tell me humans are maddened by death," she said. "It comes too quickly, severing love. People need time to become accustomed to it. Either they dwell on it all the time, worrying their lives away to make monuments to themselves, or they refuse to think of it at all, like Queen Fibji's young warriors. It becomes an obsession with men, one way or the other, so they forget to live. Like you, Thrasne."

"I don't understand," Thrasne said in his dream. "What has that to do with me?"

"Your mother died, Thrasne, and you could not bear that she was gone. So you created her again, as Suspirra, a carving, which was safe because it could not die. And then you found the drowned woman, and she was safe, too, because she was already dead. Then, when she fell into dust—I know; I was there—when she fell into dust you chose Pamra to continue to be Suspirra. You told yourself you wanted her to love, to bear your children. In truth you only wanted her never to change. You wanted her to be Suspirra."

"It is easier to honor the dead than it is to love the living."

"That's crazy," he said in his dream, but weakly.

"Oh, but men are crazy," Lila said in her bubbling voice.

"Only crazy people would have had things like Awakeners and workers. Only crazy people would dream of an eternal life in Potipur's arms." She laughed. "A baby, held in arms, rocked to and fro, unchanging. Ah, ah, that is not eternal life, Thrasne. That is eternal death. Only a crazy man would have loved Pamra. . . ."

"But I did love her," he argued, angry even in his dream, knowing he did not quite believe it.

"Only because she was Suspirra. What was she otherwise? A narrow, ignorant woman. Maddened by death into rejecting life. Holding fast to a childish naiveté which protected her from seeing reality. A believer in impossible futures. A simple, totally selfish woman who saw no one's need but her own, who invented a doctrine to meet that need and voices to validate it, who walked a way upon the world convincing others her myth was better than their myths, letting others suffer and die in the service of her madness, starving herself into spasms of self-generated rapture, not seeing, not hearing, only to be burned at last by that which she would not hear or see."

"She wanted to free the slaves. She wanted to stop the workers. She was a saint," he muttered.

"There are those who say so now. There are those who will say so," Lila whispered. "What is a saint? Delia was a saint."

"You're saying she never could have loved me!" he cried, angry at this in the dream, though he knew it was true.

"I'm saying you never should have loved her," Lila said, her voice somehow changed into something remote and terrible. "For she was like the blight, a terrible thing that kills. . . ."

"And preserves," whispered Thrasne in his dream.

"And preserves," whispered Lila as the dream whirled about him, giving way to the sounds of the River, the soft, eternal sluff of water.

He woke then, the dream at first clear, then fading from his mind. Medoor Babji lay heavily beside him, her cheek flushed and warm where it had rested against his own. He rose without waking her and went out of the owner-house onto the deck. In the dawn light the Island of the Dead loomed to the south, mist and tree behind mist and tree and yet again, mist and tree to the limit of sight, with the blessed ones—for so he now called them in his mind—the blessed ones moving slowly in the mists, like swimmers. There on the water the strangeys danced, calling to one another in their terrible voices, and among them their young sported themselves, standing winged upon the waves.

One of these came very close to the ship and looked up at Thrasne with eyes that seemed somehow familiar.

"Thrasne," it said to him in a bubbling voice. "Kesseret is here, Thrasne. And Tharius Don. They have been given the time we created for them. They live. You live, too, Thrasne. And come to us." It sank beneath the flowing surface, its eyes still fixed on Thrasne's face.

There was a hand on his shoulder.

"Come," said Medoor Babji, her dry and watchful eyes on the waves where the strangeys danced. "Let us go on to Southshore, Thrasne. This is not the place for us."

He heard the rattle of the anchor tackle, the call of the sailors as the sails were raised. On the shore of the island, one of the blessed raised its hand to wave. Tharius Don? Too soon for Tharius Don. Someone else. Bending across the rail, Thrasne let a few tears come and fall and wash away the last of whatever thing there had been tight inside himself.

And then he stood to take Medoor Babji's hand and nod acceptance. "To Southshore."

· 31 ·

As they sailed on into the south, Thrasne rigged a chair over the bow and laboriously chiseled away two of the three words that had been carved into the prow of the ship. The *Gift of Potipur* became simply the *Gift*. The winged figure that had leaned into the wavelets of the River for decades was replaced with another carving, one that Medoor Babji called, only to herself, "Suspirra in ecstasy," taking comfort in the fact that Thrasne had carved it, for it was not a face or figure any living man would lust for. It was Pamra's face, but a face beatified, glorious, and inhuman, the face of a departing spirit. Before her in her wooden hands she held the gift, a strangely shaped being that might have had either wings or flippers and was carved as though eternally poised to drop into the waters below. Tharius Don, before his death, had told Thrasne about Lila as he had seen her, Lila transformed, the child of the strangeys.

On a calm and starry night when there were no moons, the child was born. When it had been cleaned and wrapped and laid in a blanket, Thrasne stood by the basket and the baby grasped his hand, curling infant fingers around one of his own in a gesture as old as time and demanding as life itself. "Mine," said Thrasne wonderingly. "This is mine."

"Ours," said Medoor Babji firmly. "He belongs to us, and to the Noor."

"And to the *Gift*," said Thrasne stubbornly. "And to Southshore."

"That, too. I pray we find good fortune there, for our ancestors alone know what is happening behind us." She reached for

Thrasne's other hand. The birth had been more than she had expected; more in the way of pain, of effort, and of fulfillment when it was done. It was time to say. Time for words. "And what of the baby's mother, Thrasne? Do you claim her, too, or only the child?"

"Oh, yes," he said, suddenly surprised that it should need saying. "Oh, yes! She, too, is mine if she will be."

"And Suspirra?"

He shrugged, rather more elaborately than the question warranted at this stage, but he needed to be sure that both of them understood what he meant. "At the prow of the *Gift,* Doorie. Where dreams are put. That was a different thing from this."

She was content, and Queen Fibji, hearing this exchange from outside the door, sighed a great sigh of relief.

They had come to the baby's tribal day, that day on which he was to be given a name, when the hail came from the steering deck. They thought it might be only another island and sent someone scurrying up the mast to spy out the cloudy land. He came back down to say there was no end to the land he could see, not south nor east nor west, but ahead of them were white beaches and a great, towering smoke. They gave up any thought of ceremony then, preferring to crowd the rails for the earliest glimpse of the new land.

By the time dusk came they had anchored in a shallow bay rimmed with pale dunes. On the beach were three boats that Thrasne recognized, and scattered across the dunes were the tents of many earlier arrivals. High above them to the west was a towering scaffold bearing a clay firefox, and in this a great beacon burned, smoke roiling above it as from a chimney.

Some of those aboard the *Gift* splashed into the water and swam ashore while others plied to and fro on hastily rigged rafts. The *Cheevle* bore Queen Fibji, Medoor Babji, Thrasne, and the child, with Strenge plying the rudder as they ran the little boat up on the sand. The Noor crowded around, not too closely, making obeisance, pointing at the child, who regarded them with wide, wondering looks from his not altogether Noorish eyes.

"Let me see this land," the Queen called, waving them aside as she staggered toward the tops of the dunes to peer inland, seeing there a vast prairie of grass and scattered copses in the light of the moons.

Thrasne came up behind her, one arm around Babji's shoulders, the baby in the other. From behind them, far down the beach, came a hail, and they turned to see another ship against the darkening sky, and beyond that one still another.

"The Noor are gathering. On Southshore," said the Queen. "We have made landfall. All my hopes, Doorie. All my hopes. I feel—oh, I feel I might die now, knowing the best thing I could have done is done."

"Do not talk of dying," said Thrasne, shaking her by one shoulder, much to her astonishment, for the Noor did not presume to touch their Queen. "There is much planting to do if all this mob is to be fed, and who will see to that if not you?" He sounded, she thought, really angry at her. "And this one is a month old today and still has no name. Who will name him if you go dying?"

"Ah, babe, babe." She laughed, half crying as she turned to take the child. "Your father speaks the truth. You have no name." She held the baby high so he might peer away, as she did, toward the wide plains before her and the nearest line of hills. She wondered what mysteries would lie behind them, for it was sure that something wonderful awaited, just beyond the horizon. Then she turned to look into Medoor Babji's eyes, full of trust and pain, wonder and joy intermixed, then to Thrasne's craggy face, which held the same mixture of feelings. So they stood for some time, regarding each other without speaking.

"I name this child Temin M'noor," she said at last, passing him into Thrasne's keeping as she moved away from them down the hill. "Temin M'noor," she called again, her voice like that of a shore bird, hunting.

"What does it mean?" Thrasne asked, thinking he had heard the words somewhere before.

Medoor Babji was smiling at him, holding out her arms for the child, her eyes swimming with tears.

"Temin, which is to say *a key*, and M'noor, that which is *spoken*. . . ."

He did not understand, and she explained it to him.

"We have given him to one another between our worlds, Thrasne.

"His name is Password."

SIGNIFICANT INDIVIDUAL PEOPLE

Arbsen: One of the Treeci of Isle Point, Saleff's sister, Taneff's mother.

Binna: One of the Treeci on Strinder's Isle.

Blint: Owner of the Riverboat the *Gift of Potipur*.

Bormas Tyle: Chancery official, Deputy Enforcer to Tharius Don, conspirator with Shavian Bossit.

Burg: A human resident of Isle Point.

Chiles Medman: Governor General of the Jarb Mendicants. A frequent visitor at Chancery.

Delia: Nanny to Pamra Don, called Saint Delia by the townsfolk of Baris.

Drowned Woman, the: The drowned wife of Fulder Don, taken from the River in a blighted state and kept by Thrasne. Her given name was Imajh.

Eenzie the Clown: Member of a group of Melancholics to which Medoor Babji belongs.

Esspill: A flier, blown by storm to an island far in the River.

Ezasper Jorn: Ambassador to the Thraish; member of the Council of Seven in the Chancery. Conspirator with Koma Nepor.

Fibji: Queen of the Noor.

Fulder Don: A man of the artist caste in the town of Baris. Father of Pamra Don.

Gendra Mitiar: Dame Marshal of the Towers, member of the Council of Seven in the Chancery. Conspirator with Ezasper Jorn.

Glamdrul Feynt: Master of the files in the Bureau of Towers, Chancery. Conspirator with Shavian Bossit.

Haranjus Pandel: Superior of the Tower in Thou-ne.

Ilze: Senior Awakener in the Tower of Baris, mentor to Pamra Don. Becomes a Laugher.

Jhilt: Noor slave of Gendra Mitiar.

Jondrigar: General Jondrigar, member of the Council of Seven in the Chancery; leader of the armies of the Protector.

Joy: Surviving resident of Strinder's Isle.

Kesseret: "Kessie," "the lady Kesseret," Superior of the Tower in Baris.

Koma Nepor: Director of Research, member of the Council of Seven in the Chancery.

Lees Obol: Protector of Man, member of the Council of Seven in the Chancery.

Lila: The slow-baby. Born from the drowned woman.

Martien: Musician, close friend and follower of Tharius Don.

Medoor Babji: Daughter of Queen Fibji; chosen heir of the throne of the Noor.

Murga: Wife of owner Blint. Called Blint-wife.

Neff: A young male Treeci living on Strinder's Isle.

Obers-rom: Thrasne's trusted assistant, first owner's man after Thrasne takes over the *Gift of Potipur*.

Pamra Don: Awakener in the Tower of Baris, who leaves the Tower to begin the great crusade.

Peasimy Flot: Resident of Thou-ne, childlike adult son of the widow Flot. Follower of Pamra Don. Also called Peasimy Prime.

Prender: Half sister to Pamra Don.

Raffen: A Riverman in the town of Zephyr. Second husband to Murga, Blint-wife.

Saleef: A Treeci talker, resident of Isle Point, brother of Arbsen and son of Sterf.

Shavian Bossit: Maintainer of the Household; member of the Council of Seven in the Chancery.

Shishus: A semimythical typical flier of the past, used as an eidolon for young Talkers.

Sliffisunda: A Talker of the Sixth (highest) Degree among the Thraish.

Slooshasill: A Thraish talker of the Fourth Degree, blown by storm to an island in the River.

Sterf: A Treeci resident of Isle Point, mother of Saleff and Arbsen.

Stodder: Resident of Strinder's Isle.

Strenge: Favorite consort of Queen Fibji.

Suspirra: The idealized woman of Thrasne's dreams. A carved image of that woman.

Taj Noteen: Leader of a group of Melancholics to which Medoor Babji belongs.

Taneff: Young male Treeci, resident of Isle Point, son of Arbsen.

Tharius Don: Propagator of the Faith; member of the Council of Seven in the Chancery. Ancestor of Pamra Don. Leader of the cause.

Thoulia: Semimythical "Sorter," the Talker who first discovered the efficacy of the Tears of Viranel.

Thrasne: Third assistant owner's man aboard the Riverboat the *Gift of Potipur*. An orphan, adopted by the owner, Blint. Later, owner of the *Gift*.

Threnot: Servant to Kesseret.

Werf: One of the Treeci on Strinder's Isle.

GROUPS, PLACES, AND THINGS

Abricor: Male, second god in the Thraish trinity. Also the second-largest moon.

Awakeners, the: Religious order living in the Towers who oversee disposal of the dead.

Baris: Township. Homeplace of Pamra Don, Tharius Don, and the lady Kesseret.

Blight, the: A fungus living in the World River that seems to turn living flesh to wood.

Boatmen: Those who make their living on the boats that travel westward on the World River. Merchants. Not to be confused with Rivermen, q.v.

Chancery, the: The administrative center of Northshore, including the officers, buildings, and bureaucracy, located at Highstone Lees, behind the Teeth of the North.

Direction of Life, the: Movement to the west, as the sun, tides, and moons move. Movement to the east is considered antilife and forbidden.

Flame-bird: A species of Northshore bird that sets its nest afire in order to hatch its eggs.

Fliers, the: Ordinary—nontalker—members of the Thraish.

Gift of Potipur: Riverboat belonging first to Blint, then to Thrasne.

Glizzee; Glizzee spice: A euphoric substance of pleasant flavor, provided by strangeys, sold in the markets as a food additive.

Highstone Lees: The name given to the Protector's palace, as well as the Chancery offices and residence grounds in the lands behind the Teeth.

Holy Sorters: Those human or superhuman creatures who sort the dead into categories of worthy or unworthy.

Isle of the Dead: Any one of many islands to which the Strangeys bring blighted humans.

Isle Point: An island of mixed Treeci, human population in mid River.

Jakes Island: An island of mixed Treeci, human population in mid River.

Jarb Houses: Places of residence set up by the order of Mendicants for the treatment and housing of madmen.

Jarb Mendicants: Madmen enabled to see the truth by smoking Jarb root; visionaries; oracles.

Jarb Root: A food root often eaten by the Noor whose toasted peel contains an anti-illusory drug.

Jondarites: The military personnel under the command of General Jondrigar.

Laughers: Pursuivants and inquisitors sent from the Chancery to find heretics in Northshore.

Light Bringer, the: The name given to Pamra Don by the crusaders, particularly by Peasimy Flot. Also, "Mother of Light."

Melancholics: Wandering pseudoreligious bands of the Noor who collect coin for the Queen of the Noor in the cities of Northshore.

Noor, the: The black people of the northern moors, from whom the Melancholics come.

Northshore: That area of land immediately to the north of the World River which is occupied with separated townships.

Pamet: A fiber crop in which armlong pods open to reveal sheaves of white strands used in making cloth.

Potipur: Chief god in the Thraish trinity. Also the largest moon.

Priests of Potipur: Awakeners assigned to Temple duty, distinguished by blue-painted faces and mirror-decked garb.

Progression: The circumnavigation of the planet done once every eighteen years by the Protector of Man. Ship of the Progression: The gilded and highly ornamented ship on which this journey is made.

Puncon: A spicy fruit, most often used in jam and confections. The bloom of the puncon tree.

Rivermen: A heretical group who put their dead in the River.

Servants of Abricor: Another name for the fliers who frequent the bone pits. The Thraish.

Shorefish: Derogatory term used by the Noor to describe the non-Noor inhabitants of Northshore. Term also used by the Talkers to describe all humans. The implication is of a thing which can be easily caught or eaten.

Song-Fish: A shallow-water fish that grows to great size and which sings in the evenings and early mornings, the pitch and tempo dependent upon the size of the fish (smaller fish having higher, more frequent tonal eruptions).

Sorting Out: Theologically, that process by which the dead are sorted into categories of worthy and unworthy.

Southshore: The land to the south of the World River, considered almost mythical.

Split River; Split River Pass: A river originating in a mountain lake in the Teeth of the North, running both north and south from that point. The pass cut by that river. The shortest route from the Chancery to Northshore, ending in the town of Vobil-dil-go.

Stilt-lizard: A lizard with very long rear legs that stalks the shallow waters of the River or swamps, snapping up small fish or aquatic bugs.

Strangeys, the: Creatures of vast size and unknown habits living in the World River.

Strinder's Isle: An island not far from Northshore that is occupied by a tribe of Treeci and a few surviving members of the Strinder family.

Talkers, the: Infrequently hatched members of the Thraish who have the talent of articulate speech over and above that found in ordinary Thraish.

Tears of Viranel: A fungus that reanimates recently dead bodies or takes over live ones, changing the composition of the flesh.

Teeth of the North: The mountain range separating Chancery lands from the moors of the Noor and Northshore.

Thou-ne: Township. Birthplace of Peasimy Flot. Site of the origin of the crusade.

Thraish, the: Race of large, carnivorous fliers in the world north of the World River. A flier can lift a small person easily. Two or more of them can carry a large adult human. While light-boned, their talons and beaks are formidable weapons.

Towers, the: One in each township, residences of the Awakeners.

Towns, the: Areas along Northshore, each approximately thirty miles wide, largely agricultural, usually centered on a village or urban area, extending northward into unsettled or Noor country. Typical towns are Thou-ne, Baris, Cheeping Wells, Xoxxy-Do, and so forth. There are 2,400 towns on Northshore.

Treeci: A race of ground-dwelling Thraish whose wings have atrophied because of their diet. Their wings, however, are still large and their wing-fingers are capable of adroit manipulation.

Viranel: Third, female, deity in the Thraish trinity. Also the third moon.

Vobil-dil-go: Township. Some distance west of Thou-ne. Historically called the site of the embarkation of the Noor.

Xoxxy-Do: Township. Birthplace of Thrasne.